BETWEEN HIS LOVER AND THE DEEP BLUE SEA

MERRY FARMER

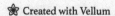 Created with Vellum

YORKSHIRE, NEAR HULL – MAY, 1816

A t last, the war was over. That bastard Napoleon was rotting away on a tiny island in the middle of the Atlantic, order was being restored to Europe and the Americas, and Septimus Bolton was suddenly homeless and without a damn thing to do. The *HMS Majesty,* Septimus's home for the past three years, had been decommissioned almost as soon as the treaty was signed and ordered to sail home from Canada, where it had been enforcing blockades and chasing privateers, along with her sister ship, the *HMS Hawk.* The officers of both decommissioned ships, Septimus among them, had been thanked for their service, given a final pay packet, and sent on their way.

It was the most miserable situation that Septimus could have imagined himself falling into. No employment, no purpose, and effectively no home. The only things he did have—the thing he was eternally grateful for—were his friends.

"There it is, lads," Lord Redmond Wodehouse, Viscount Beverley, said, slapping Septimus on the back. He pointed with his free hand to the sprawling manor house as they made their final approach. "My brother, the Duke of Malton's, grand and glorious estate, my childhood home, and your convalescent home for the summer."

Septimus managed a faint smile for his friend's sake, but all he could really think about was how ridiculous it was that Red had been in such a hurry to get home that he'd secured the three of them a ride in the back of a farmer's wagon. A wagon for two viscounts and a—well, Septimus was nobody. Nobody but a sailor barred from the sea, without a ship and without an identity. He would rather have traveled in the leakiest of skiffs than in any sort of conveyance over land.

"We're hardly convalescing," their other friend, Lord Barrett Landers, Viscount Copeland, laughed, craning his neck to get a good look at the estate and its grounds as the wagon rattled its way up a slope toward the house. "It's not as though any of us were injured, or even made ill, in what passed for a war these last few years."

"Blockading is hard work," Red argued with a mischievous glint in his eyes. "Canadian winters were even harder work, if you ask me. I think we all deserve a good Yorkshire summer before moving on to whatever's next."

"God only knows what that will be," Septimus muttered, kicking his toe against one of several barrels riding with them in the wagon.

It wasn't that he minded riding, like just another bit of provisions, in the wagon. It was the feeling that once again, he was little more than cargo, being carted around at yet another nobleman's command. At least Red wasn't the sort of nobleman who thought Septimus should know his place and keep to it. His friends were sympathetic to his plight.

"No word from the Admiralty yet?" Red asked with a hopeful look.

Septimus sighed and shook his head. "I was hoping a letter would be waiting for me in Hull. I told them this is where I would be staying until hearing from them."

"But nothing yet?" Barrett asked.

"Not a blasted thing," Septimus grumbled.

Red and Barrett exchanged looks. "The war is only just over, all things considered," Barrett said. "I am certain that once the Admiralty has a chance to reconfigure, they'll be hungry for experienced sailing masters like you."

"Yes," Red agreed. "Lieutenants like the two of us don't stand a chance of being given another royal commission, whereas you—"

"—were never granted a royal commission in the first place," Septimus finished Red's sentence for him.

"That didn't stop the rest of us from knowing who truly ran that ship," Barrett argued. "Captain Wallace depended on you for everything."

Septimus would never have said it aloud, but Captain Wallace was a vain, wool-headed fool who had purchased his commission—the same as his friends had—then bought his way up in the ranks until he captained a ship. Nearly every officer in the British Navy had come from the same aristocratic background, though some, like Red and Barrett and a few of their friends from the *Hawk*, had worked hard to earn their position.

Septimus, on the other hand, was as far from nobly-born as it was possible to get. He was the son of a Cornish fisherman, albeit a prosperous one. Septimus had worked the sea with his father from the time he was in leading strings. His father had arranged for him to serve as a cabin boy with the British Navy when he was but eight years old, and from there, Septimus had toiled his way up the ranks to become master, the highest rank possible without a royal commission.

And that was as far as it had been possible for him to go. Which he'd been reminded of by men like Captain Wallace, with whom he'd served over the years. Constantly. They'd never let him forget.

"I thank you for your faith in me," Septimus said, squaring his shoulders and reminding himself that pouting was unbecoming for a man, "and I thank you also for your hospitality this summer."

"It is my brother's hospitality, really," Red said, his mischievous smile returning. "Anthony will be away in London for another few weeks, which is why we must make the best of things before he returns."

"The best of things?" Septimus asked, one eyebrow raised.

"Is your brother an ascetic sort?" Barrett asked as well.

"No," Red laughed. "Not at all. But he is a widower who constantly harps about having two children to raise and an estate to run and make profitable, and he's not used to, nor does he enjoy, company."

"Are you certain we're truly welcome here, then?" Septimus asked. It wouldn't have been the first time a nobleman said he was welcome, then turned around and treated him shabbily.

"I am certain," Red said. "Anthony adores me. I'm the baby of the family, and he would never deny me anything."

Barrett laughed at that. Red had always kept things lively on the *Majesty*, that much was certain. Red on the *Majesty* and Lucas Salterford on the *Hawk*, and the two of them conspiring together whenever the two ships patrolled in concert. Sebastian could only manage a small smile for his friend's good humor.

"So what sort of trouble do you plan for us to get into before your august brother returns home?" Barrett asked, glancing out over the lawns and gardens of the estate as the wagon neared the front of the massive house.

"Oh, the possibilities for trouble are endless," Red answered with a shrug. "The house itself has enough half-concealed nooks and secret rooms to get up to every sort of mischief. It was constructed during the time of the Young Pretender. Some misguided ancestor of ours believed Bonnie Prince Charlie had a chance, and constructed this house with all of its hiding places in the hopes it could serve as a stronghold for the Jacobites. That never happened, of course, but we gained a truly fascinating home out of it."

"So the Wodehouses have a history of rebellion, do they?" Barrett asked with a laugh.

"The Wodehouses have a history of unconventionality and mischief," Red answered. "Which unfortunately passed over Anthony entirely. But not to worry. In addition to the mysteries of the house itself, we have a delightful stretch of woods that has been home to brigands and smugglers in the past, miles of fields and moorland for anyone with a poetical bent to wander over, and for you, Septimus, we have a rather large and diverting lake down that way, complete with a small boat house, several pleasure craft, and enough fish to satisfy your pining for the sea. You can even walk to the beach along the North Sea within an hour, if you are so inclined. I would recommend the lake over the beach, though. There is less chance of melancholia-induced weeping at the lake."

Septimus knew Red's teasing was meant to make him feel better, and he managed a pretend laugh for his friend's sake, but a lake, no matter how large or diverting, was not the sea.

He twisted to glance over his shoulder at the vista from the top of the slope, where the house stood. At least his home for the summer had a view of the sea. Everything within Septimus longed to feel the pitch and roll of the ocean under him, to breathe in the salty air, and to hear the gentle lap of the waves against a strong hull and the cries of sea birds above him. His soul belonged to Poseidon, and he was convinced that saltwater ran through his veins instead of blood. He'd only been on dry land for a handful of days, and already he felt as though he'd lost a lover.

He would do anything, absolutely anything, to find himself standing on a deck again, a ship's wheel in his hands, sails flapping above him, and the promise of adventure on the horizon.

"Gentlemen," Red announced, standing as the wagon came to a stop at the juncture where the gravel drive branched toward the front of the house and around to the more serviceable areas at the back, "we are home."

"It's brilliant," Barrett said, standing with Red then hopping off the back of the wagon.

Septimus sent one last look over his shoulder at the sea, sighing as his chest constricted with loss, then climbed down from the wagon. Home was a hundred leagues behind him, where the water met the horizon, not at some land-bound estate, all full of greens and browns.

"You'll make certain our things are taken up to our rooms?" Red asked the wagon's driver, handing the man a small coin in thanks for the ride.

"I will inform your staff, my lord," the man answered in his peculiar, Yorkshire accent—something Septimus didn't think he would ever get used to.

"Come along, mates," Red said, clapping a hand on both Barrett's and Septimus's shoulders. "Come and see the curiosities and wonders of the home I was raised in."

In spite of his own gloom and sense of loss, Red's joy and enthusiasm at returning to what must have been a happy home was contagious. Septimus gave the house a second look, trying to be fair about it. The building was grand and intriguing, from its three stories to its warm, tannish brick, to its surprisingly large number of tall windows. Unlike some of the manor houses Septimus had seen that appeared to be nothing more than large, uniform blocks plopped down in the middle of the countryside, Wodehouse Abbey was a riot of alcoves and towers that reflected both the more popular classical style and bits of earlier styles that had gone out of fashion. There was something clever and welcoming about the unusual design that reminded Septimus of Red. It wasn't the sort of home he would have built for himself, but he had to admit that the building held the promise of being comfortable.

The interior was just as eclectic and unusual as the façade, as Septimus discovered when Lord Malton's butler greeted them at the door and showed them in.

"Welcome, my lord," the middle-aged man said with a gracious bow. "We weren't expecting you this early."

"We couldn't stay away for another moment, Worthington." Red greeted the butler with a smile. He turned to gesture to Barrett and Septimus. "My friends, Lord Copeland and Mr. Bolton."

Barrett seemed to know exactly the right way to greet a butler with grace, but Septimus was left sketching a clumsy bow, then wondering if that was even right. He detested the trappings of the nobility. Rank and office aboard a ship, he understood, but not the frippery that came with hereditary titles and men who were born into a world where they were assumed to be better than everyone else, the sort of world Captain Wallace loved.

"Would you and your friends care for refreshment after your journey, my lord?" Worthington asked, following Red as he led Septimus and Barrett deeper into the house.

"That would be splendid, yes," Red said. "But I think I'll just show my mates around the house a bit to start."

"Very good, my lord." Worthington bowed, then walked off down the long front hall with more dignity than Septimus figured he could ever muster.

"Worthington was first footman when I was a lad," Red told Septimus and Barrett as they stepped off in the other direction, toward the entrance to what looked like an ornate parlor. "I fancied him something fierce right before being bundled off to Oxford."

"I can see why," Barrett laughed, keeping his voice low. "Does he...?"

"God, no," Red shook his head. "Straight as an arrow, that one. But a man can dream, can't he?"

The two of them shared a laugh. Septimus cracked a smile as well, but he'd never been the sort to joke about such things. He glanced back over his shoulder as they stepped into the parlor, just to be certain that the kind butler hadn't overheard Red.

He stopped with a jolt, nearly tripping over himself, at the vision he spotted coming down the grand staircase in the middle of the front hall. Septimus had never seen such a beautiful man in his life. Beautiful was the only word for him. Whoever he was, he couldn't have been more than one-and-twenty years old. He still had the glow and smoothness of youth about him. His blond hair had just a bit of curl to it and framed the solid yet delicate lines of his face perfectly. He wasn't particularly tall, but his form and carriage were elegant. Even though they weren't particularly elaborate, the man's clothes fit him perfectly, his breeches showing off strong thighs and shapely calves. But it was the man's sensual mouth that grabbed Septimus's attention, and the blue-green of his eyes when the young man glanced casually across the hall and caught him looking.

The lad stopped on the stairs as well, his eyes widening slightly and his fresh complexion pinking a bit, before continuing down. A smile formed on his face as he glanced away for a moment, as if checking the stairs to make certain he wouldn't tumble the rest of the way, then peeked up at Septimus again. Septimus's cock stirred in reaction to that coy smile, and before he could do anything he would regret, he rushed into the room after Red and Barrett.

"...had that commissioned by Reynolds, I believe," Red was in the middle of telling Barrett as he pointed up at a portrait of a lovely young woman to whom Red bore a resemblance. "I know it is sentimental silliness, but I came here to say goodbye to her before taking up my commission, as if she were still alive and I were still a babe in her arms."

The sweet emotion radiating from Red somehow unsettled Septimus. He was used to the gruffness and crude behavior of sailors, but in the space of the last minute, he felt as though he'd plunged into a world of softness that he was anything but prepared for. He cleared his throat and tugged at the hem of his jacket to stop himself from turning into a puddle of feeling. And yet, that didn't stop him from glancing back over his shoulder to see if he could catch another glimpse of the gorgeous creature he'd spotted earlier.

"Something wrong, Bolton?" Red asked, addressing him more formally than usual, which indicated Septimus was in for a thorough teasing.

Septimus cleared his throat again. "Er, no. I was just...." He glanced into the hall again, scrambling for some sort of excuse for his behavior. "I was curious as to whether the day's post had arrived yet."

"Expecting your letter from the Admiralty already?" Barrett asked, exchanging a glance with Red that said he would be up for whatever teasing Red had in store.

"Or any of the other inquiries I made," Septimus said.

He tried to stand straighter and deport himself like the weathered sailor he was, but a melodious tenor voice behind him said, "I came down to inquire after the post myself."

Septimus's cock twitched in interest again, and he turned to find the beautiful man from the stairs standing only a few yards away from him. It portended nothing good that the sound of the man's voice could cause a reaction in him. Septimus absolutely did not consider himself the sort to work himself into a frenzy over any man that he'd just met, particularly not one as sweet and effeminate as whoever the new

arrival was. He'd fancied a bloke or two in his day, and
in spite of the laws, there was never a lack of release
when it was needed aboard a ship, but never had he
been captivated by a man he didn't even know.

The only thing that saved him from utter, stumbling embarrassment was the fact that Red didn't
seem to have a clue who the man was either.

"I do not believe we've met," he said, striding back
across the parlor with his usual, open and friendly
smile. "Redmond Wodehouse, Anthony's youngest,
errant, miscreant brother, returned home from adventures on the high seas." He extended a hand to the
stranger.

Septimus was tempted to roll his eyes at Red's
flowery introduction—and to clench his fists in jealousy that the gorgeous young man seemed amused by
it—but before he could react and before the stranger
could answer, two wide-eyed, finely dressed children
flew down the grand staircase and flung themselves
across the hall toward Red.

"Uncle Red, Uncle Red!" both of them exclaimed,
as Red stepped past the stranger and extended his
arms. "You're home at last!"

"Francis! Eliza!" Red greeted the children with a
fierce hug as they dashed into his arms. "I've missed
you so. Did you receive the parcel I sent from
Halifax?"

"We did," the girl, Eliza—who looked to be about
ten—said, kissing Red's cheek enthusiastically. "Did
you bring more of those maple sweets?"

"Yes, they were delicious," Francis, the boy—who
seemed about eight in Septimus's estimation
—followed.

"I did bring more," Red said, "and I'll give them to
you later."

"After your lessons," the beautiful stranger said, smiling at the children.

Both children made disappointed sounds, and Eliza said, "How can we concentrate on French verbs when Uncle Red is home?"

With a blink, Septimus realized the beautiful man must have been the children's tutor. One who was easily swayed, judging by the pinch in his expression that hinted the children were about to get their way.

"I suppose those French verbs will still be there tomorrow," the tutor said, just as Septimus predicted he would. The man rested a hand on Eliza's head for a moment. "It isn't every day one's uncle returns from adventures on the high seas." He sent Red a friendly smile.

Septimus found himself wishing that smile were for him.

A moment later, he was caught unprepared when the man did, in fact, turn that smile to him. "Adam Seymour," he introduced himself, extending a hand to Septimus, since Red's arms were filled with his niece and nephew for the moment. "I am the children's tutor," he said, confirming Septimus's suspicions.

"I'm glad my brother didn't leave these two hellions without supervision while taking care of his business in London," Red said, kissing each of the children's heads as he straightened.

Seymour had his hand extended toward Septimus, so the only polite thing to do was to take it. He did his best to ignore the jolt of lust that came from his rough and calloused hand sliding against the smooth skin of Seymour's, or from the surprising firmness of the man's handshake. It was an unusually open gesture, reserved for more informal acquaintances, which stirred Septimus's blood. So much so that he barely managed to blurt out, "Septimus Bolton."

"Mr. Bolton and I recently served together on the *Majesty*," Red explained to his niece and nephew. "Mr. Bolton was sailing master. That means he was the one who steered the ship, carrying the rest of us wherever we needed to go."

The children hummed and cooed, as if impressed. Seymour looked impressed as well, which did absolutely nothing to calm the utterly inappropriate excitement Septimus couldn't seem to tamp down in the man's presence.

"And this is Lord Barrett Landers, Viscount Copeland," Red continued his introductions, blessedly removing the pressure from Septimus's shoulders.

As Barrett bowed to Seymour with a polite, "How do you do?" and a smile, Septimus took the much-needed opportunity to step away from the gorgeous man so that he could breathe again. What was he thinking, allowing his feelings to spin away from him so swiftly, and why? Because the young man was pretty to look at? He was years too young and far too refined for Septimus to even consider being tempted by.

"It is a pleasure to meet you," Seymour nodded to Barrett, then stole another glance at Septimus. "We have been anticipating your arrival for days now."

"Yes," little Francis rushed on, cutting off whatever else Seymour had been about to say. "Papa sent a letter saying you and your friends would be staying with us for the summer, and I've been ever so excited about it."

"I can see," Red laughed, clapping a hand on Francis's head to stop him from jumping up and down.

The sound of a throat being cleared from the hallway snagged everyone's attention, and they turned to find Worthington standing a few yards away in the hall. He held a salver that appeared to have two letters on it, and said, "The correspondence you have been waiting for has arrived, Mr. Seymour. And a letter for you as well, Mr. Bolton."

Almost in unison—which Septimus found more than a little unnerving—he and Seymour stepped into the hall to retrieve their letters from Worthington. They both reached for the salver at the same time, which brushed their fingers against each other. It was somehow a thousand times more intimate than shaking hands, and Septimus felt heat rise to his face in concert with the attractive blush that painted Seymour's pretty face.

"I beg your pardon," Seymour said, taking his letter.

Septimus merely nodded, suddenly seized by the wild imagination of the man begging for much more. Perhaps on his knees. Without the benefit of the fine clothes he was wearing.

Those thoughts were so errant and plainly wrong that Septimus turned away, stepping closer to the window, as soon as he had his letter in hand. He put as much distance between himself and the temptation of Adam Seymour as he could, tearing open his letter with a bit more force than was necessary.

As soon as he read the short message it contained, all thoughts of carnal mischief, indeed, all thoughts of happiness of any sort, were thwarted. "*Dear Mr. Seymour,*" the letter read. "*In response to your inquiry as to open positions and the possibility of a royal commission in His Majesty's Navy, we regret to inform you that we will be unable to satisfy your request as no commissions of any sort are available for sailing masters at this time."* It was signed by someone who Septimus was convinced had to be a minor figure in the Naval Office.

Either way, that was it, the end of his hopes and dreams of a quick return to the sea. He was stuck on land, useless and lost.

2

"*D*ear Mr. Seymour," Adam's letter read. "*Though we are impressed by your ambition and greatly approve of your endeavor to establish a school for students in need, we regret to inform you that Jacobs and Hadley believe that the risk involved in patronizing said school is not in the best interest of our offices, and we will be unable to accommodate your request for funding at this time. Your youth and inexperience do not appeal to serious speculators such as ourselves. We suggest you rely on your esteemed family connections in this matter.*" It was signed "*E. Jacobs,*" one of the office's partners.

Adam let out a disappointed breath, read the curt letter one more time on the off chance the words might change, then dropped his shoulders despondently. He'd had such high hopes for Jacobs and Hadley. They were distantly connected to his family, and they were the fifth entity he'd approached about his idea for a school catering to young men in need. Now they were the fifth rejection he'd received. It was always the same message, always the same advice— you are too young, too impetuous, and not to be taken seriously, and should remain under the thumb of the family you were born into, regardless of your personal ambition.

He refolded the letter with a sigh and tucked it into his waistcoat pocket, then glanced around, searching for something to take his mind off of the long stretch of disappointments he found himself in the thick of. Which meant his gaze flew straight to his employer's new houseguest, Mr. Septimus Bolton.

Adam had only recently been informed by Lord Malton that his brother and a few friends from the newly decommissioned *HMS Majesty* would be arriving at Wodehouse Abbey for the summer soon, and would he see to it that the children stayed out of their way. It had seemed like a straightforward request at first. Adam had expected a pack of swarthy sailors to invade the house, who would be more interested in drinking and carousing in Hull than lounging around, interrupting the children's lessons. He hadn't expected the guests in question to be refined officers and gentlemen. For some reason, he hadn't expected the children to adore their uncle so much. And he most certainly hadn't expected to have a vision of masculine perfection like Mr. Septimus Bolton crash into his presence, as if Hercules had come to the Abbey to accomplish one of his great labors.

Bolton was everything Adam liked in a physical specimen of manhood. He was tall, with broad shoulders and arms corded with muscles from working hard. He had a trim waist and powerful thighs under his breeches. Thanks be to the current fashion of tight-fitting breeches, as they allowed Adam to ascertain another feature that Bolton had nothing to be ashamed of. Adam didn't even feel sheepish at his reaction to the way the fit of Bolton's breeches made his own decidedly uncomfortable.

He snapped his eyes up to study Bolton's face again, deeply aware that Lord Francis and Lady Eliza were nearby, chattering like magpies to their uncle. There was something about Mr. Bolton's dark eyes and creased brow that reminded Adam of thunderclouds over the sea. The content of the letter he had received appeared to be as much of a disappointment as Adam's own letter. A palpable sense of frustration and desperation hung over Bolton that Adam instinctually wanted to soothe. He went so far as to take an impulsive step toward the man, as if giving in to the irresistible attraction he felt for him.

"Has my brother sent any word about when he plans to return?" Lord Beverley called from the doorway to the parlor, where he now had his niece and nephew clinging to his sides and searching through his coat pockets, as though the promised maple candy was hidden there.

Adam sent a fleeting glance to Bolton—his breath hitched when Bolton looked up, caught him staring, and locked eyes with him for a heartbeat—then turned and marched toward Lord Beverley and the children on unsteady legs. "The last missive he sent home was to inform us all that you and your friends would be coming to stay, my lord," Adam reported. "And that only arrived a week ago."

"Good heavens, but the post is slow this far north," Lord Beverley said, still as cheery as could be as he hugged the children. "I must have posted that a month ago. Which means Anthony could have sent word of an early return weeks ago, and we simply have yet to receive it."

"It is possible," Adam said with a shrug. "But I understand his business in town is quite pressing at the moment."

Lord Beverley made a crude but good-natured sound that had the children laughing. "No business is ever as important as family."

Adam smiled, mostly because that was the reaction which was expected of him, but his chest tightened at the mention of "business" and "family" in the same sentence. He loved his family, but their idea of a business appropriate for the son of a baron was to join the church—which he didn't have a taste for—or the army—which he didn't have the constitution for—or to explore one of the new avenues of industry and production that were sweeping the north. Instead, Adam had thwarted his father's ambitions by developing a passion for forming and educating young minds, combined with an altruistic streak that baffled every potential patron he'd approached with his idea for a charity school. He was exceptionally fortunate to have found a position as tutor for Lord Malton's children upon leaving university, though it would take years for him to save up the capital he needed to open a school with the salary Lord Malton paid him alone.

"I was just hoping to give my friends a tour of the house and grounds," Lord Beverley went on, scrubbing Lord Francis's hair before taking a step away from the children. "Seeing as this will be their home for the summer, I thought I would show them all of the delightful oddities of Wodehouse Abbey and educate them about all of the hiding places for getting up to no good." He winked at Lord Copeland.

"Are you certain you wouldn't like to be shown to your rooms first?" Adam asked. "I could have Worthington take you up."

Mr. Bolton stepped forward, as if that were precisely what he wanted in that moment, which seemed a bit of a letdown to Adam, but Lord Beverley said,

"Nonsense. The rooms aren't going anywhere, and we've been jostled around a wagon for the better part of the last hour. Now is the time for exploration, not rest."

"Can we come with you?" Lady Eliza asked, slipping forward to grasp her uncle's hand.

"Yes, we haven't seen you for years and years and *years*," Lord Francis added.

Lord Beverley laughed. "Of course you can accompany us."

Adam stood a little taller, seeing the opportunity in front of him. "We've been studying the history of the house and the events surrounding its early occupants," he said. "Perhaps the children could give you a guided tour as a means of ascertaining whether they remember their lessons."

"Yes," Lord Francis said, so excited he gave a short jump. "Eliza and I will tell you all about the house, beginning with the front hall. Did you know that suit of armor over there belonged to our great-great-great-great, I forget how many, grandfather, who fought with the cavaliers against that horrid Cromwell?"

"Did it?" Lord Beverley asked, laughing.

"It most certainly did," Lady Eliza said. "And Oliver Cromwell was a wicked man who went about lopping off the heads of kings without any reason." She grasped Lord Beverley's hand and led him into the parlor, which would likely begin a circuit through the house.

"No reason at all?" Lord Copeland asked following Lord Beverley and the children on their tour.

"Well, I don't think he had any reason," Lady Eliza explained.

Adam held back for a moment, glancing hopefully toward Mr. Bolton. "Will you be joining us?" he asked.

Bolton seemed a bit nervous. He glanced at his letter again, finally folding it and tucking it into a pocket. "I don't see as I have any choice," he said in a rich, gruff baritone.

Adam tried to tamp down the thrill that zipped through him as he and Bolton fell into step several yards behind the others. Dash it, but the man appealed to him on every level. He wasn't used to such a swift attraction. Instinct urged him to make the most of it, draw the man in, learn more about him, perhaps drop to his knees and offer to swallow his cock.

No, no, that was utterly inappropriate and out of the question.

Wasn't it?

"I take it you received disappointing news?" He asked, nodding to the pocket where Bolton had stored his letter.

Bolton took his time replying, sending Adam a wary, sideways look, as if he didn't quite trust the unusual openness Adam had approached him with. Openness and informality had always been two of Adam's shortcomings, if those things could even be considered as such. Adam had always been friendly, even as a child, and quick to engage new acquaintances, even though his family had constantly warned him too much affability was off-putting. He'd ignored their stodgy ways, and openness had always served him well in the past, even if men like Bolton found it alarming.

Finally, Bolton cleared his throat and said, "The Admiralty doesn't have a ship for me, which means I have no chance of a royal commission at this time."

"Oh, I'm sorry." Why the man's misfortune should make him want to smile was beyond Adam. Except it meant that those handsome eyes and strong arms would be around Wodehouse Abbey for some time to come. "I take it you were hoping to go back to sea?"

Bolton nodded. "I was born and raised by the sea. I've spent more of my life on the ocean than on dry land. I am at a loss as to what to do with myself now." He stumbled slightly as they crossed into the music room along with the children and their rapt audience. "Forgive me," Bolton muttered. "That was too forward of me. We've only just met."

"Think nothing of it," Adam said with a shrug and a smile. "I have found that people consider me easy to converse with and whisper secrets to. I can assure you, I am as silent as the grave when it comes to keeping those secrets."

Bolton continued to look deeply uncertain. More than that, the man practically vibrated with an energy that was almost sensual.

It was Adam's turn to nearly miss a step as he suddenly recognized the heat in Bolton's stolen glances. The man couldn't actually find him attractive, could he?

"I've just received a bit of a disappointment myself," Adam confided, a bit breathless because of his realization, as Lord Francis dashed to the corner of the music room to demonstrate how one of the panels behind a tall cabinet was actually a secret passage that led to the library on the other side of the wall.

Bolton's brow rose in shock—for the passage, no doubt, and not Adam's confession. Lord Copeland seemed to find the secret passageway fascinating as well, and they all crossed through into a vast and comfortable library.

"This was supposed to be a way for anyone who supported Bonnie Prince Charlie to escape from the crown," Lady Eliza explained as they sneaked through.

"So your family supported the crown in the Civil War, then went against it a hundred years later?" Lord Copeland asked with a laugh.

"We Wodehouses tend to change our minds about things from generation to generation," Lord Beverley explained with a laugh.

"And this is the library," Lord Francis rushed straight to one of the windows. "You can see the lake from here. My great-grandfather built that lake all by himself and stocked it with fish so he didn't have to take a boat out on the ocean to catch supper."

Lord Beverley laughed. "More like Grandfather enjoyed taking a skiff out to the middle of the lake, away from Grandmama, so that he could nap in peace now and then."

Bolton walked over to view the lake, so Adam followed him. There was so much sadness in the man's eyes as he glanced out over the estate's grounds and beyond, to the sea. Adam's heart hitched in his chest. He could only imagine what it might be like to miss something so fervently. The contrast between the stoic set of Bolton's jaw and the longing that radiated from him left Adam feeling as though he would do anything to ease the man's pain and put a smile on his face.

Anything.

He sucked in a breath and stepped back, shocked at himself. He wasn't the sort to go throwing himself at a complete stranger, even if he was as handsome as the devil.

Bolton breathed in suddenly and pulled away from the window as well. "Forgive me, you told me you, too, have suffered a disappointment?"

"A small one," Adam admitted with a sheepish look—though the look was more for the rush of feeling he had for Bolton than for his own troubles. "I am attempting to establish a charity school," he said as the two of them headed across the room to where the children were telling some wild tale about a series of portraits between two bookshelves to their uncle and Lord Copeland. "I was just denied funding, yet again," Adam finished.

"A charity school?" A spark of interest lit Bolton's eyes.

Adam half wished that interest was for more than his educational endeavors. "Yes. When I attended the University of York, I discovered quite by accident that several of the brightest of my peers were only able to attend because of special scholarships, as I was. Upon further inquiry, I learned that they believed some of the brightest minds in the land never have a chance of advancing themselves because they cannot afford basic education. I was so damnably struck by that unfairness that I have made it my mission to champion the less fortunate and enable bright young minds to flourish, in spite of their family's position or finances, or lack thereof, no matter what difficulties I encounter along the way." He was breathless with zeal by the time he finished.

Bolton's brow went up, and he blinked in surprise.

Adam immediately felt embarrassed. "Forgive me, this is a subject I am rather passionate about. I tend to prattle on, when given half a chance."

"No, no, I don't mind," Bolton said, his deep voice laced with more emotion than Adam would have expected. He cleared his throat as their entire group walked on, back into the hallway and across to a long portrait gallery. "I was one of those lads who was never given a chance, you see," he went on. "It has... held me back."

Bolton's face clouded over again, and he stepped on, ahead of Adam. Adam cursed himself for... he didn't know what. He didn't think anything he said had upset Bolton particularly. For a moment, they'd teetered on the edge of some sort of deeper connection, but it felt as though that opportunity had slipped through his fingers.

He wouldn't stand for that.

"You were the *Majesty's* sailing master?" he asked, catching up to Bolton.

Bolton hung back, waiting for Adam, though Adam could feel some reticence from him. "I was," he said. "For three years."

"And before that?" Anything Adam could do to keep the man talking was a good thing, as far as he was concerned. He couldn't get enough of the sound of Bolton's voice—or the impression of how much bigger and more powerful than him Bolton was as they walked side by side down the long gallery. The more he prompted the man to talk, the sooner they could consider themselves friends.

All the same, Bolton continued to bristle with nervous energy as he said, "I've served in the Royal Navy since I was a lad of eight, starting on the *Indefatigable* and working my way up to the position of noncommissioned officer on the *Majesty*."

Adam sent him an almost teasing smile and asked, "Were you at the Battle of Trafalgar?"

Bolton paused as the others studied a series of portraits, and said with perfect honesty, "In fact, I was."

Something in the proud way Bolton spoke, the way he squared his broad shoulders, and the hint of a grin that pulled at the corner of his mouth had

Adam's cock twitching with interest. He hadn't thought he was the sort to be swayed by the hint of fame that came with being a part of such a notable event, but participation at Trafalgar would have appealed to the imagination of even the most stoic Englishman.

"I was only a seaman at the time," Bolton went on, "but I was there, serving on the *Leviathan*."

"So you were right in the thick of the action?" Adam's pulse sped up even more.

His heart—or perhaps a lower organ—nearly burst when Bolton's grin turned impish and fiery at memory. "Very much so," he said.

"I would love to hear all about it," Adam said, all too aware of how enthralled he sounded, and of the way his face heated as he gazed up at Bolton. The man had a good six inches on him, which only tickled Adam's fancy all the more.

He knew he'd come on too strong when Bolton's grin faltered and he took a step back. "All of that is in the past now," he said, the storm clouds closing in around him again.

Adam wanted nothing more than to chase those clouds away permanently. "Perhaps you could join me —that is, join me and the children—in the schoolroom at some point during your stay at Wodehouse Abbey to teach a lesson about the battle and about Nelson."

Bolton flinched. "Me? Teach a lesson?"

"I'm certain you have a great deal that you could teach a willing student," Adam blurted, glancing up at the man as boldly as a coquette, twitching to brush his fingers against the back of Bolton's hand.

No sooner had he made that flirtatious gamble than he regretted it. Bolton's eyes widened and smoldered, but he took a step back. "I am hardly qualified to teach anything," he said, glancing away.

Adam clenched his jaw to keep himself from blurting out more that he would regret. Not every man was as bold about what they wanted as he tended to be. Truth be told, it had been a long time since he'd wanted the sort of things that meeting Septimus Bolton had instantly inspired in him. A long time indeed.

"I think the children would greatly appreciate a history lesson from a man who was there when it happened," he said, pulling back with his flirtation, but keeping his suggestion firmly in place. Perhaps reminiscing about the sea for two intelligent children would help remove the wistfulness from Bolton's spirit.

"I thought he looked familiar." The statement came from Lord Beverley at the end of the gallery.

Adam was alarmed to find Lord Beverley, Lord Copeland, and both children watching him and Bolton with delighted smiles. He was immediately self-conscious, wondering how much of his flirtation with Bolton they'd seen, until he recognized the portrait they'd all been standing around.

"Ah," he said, glancing to Bolton, then walking past him to join the others. "I see you've found Great-Uncle Stephen."

Adam caught the edge of Bolton's confused frown as the man strode over to join the rest of them.

"When you introduced yourself, you did not tell me you were Baron Laytham's son," Lord Beverley said.

Adam winced, but turned the expression into a smile. "I find the detail to be irrelevant, seeing as I am the youngest of six sons and in no danger of inheriting the title or the estate," he said. "Or even my father's approval."

"You're gentry?" Bolton asked, more shock in his question than Adam would have expected.

"Only in the broadest possible definition," Adam said apologetically.

Much to his distress, every bit of the easiness and friendship that had just begun to blossom between them withered, and Bolton's expression closed up. He didn't make any further comment, but neither did he look at Adam again as their group walked on.

An odd sort of pain radiated through Adam as Lady Eliza said, "The dining room is next. Let me show you the silver platter that Queen Anne gave to my great-great-grandmother as a wedding gift." He didn't know what he'd done, but Bolton was behaving as though Adam had insulted him. And things had started off so well between them.

Whatever it was, Adam wasn't having it. He'd felt the spark of something exciting ignite between him and Bolton, and he wasn't simply going to ignore that because a portrait had given the handsome naval officer second thoughts. They had the entire summer to explore whatever force it was that seemed to exist between the two of them, urging them into each other's orbit, which meant Adam had more than enough time to bring out the vibrant part of Bolton he'd seen at the mention of Trafalgar, and to see what might happen because of it.

had spent the better part of the day in Seymour's company. Since he wasn't one to engage in idle chatter

3

S eptimus's first night at Wodehouse Abbey was
every bit as restless and unsettled as he'd expected it to be. He still wasn't used to sleeping on dry
land, without the constant pitch and lap of the sea
lulling him into sleep and keeping him there. Every
time he managed to doze off, he jolted awake again
only an hour or so later with the sensation that something was terribly wrong. He told himself that the
state was temporary, that he would find solace in sleep
again once his body adjusted to the solid, motionless
oddity that was land.

His mind had an entirely different set of problems,
however. Every time he closed his eyes, his imagination conjured up images of Mr. Adam Seymour. The
young man was physical perfection, as far as Septimus
was concerned—slender but masculine, with expres-
sive eyes and a mouth made for sin. Seymour had
spent the better part of the afternoon with him, Red,
Barrett, and Red's niece and nephew, touring the
house and estate, taking tea on the lawn. Seymour had
prompted the children to report on all the things they
were learning in their lessons, amusing Septimus to
no end. They had all then enjoyed what had to be the

most wildly unusual supper Septimus had ever sat down to. Septimus was under the impression that the children of the aristocracy never dined with their adults, but Lord Francis and Lady Eliza sat with them in the grand dining room, continuing to regale their uncle with every bit of news that had happened since the last time he'd seen them, at Christmas over a year ago.

All of this communal activity meant that Septimus had spent the better part of the day in Seymour's company. Since he wasn't one to engage in idle chatter about new calves that had been born, odd things a certain Lady Croundland had said, or the curious ways of the estate's gamekeeper, a Mr. Declan Shelton, Septimus spent most of the day quietly observing Seymour.

The man was all grace and beauty, intelligence and wit. He was everything Septimus liked, and everything he was not. When they'd strolled around the gardens of Wodehouse Abbey, Seymour's hair had filled with golden highlights, as though he were an angel of some sort. When he was elaborating on something one of the children had reported to their uncle, his blue-green eyes flashed with quick wit. And when Red had challenged the children to an impromptu race down the slope of the lawn to the lake, Seymour had run with them, giving Septimus a view of his body in motion that proved the tutor was athletic as well as intelligent.

If only he weren't a bloody nobleman.

By the time morning rolled around, Septimus's body ached from lack of sleep—and lack of release. His cock had had its own opinions of Seymour's many fine qualities throughout the night, opinions that Septimus had refused to acknowledge by relieving himself. The whole thing was maddening, and there was not a damn thing he could or intended to do about any part of the situation he found himself in. The only solution he managed to come up with for his physically and mentally tormented state was to throw on a pair of breeches and a shirt, take up the towel hanging off the side of the washstand in his guest room, and to creep out of the house in the dawn light to head down to the lake. It wasn't the ocean, but any body of water was bound to soothe the sensation he had that everything was wrong in his world.

It was early enough in the year that the lake was still cold, but not only was Septimus not bothered as he shed his clothes and stepped out onto a jetty stretching into the shimmering water, he welcomed the chill as he dove in. The slip of cold water across his body as he glided for as long as he could hold his breath felt as though it peeled away the layers of anxiety and disappointment that had built up over the past few weeks. He reveled in the strain of his muscles as he broke the surface and began to swim, reaching his arms over his head and in front of him, kicking his legs, and reminding his body what it was there for.

Of course, in spite of the chill of the water, his body still wanted to remind him of other things it was there for. The furnace of desire for Seymour that smoldered in him refused to go away. He couldn't shake the memory of Seymour's easy smile and melodious laugh, no matter how hard he swam toward the lake's opposite shore. What was wrong with him? It wasn't as though he'd been without male company of late. In fact, that was practically the only company he'd had for the years of his naval service. And among that company, there had always been a likely fellow willing to help satisfy his lusts. He'd only just met Seymour. The man should not have such a hold on him already.

By the time he reached the far end of the lake and turned to swim back, Septimus had decided that he must be suffering from some sort of land sickness, just as men who were not used to the ocean spent the first few days out to sea casting up their accounts whenever the ship rolled even a little. He told himself the distraction Seymour presented was merely a symptom of how off-balance he felt because of the change in his own situation, and that as soon as he appealed again to the Admiralty and was given a new commission so that he could return to sea, his thoughts and feelings would sort themselves out.

He was almost convinced of the fact as he neared the jetty once more.

"You have excellent form."

The comment, called out to him from the end of the jetty as he approached, nearly caused Septimus to flinch and sink. His imagination must have had stronger powers than he knew, because there was Seymour, standing on the dock in the morning sunlight, wearing nothing but a simple pair of breeches and shirt, looking like some sort of favorite of Apollo.

"I beg your pardon?" Septimus asked, knowing full well his voice was gruff and he sounded like a whale with a stomach ache. He stopped swimming several yards away from the jetty and treaded water, half of him hoping Seymour would vanish or turn and go away.

The other half of him was a rebellious arse whose insides shivered at the sight of the young man.

"I was admiring your form," Seymour said, more of a glint in his eyes than Septimus wanted to see. "As

you swam," he clarified. "You're an excellent
swimmer."

Septimus was at a loss as he bobbed, neck-deep, in
the lake. Was the man actually using that observation
as a way to begin a conversation? He wasn't some rube
who had fallen off the turnip truck yesterday. He knew
what Seymour was truly saying. He'd sensed almost
from the first sight of the man where his interests lay.

"I've been swimming my whole life," he answered
after too long a pause.

"I can see that," Seymour said, still smiling, then
proceeded to toe off his slippers and tug his shirt off
over his head. "I've been swimming most of my life as
well, but likely not as much as you."

Septimus's mouth dropped open wordlessly as
Seymour tossed his shirt aside, revealing a trim waist
and a surprisingly fit and muscular chest, with just
enough hair to prove he was a fully-grown man and
not the youth he appeared to be at certain angles. Septimus's own body heated and tightened, and his sense
of modesty—one he hadn't known he possessed—
urged him to turn away. But he couldn't. Not even
when Seymour undid the fastenings of his breeches
and pushed them down his legs.

"You've stolen my idea, I see," Seymour said, as
easy as you please, as he straightened, showing off his
beautiful nakedness to Septimus. The man had
shapely thighs and calves, but Septimus barely noticed them with such an enticing cock and perfect
balls suddenly on display. A thousand wild notions of
all the ways he could make use of that cock and those
balls roared through Septimus. So much so that he
almost didn't hear Seymour go on with, "I come down
here for a morning swim myself whenever the
weather permits."

Before Septimus could answer—if he was even capable of answering with the undertow of lust pulling at him and threatening to decimate him—Seymour dove into the water, like some sort of elegant dolphin. Septimus watched the lithe, pink shape of him rippling under the water until he emerged a couple of yards away.

Seymour pushed his wet hair out of his face as he bobbed above the surface, smiled, and said, "It will make a nice change to have a partner to swim with. I am usually the only one up so early in the morning."

If not for the temperature of the water, Septimus was certain he would be as up as it was possible to be. Even with the cold, he was halfway there.

"Do you not find it dangerous to swim alone in the mornings?" he asked, starting toward the opposite side of the lake once more, if only to indulge the instinct he had to flee from the temptation Seymour presented.

Seymour shrugged, then swam after him. "I suppose. One never knows when a cramp or sheer exhaustion will take over and drag one down."

"Yes," Septimus agreed in a low growl. "Letting one's guard down can lead to every sort of disaster. It is best not to venture into danger." It was a much bolder statement than Septimus was wont to make. He peeked sideways at Seymour to see if he understood his true meaning.

Blast the man, but he laughed in that mellifluous way he had, heating Septimus's blood even more. "Danger is the best place to venture into," Seymour said. "Without a bit of a gamble now and then, life becomes nothing but a dull succession of eating, sleeping, and listening to family members tell the same exhausted story over and over."

Septimus's mouth quirked into a half smile in spite of himself. "You've met my mother, I see."

Seymour laughed again. The man was uncommonly free with his laughter. "I believe everyone's mother is the same, high or low, rich or poor."

Septimus lost his smile at the reminder that Seymour was above him, or probably thought he was. Just like every other nobleman who'd bought his way onto Septimus's ship and ended up standing in his way. He concentrated on swimming, on the movement of his arms and legs, and not the twist of disappointment in his gut.

"Have I offended you somehow?" Seymour asked as they neared the center of the lake. "Only, I noticed that you seemed reluctant to speak with me after the portrait gallery yesterday."

"You've done nothing, sir," Septimus said. "Or should I refer to you as 'my lord', since your father is a baron."

"Ah," Seymour said, as though Septimus had said far more than he intended to. "It's 'Adam', not 'my lord', and not even 'sir', if you please. I am not one to stand upon ceremony."

Septimus eyed him sideways, wondering if referring to the man by his Christian name would help ease things between the two of them or whether it would merely provide another facet to the fantasies that had kept him up all night long.

"May I ask," Adam went on, "do you have some sort of grudge against the nobility?"

Septimus nearly missed a stroke as he swam. With one blunt question, he suddenly felt as though he'd been turned inside out and called out for behaving like a sullen child. He forced himself to loosen his grip on his disappointments and failures. If Adam was

open enough to insist he be called by his Christian
name, the least Septimus could do was be honest
with him.

"I have come to distrust men with titles," he admitted, though it was difficult. "Particularly as they tend
to be promoted among the ranks of His Majesty's Navy
at a far greater frequency than men who have served
most of their lives at sea."

As Septimus knew he would, Adam let out a hum
of understanding. "I take it the sting of seeing men
less competent and less experienced than you being
given the reins of a ship on which you serve, simply
because they have the blunt to buy the position, is
acute."

Adam's seemingly genuine sympathy did nothing
at all to help Septimus wrestle against the lust that the
man inspired in him. "Ships don't have reins," he
mumbled instead of giving a more honest answer.

Unsurprisingly, Adam laughed. "I shall have to
learn the correct terminology."

"I thought you were the teacher and not the student," Septimus said.

"A good teacher must always continue to be a student," Adam answered, sending Septimus a flirtatious
look as they came close enough to the lake's opposite
shore to turn and swim back. "Which is why I think
you and I could be the best of friends, Mr. Bolton."

Shivers of a dozen different kinds passed through
Septimus. He was mad to allow Adam to flirt with him
the way he was. For one, their positions in life were
too disparate. For another, there must have been at
least ten years between them. Adam still had the
freshness of youth about him, and Septimus was well
into his thirties, with experience of life that made him
feel decades older. Even if the man were game for

something more than flirtation—which it was obvious he was—it would have been unthinkable. What could a salty old sailor like him have to offer a lithe and beautiful son of a baron?

But fool that he was, the next thing that came out of Septimus's mouth was, "If you insist I call you Adam, it's only right that you call me Septimus."

A moment later, Septimus prayed the lake would open up and swallow him.

A moment after that, Adam smiled, and Septimus found himself wondering if it was possible to swim with a full cockstand.

"I was serious yesterday when I said that you should come teach a lesson to Lord Francis and Lady Eliza, Septimus," Adam went on, as if that were the only thing he'd meant by his flirting and not something that was most certainly not fit for children. "I would wager you could teach us all far more than history. Would I be correct to assume that your post as sailing master involved the calculation of coordinates and positions, as well as the use of a sextant?"

Every part of Septimus heated at the way Adam made such innocent terms like "positions" and "sextant" seem suggestive and dirty. "Yes, that would be correct," he said, wishing he could concentrate on swimming. Their progress back across the lake had slowed, since their initial burst of energy had worn itself out. "But why would the children of a duke need to know anything about seafaring calculations?" He absolutely could not bring himself to say the word "sextant" in Adam's presence.

Adam managed to shrug while swimming. "Lord Malton wishes for his children to have as well-rounded an education as possible. He believes knowledge is key to the running of an estate such as this one." He paused before saying, "Knowledge is the key to improving a great many things, and it is scandalous that so much knowledge is withheld from anyone unfortunate enough not to be born with a steady income."

The way Adam grew serious as he talked about the impetus behind the school he'd mentioned wanting to start was even more of an aphrodisiac to Septimus than flirtatious looks and suggestive statements. It was an unsettling reminder that, with all the differences between the two of them, they had at least one belief in common. One very important belief.

"We agree on that much," he said, wondering if he were mad for opening himself up that way. For all the things that set him and Adam apart and for all the reasons he knew he couldn't entertain the idea of misbehaving with the young man, he was devilishly attracted to Adam's kind spirit. It was something he'd been missing in his harsh, naval life.

"You have no great love for the aristocracy," Adam went on, glancing sideways at Septimus with a sparkle in his eyes, "but that does not mean every one of them should live down to your expectations. I believe—and Lord Malton shares my beliefs—that a responsible peer understands the lives and needs of all men, not just those of his social standing. The more Lord Francis and Lady Eliza learn about practical things, in addition to French grammar and the classics, the better equipped they will be to guide the future of the Empire."

"Lord Malton believes that?" Septimus asked in surprise.

"He does," Adam answered. "As do I. So please do say you will come and teach a lesson in navigation or ship construction or our recent history to the children, and to me."

The combination of invitation, expectation, and blatant, carnal interest in Adam's eyes had Septimus's senses reeling. He couldn't possibly give in to what every fiber of his body was screaming at him to do. He hadn't come to Wodehouse Abbey to have a summer tryst with his host's children's tutor. He'd only come because he had nowhere else to go while waiting for the Admiralty to contact him that would impress the Naval Office into deeming him worthy of the commission he so desired. The last thing he needed was something—or someone—as intriguing and irresistible as Adam was to anchor him to shore.

He was spared from answering by the sight of Red and Barrett coming down the slope from the house and appearing around a small stand of trees, which had shielded them from view until that point.

"Hello," Red called out to Septimus and Adam, prompting them to pick up speed and swim toward the jetty. "Worthington said he'd spotted the two of you down here."

"What possessed the two of you to rise so early for a swim?" Barrett asked, putting far too much emphasis on the word 'rise'. The last thing Septimus needed was his friends getting wind of any sort of attraction between him and Adam. If they suspected a thing, he'd never hear the end of it, and being made fun of for having designs on a young, bright, and nubile baron's son was not how Septimus wanted to spend his summer.

"I always come down to the lake for a swim in the morning, my lord," Adam answered once they were close to the jetty. "As I've discovered, Mr. Bolton does the same."

"Yes, that one has always been part fish," Barrett said.

The corner of Red's mouth quirked up. "Part fish, part man. I suppose that makes him a merman."

"Or a selkie," Barrett suggested. "Do you suppose he is in danger of anyone stealing his skin and keeping him ashore?"

Septimus's brow dropped into a deep scowl as he swam to a stop by the jetty. So the teasing had begun already, had it?

He didn't help his own cause where the teasing was concerned as Adam grabbed hold of the jetty, hefting himself out of the water, sun-kissed droplets sluicing down his gorgeous body, by staring at the young man with hunger he couldn't conceal. Sure enough, after widening their eyes at the picture Adam made as he walked over to fetch the towel he'd brought down with him, Red and Barrett glanced to Septimus with impressed looks, as if he'd already made a conquest.

Septimus scowled even deeper at the two of them and asked, "What do the two of you want? Isn't it overly early for you to be up and about as well?"

"We've heard word that there's a festival of some sort in Hull today," Red said.

"I've been promised food, games, dancing, and attractive company," Barrett added, peeking at Adam's arse without an ounce of shame.

"Hull is always having some sort of festival," Adam said as he toweled himself dry, doing a bit—but not nearly enough—to hide his body as he did. In fact, at one point he bent at the waist to dry his calves, giving Septimus far more of a view of his arse and balls than was good for him. Septimus wouldn't be coming out of the water anytime soon.

"How could anyone resist a promise like that?" Red asked with a broad grin, his eyes flashing as he all but winked at Septimus. "A festival is a grand thing," he said, as if his first statement were as innocent as could be.

"Are you coming, Septimus?" Barrett asked with the same sort of cheeky inuendo.

"I do not suppose I'll hear the end of it if I cry off," Septimus growled. He hesitated, checking the state of his body, and when he figured he was safe to muscle himself out of the water, he pulled himself up onto the jetty.

He was well aware of Adam glancing casually in his direction and raking his form with an appreciative glance. There was nothing Septimus could do about that but stride over to his towel and clothes and work to dry off and cover up as fast as possible. At least if he spent the day in Hull with Red and Barrett, he wouldn't have to worry about the lithe, clever temptation that was Adam Seymour.

"I think I might just bring the children and accompany you into Hull," Adam said, immediately squashing Septimus's notion and sending his pulse soaring. "If that would be acceptable with you." He glanced to Red.

"I wouldn't mind," Red said with a shrug. "Would my brother consider the outing as his children shirking their lessons?"

"Not at all," Adam said as he tossed his towel aside and reached for his breeches, bending over again just as Septimus glanced in his direction. Did the man have no shame? "I always find a way to turn any event into a lesson," he explained.

"Then you and the children are more than welcome to join us," Red said. He peeked past Adam to send Septimus a teasing look.

"Thank you, my lord." Adam nodded to Red as he fastened his breeches.

Septimus wished Red had forbidden the man to come along, and perhaps that he'd ordered Adam locked in a tower somewhere. It seemed as though one sleepless night wasn't going to be the end of things where his cock and Adam Seymour were concerned.

4

A dam was surprised and somewhat embarrassed at how adept he'd proven at lying. It wasn't a horrible lie. He did get up early to swim in the lake now and then in the warmest summer months, but certainly not so early in the summer, or so early in the morning. His one and only motivation for throwing on some clothes and dashing down to the lake when the sun had barely peeked above the horizon was because he'd spotted Septimus strolling down the hillside through his window when he'd crawled out of bed to relieve himself. He'd intended to crawl right back into bed for an hour or so, since the children generally didn't start their lessons until late in the morning, but the opportunity to become better acquainted with Septimus had been too much to resist.

Several hours later, as their odd group stepped down from the carriage Lord Beverley had commandeered from his brother's collection and onto one of the main streets of Hull, Adam was deeply grateful that he'd taken the gamble and had his time alone with Septimus before the madness of the festival.

"Now, Lord Francis, Lady Eliza, do you have your lists?" Adam asked as he led the children away from the bustling road and into the shade of a shop. Lord Beverley and Lord Copeland stepped down from the carriage but remained close to the road, glancing up and down as though deciding on what sort of mischief they might cause. Septimus, however, glanced uncertainly between his friends and Adam and the children before moving subtly to the side, almost as if he would choose to follow along with the lesson Adam had planned instead of running off to cause havoc with his friends.

"I have my list right here." Lord Francis held up the scrap of parchment Adam had prepared for him in a hurry that morning, after plans had been made.

"And here is mine," Lady Eliza added.

"Good." Adam clapped his hands together. "Now, here is your assignment. You must find each of the items I have listed for you without the help of any adults." Adam sent Septimus a crafty smile, as though he were in on the lesson as well, then glanced on to Lord Beverley and Lord Copeland, who actually seemed interested in what the children would be doing. "When you find an item from the list, use your pencil to mark it off."

"What sort of things will these little rapscallions be searching for?" Lord Beverley asked.

"Something written in French," Lady Eliza said, showing him her list and pointing at the first item. "And I must translate it as well."

"Mine says two numbers of greater than three digits, and then I must add them together," Lord Francis said.

Lord Beverley checked the lists, then smiled at Adam. "Very clever, and highly unusual," he said. "No wonder my brother hired you as a tutor."

"I believe that life is the greatest tutor any child

can have," Adam said, "and since life is all around us, why not become accustomed to it at an early age?"

"It is certainly an improvement over idling away in a schoolroom," Lord Copeland said. "Wouldn't you agree, Bolton?"

The intention behind the teasing smile Lord Copeland sent Septimus wasn't lost on Adam. His own face heated at the look. He knew full well that he'd been too bold that morning, made his intentions a bit too obvious. But how could he have held back with a man as magnificent as Septimus right in front of him? Septimus wasn't just a hero, he was a vision. It had been all Adam could do to get himself into the cold water of the lake quickly to avoid the embarrassment of Septimus ogling what would have been an enormous cockstand after taking in the sight of the man's powerful body gliding through the clear water of the lake. Adam had enjoyed every part of Septimus that he'd seen, from the thick muscles of his arms and shoulders to the tight mount of his arse, to the fleeting and devilishly tempting glimpses of his prick under the water.

None of which were even remotely appropriate for him to be contemplating with Lord Francis and Lady Eliza glancing hopefully toward him for further instructions about their lesson. Adam should have been thankful for the children's presence, just as he should have been thankful that Lord Beverley and Lord Copeland had arrived at the lake that morning before he let his impulsiveness land him in a situation that could have proven disastrous.

"It is a clever lesson," Septimus mumbled, glancing toward Adam in a way that seemed to indicate he was trying exceptionally hard *not* to look at him. "If you will excuse me, seeing as the post office is just across the way, I need to inquire after any letters."

Adam's heart squeezed for the man as Septimus nodded toward Lord Beverley, attempted a small smile for the children, then strode quickly right out into the middle of traffic, nearly being bowled over by a cart filled with barrels, and across the street. Adam was aware that he made Septimus uncomfortable, likely for several reasons, but he had also deduced that everything about the man's life at the moment was a source of discomfort.

"How do we go about completing these lists?" Lord Copeland asked, glancing over Lord Francis's shoulder at his parchment, then at Adam.

"The children must complete their lists on their own, my lord," Adam reminded him, though he was secretly happy that Lord Beverley's friend seemed to enjoy the children's company. "The best thing for it is to simply walk through Hull and the activities that are a part of this festival, searching out what needs to be found."

"Then that is what we will do," Lord Copeland said, winking at the children.

"Septimus will catch up with us when he's done," Lord Beverley said as their group started forward, almost as if consoling Adam for the man's absence.

Adam found himself falling into step with Lord Beverley, as the path they walked on was narrow and Lord Copeland seemed determined to help the children. "I should apologize for my demeanor this morning," Adam said, lowering his voice and his head slightly. "It was a bit forward of me."

Lord Beverley laughed. "It was, but I do not think Septimus minded."

Adam wasn't certain whether to wince or laugh along with Lord Beverley. "I am not usually so... bold."

Lord Beverley sent him a sideways smirk before focusing on his niece and nephew as they stopped in front of a haberdasher's shop that included a series of illustrations of bonnets with French captions under them. "Septimus is a sight to behold, and one that has turned quite a few heads before yours."

Adam's face heated even more, and his nerves frayed. "I'm not sure what you must think of me."

Lord Beverley glanced at him with a frank look as they waited for Lady Eliza to copy a few of the French phrases, then translate them. "Seymour, I've spent the last several years of my life aboard ships. Even before that, my aesthetic tastes ran more toward the Greeks than anything else. I know a hawk from a handsaw, as the bard would say." Lady Eliza finished with her translation, and they walked on. "To be honest, if Septimus hadn't been so keen right from the start, I might have had a go myself."

Adam's mouth fell open, and he worked his way through several clumsy, gaping syllables that never quite formed themselves into words before sputtering, "Oh." That hardly seemed adequate for the confession Lord Beverley had just made, so he shook himself and went on with, "If it does not bother you, then."

"Never has, never will," Lord Beverley confirmed. He nodded to Lord Copeland's back. "We're all of the same mind here."

It took Adam a few beats to sort the surprising new information in his thoughts. He was given an additional few moments to reconsider what he wanted to say as they crossed the street and entered a wide square that was decorated with flags and bunting, and which held tables and booths of all descriptions. The scents of everything from roasting meat to sweets to flowers crowded the air, along with the excited chatter of what seemed like half the population of Yorkshire. In a backwards way, Adam was glad for the crowd. The only thing better than speaking discreetly in isolation was talking in a crowd, where no one was interested in listening to anyone else and everyone had something to say.

"I was wondering if you could tell me something," he began, glancing seriously at Lord Beverley. "I feel as though I offend our friend, Mr. Bolton, in some way." He had never been particularly good at disguising his speech so that only someone in the know would understand what he was talking about, but was satisfied those words wouldn't sink any ships. "As I understand it, he doesn't care for the aristocracy, and yet the two of you, and Lord Copeland, seem close."

"Septimus says he despises nobs," Lord Beverley laughed, "but he only harbors true prejudice against those who have thwarted his ambition for no other reason than their rank at birth. And with good reason. Septimus is the most competent and experienced seaman I've ever met. He steered us, and the *Hawk*, through more storms and dangerous encounters with privateers than I can count and brought everyone out safe in the end. He was even instrumental in the capture of a French privateer off the coast of Nova Scotia last autumn. But the *Majesty's* captain, a Captain Wallace, took credit for every action and every maneuver Septimus executed in his reports to the Admiralty. The result was that Wallace was lauded as a hero, he was granted the prize money that should have gone to Septimus, and Septimus was prevented from advancing to a lieutenancy or captaincy of his own, as is his dream."

"That is horrible," Adam said, his heart breaking for Septimus.

"It is. The only reason Septimus likes me and Barrett—and a few other officers from the *Hawk* who formed our circle—is because we proved ourselves to him, in battle and by standing up for him against Wallace's assertions, not that it did any good in the end."

"Might I assume his ambitions have been thwarted multiple times because the higher ranks of the Royal Navy are filled with noblemen who purchased their commissions?" Adam asked. He might not have known much about the Navy, but everyone knew that.

"Precisely." Lord Beverley nodded. "For most men of Septimus's birth, attaining the position of sailing master would be the finest feather they could possibly put in their cap. Septimus bears the curse of being intelligent beyond his class and ambitious beyond the expectations of the sods in charge of things. If he had spoken out against Wallace, knowing Wallace, he would have accused Septimus of mutiny. That would have killed any hope of a commission in the future."

Adam hummed and nodded as they followed the children from a cart selling seasoned nuts to an impromptu puppet show near the corner of the square. "This is precisely why I wish to establish a school that will foster the ambition of boys like Septimus who wouldn't otherwise be given a chance to use their native skills."

Lord Beverley turned to Adam with a look of surprise. "How very ambitious of you." The corner of his mouth twitched, and he added, "For a baron's son."

Adam sent him a sardonic look. "My father's barony is small and unimportant. Half of the farmers in our county are more prosperous than we were. I was only able to attend university because of a scholarship, and even then, when not attending classes, I quite scandalously engaged in *work* to pay for my room and board."

"Perish the thought," Lord Beverley said with mock horror, though Adam could tell that he'd suddenly risen in the man's estimation. Lord Beverley smiled. "You and Septimus are more alike than I thought."

"And yet, he seems reticent to befriend me," Adam went on, applauding when everyone else did, though he wasn't certain why, other than that the puppet show had concluded.

Lord Beverley laughed. "I'm not certain what your standard of friendship is, Seymour, but from what I've observed within the last day, Septimus has warmed to you far more quickly than he usually does with men he doesn't know."

"Truly?" Adam asked, hope blossoming within him. He tilted his head to the side and shifted his shoulders. "Mama always did tell me I was too fulsome for my own good, that I put people off."

"Oh, Septimus is by no means put off," Lord Beverley chuckled. "But he is also the most stubborn man I've ever known."

They walked on, past several stalls selling meat pies, cakes, and bread, and on toward a block of booths where local merchants and businessmen were advertising their services. Lord Francis and Lady Eliza were excited to discover several items on their lists that they could cross off by reading the signs and pamphlets those businesses displayed.

"Tell me more about this school of yours," Lord Beverley went on as they ambled over to Lord Copeland and the children. "Do you have a location for it? Funding and whatnot?"

Adam sighed and rubbed a hand over his head. "I'm afraid not. I've pursued several avenues for funding, attempted to secure patronage that would allow me to purchase or rent a building and supplies, but have yet to find a bank or group of speculators willing to patronize something as domestic as a school when there are any number of more exciting industrial endeavors seeking capital."

"And because starting a school for waifs and pickpockets is a rubbish idea," an all-too familiar voice commented from the booth right next to where Adam and Lord Beverley had stopped.

Adam winced and pivoted toward the booth, angry with himself for not being aware enough to spot Martin Goddard lurking on the other side of a small counter earlier.

"Goddard," he greeted the man with a nod.

"Seymour," Goddard smirked at him in return. "Attempting to wheedle money for your silly school out of this unsuspecting target?"

"I beg your pardon?" Lord Beverley blinked at the man.

Adam sighed. "Lord Beverley, may I introduce you to an old classmate of mine, Mr. Martin Goddard."

As if Adam hadn't said a thing, Goddard bowed sharply on the other side of the booth and said, "Martin Goddard of Hamilton, Bradley, and Associates."

Lord Beverley's brow shot up.

Adam cleared his throat and said, "Goddard, this is Lord Beverley, Lord Malton's brother."

Goddard's smug expression faltered, likely as he calculated what sort of rank the brother of a duke would have and how damning of a social faux pas he'd just committed. "We act as agents in real estate transactions and property settlements," Goddard blundered on. "If you should ever find yourself in the market for an estate of your own."

"I see," Lord Beverley said, tilting his head up and staring down his nose at Goddard. "Oh, look. My niece and nephew are moving on." Lord Beverley stepped away from Goddard's booth without another glance at him.

Adam would have snorted with laughter at the obvious snub if Goddard hadn't slipped out from behind the booth and stepped into his path before he could follow.

"What do you think you are on about, keeping company with gentlemen like that?" Goddard hissed.

"You forget, Goddard. I am a gentleman as well," Adam defended himself.

Goddard snorted. "In name only. You've no more of a right to give yourself airs by keeping company with peers than that costermonger over there." He flung his hand out to one of the other booths.

Adam sighed. He'd grown tired of the imagined rivalry Goddard had manufactured between the two of them years ago, and all because Adam had won some silly prize at their grammar school's celebration after Trafalgar.

"You know I have my eye on that parcel of land belonging to Wodehouse Abbey, that so-called woods," Goddard went on in a low voice. "Once I convince Lord Malton to sever it from his estate and sell it so that a mill can be built there, my fortune will be made. I won't have you whispering in anyone's ears, telling them not to sell."

"I have no intention of doing such a thing," Adam told him with a frown. "As I understand it, Lord

Malton simply isn't interested in dividing up his estate in any manner. And why should he be?"

"Because I could make a fortune," Goddard said, stepping threateningly toward Adam. "You're just jealous because—"

That was as far as Goddard got before a sharp shout of, "Step back!" blasted from several yards to the side.

Adam jumped as much as Goddard did at the sound, but instantly warmed when he turned to find Septimus striding toward them, his face like thunderclouds at sea. The only part of Adam jumping after that was the part that his breeches wouldn't be able to do anything to hide if he wasn't careful.

"Has this man accosted you?" Septimus asked as he came to stand between Adam and Goddard, his broad-chested, masculine presence turning Adam's knees to jelly. Goddard's too, by the look of it, but for drastically different reasons.

"W-who are you, sir? And what right have you to interfere in a private matter between friends?" Goddard asked, visibly quaking as he did. He wasted no time in leaping back behind his booth, as if it were a shield that could protect him.

"Is he your friend?" Septimus asked, his expression immediately regretful of his actions.

"In a manner of speaking," Adam murmured. "Septimus Bolton, I'd like you to meet an old acquaintance of mine from childhood, Martin Goddard."

Goddard attempted to ingratiate himself to Septimus by smiling as though nothing were amiss and asking, "Have you any need of purchasing land to build a home or business, Mr. Bolton?"

"No," Septimus answered bluntly, then cupped Adam's elbow and marched him off in the direction where Lord Beverley had caught up with Lord Copeland and the children.

A dozen wild emotions charged through Adam all at once. He crowed over the way Septimus had come to his rescue when he assumed there was a threat. He admired the way Septimus hadn't stood for any of Goddard's silly, preening behavior. And, God help him, he throbbed with arousal at the way Septimus manhandled him over to the others, almost as though he were jealous at the way Adam had been talking to another man. It went against every shred of pride and dignity Adam had to be ordered about in such a way, but it equally satisfied a deep, pervasive need in him that he was only peripherally aware of having. If he reacted so strongly to Septimus simply clasping a hand around his elbow, what would it feel like to have the man hold his arms mercilessly over his head as he pinned him down with that powerful body of his.

The only thing that snapped Adam out of his fantasy was the knowing grin he caught from Lord Beverley. Perhaps he shouldn't have been so open with the man after all.

"Mr. Bolton, Mr. Bolton, look," Lord Francis said with a bright smile, practically dancing in his place as he pointed to a large placard posted on the side of one of the booths. "There's a competition of strength down on the beach in fifteen minutes, and the prize is an entire barrel of mackerel!"

"You must enter," Lady Eliza added. "Lord Copeland says you're the strongest man he has ever known."

"I like mackerel for supper," Lord Francis added, as though that would be the deciding factor in persuading Septimus to enter the competition.

Septimus frowned at Lord Copeland and Lord

Beverley, pursed his lips, and sighed. "I wonder whose idea this is," he said.

"It could be quite educational for the children," Adam said, trying to keep his grin in check. The last thing Septimus likely needed was him teasing right along with Lord Beverley and Lord Copeland, but it was irresistible.

"Educational?" Septimus raised one eyebrow.

Adam shrugged, his mouth quivering as he lost his battle not to beam at the man. "Consider it competing for the honor of Wodehouse Abbey, then. The same as you would compete for your ship before."

That argument seemed to sway Septimus, but also to fill his expression with wistfulness that twisted Adam's heart in his chest. Septimus might have been powerful and protective, but he was also lost and hurting. The combination spun Adam's head like strong wine.

"All right," Septimus sighed, letting go of Adam's elbow at last. "I'll do it." He marched ahead, following the arrow on the sign that pointed the way to the beach.

Adam rubbed his elbow absently, missing Septimus's touch already, and followed, eager to discover just how strong his champion was.

5

By the time their group made it down to what passed for a beach, Septimus had his doubts about whether he was in his right mind. His friends, the children, and most particularly Adam seemed to think he was some sort of champion who couldn't possibly lose a contest of strength. Septimus knew better. He was more than capable of losing a great many things, and in his present company, defeat would be extraordinarily painful. At the same time, he would rather have faced defeat than disappoint the children.

No, that was a lie. As they crossed the last barrier between the waterfront streets at the edge of Hull and the silty bank of the River Humber that represented a beach for the competition, Septimus was forced to admit to himself that he was competing for Adam, and for Adam only—to show off his strength, to attempt to impress the gorgeous young man, and to win a prize for him, the way knights of old would win so that they could bestow favors on their ladies fair.

There was something both thrilling and lowering about the entire endeavor.

"Oh, look," Lord Francis exclaimed, pointing to the odd line of eight ropes extending far into the river. "Is that the competition? What sort of a competition is it?"

"I don't see much of a challenge in hauling a line in from the river," Red said skeptically.

Septimus could see at once there was more to it than that. The ropes were taut, suggesting they were affixed to something heavy under the water, deep in the river. The challenge would be to haul in whatever that was to the beach. It instantly reminded Septimus of bringing in some of the larger nets his father had cast into the ocean when he was a lad, on days when they caught so much it nearly sank the boat.

"It looks as though men are signing up to compete over there," Adam said, stepping close enough to rest a hand on Septimus's shoulder as he pointed to a table with a large keg—presumably of mackerel—at one end, and a middle-aged man taking down names at the other.

Septimus barely saw either of those things, though. The moment Adam's hand touched his shoulder, it was as though a snap of lightning passed through him. Heat radiated from the spot where their bodies connected, and even though it was nothing more than a hand and a shoulder, his entire body thrilled to the touch.

He glanced sideways at Adam's hand, but he must have worn too fierce an expression. Adam withdrew as though Septimus were made of fire and sent him a bashful smile of apology. The smile was even more potent than the man's touch. Septimus sucked in a breath, and he had to force himself to stride forward to the table before he did something he'd regret, like grasp the man's patrician face between his calloused hands and kiss him into oblivion.

"Huzzah, Mr. Bolton," Lady Eliza called after him,

even though he'd hardly done anything to deserve such encouragement yet. "You will win the prize, I am certain."

Only as an afterthought did Septimus twist to send the young noblewoman a smile. He enjoyed children. Most of the time, he found them charming and sweet. But he didn't know the first thing about how one behaved around a ten-year-old girl who ranked far higher socially than he ever would. At least Lady Eliza and her brother seemed more like normal children than future nobs.

"I can tell at a glance that you have come to register for the competition, sir," the middle-aged man sitting at the table said with an eager smile as Septimus approached. He swept Septimus with an assessing glance, as if gauging whether the winner of the contest had just arrived. "Your name, sir?" he asked, pencil poised over the sheet of paper in front of him.

"Septimus Bolton," Septimus answered, then went straight to, "Is it truly necessary to register for a simple contest?"

"I have my reasons," the man said. When he finished writing Septimus's name, he extended a hand. "Robert Carver."

Septimus shook the man's hand with a nod, impressed by how firm Carver's grip was and by the callouses on his hands. Carver was a working man, too.

"We've room for one more competitor," Carver went on, glancing past Septimus to where another burly, bearded man had just approached the table, "and it appears to be you, Malcolm."

"My Betsy has her eye on those mackerel," Malcolm, said, smiling with pride. "She gets a mighty craving for them when she's in the family way."

Carver grinned brightly and wrote the man's name

under Septimus's as though he already knew it well. "How many is this, then?" he asked.

"Six, God bless her," Malcolm said with pride. "She keeps telling me it feels like twins, but she's said that every time, and we've yet to have any."

"Best of luck to her this time," Carver said with a laugh, standing. He walked around the end of the table, approaching a group of men who'd been standing around chatting, then leading everyone down to where the ropes were affixed to the shore.

Septimus followed, though he spared a glance for his competitor, Malcolm. The man looked to be of an age with him, though perhaps not quite as weathered as he was. Malcolm raised a hand to wave to a small cluster that must have been his family waiting atop a small section of wall that bordered the silty beach. Septimus's heart squeezed at the sight of the round-faced woman and children. They were all clearly fond of Malcolm, which reminded Septimus of his own family back in Cornwall. By the looks of them, they could use a bit of feeding up. Septimus decided then and there that as much as Lord Francis loved mackerel for supper, he would purposely lose the contest, because Malcolm and his family needed the prize more.

No sooner had he reached that conclusion than his gaze shifted on, only to find that Adam had separated from the others and walked back to the roadside so that he could speak to a trio of finely-dressed young women who appeared to have come to see the show. By their bonnets and parasols and their rosy-cheeked complexions, it was clear they were gentry of some sort. It was equally clear that all three of them adored Adam.

"As you can see," Carver began in a loud voice, forcing Septimus's attention away from the scene unfolding by the road—a scene that had his throat constricting and his stomach twisting, "here we have eight ropes. They are each attached to nets containing equal weights of flotsam and jetsam. The competition is simple. At my call, whoever hauls their load to shore and carries it to the other side of that rope there—" he pointed to a rope placed farther up the beach, "—will win the keg of mackerel. And a fine catch that was too," he added with a cheery laugh. "Now, take your mark."

The competitors stepped up to a second rope that was placed close to the edge of the water. Septimus glanced back to Adam and the ladies just as the ladies burst into laughter over something Adam had said. They all seemed to know each other, perhaps quite well. One of the ladies, dressed in light blue, seemed particularly taken with Adam, and Adam stood quite close to her.

"Mr. Bolton, if you please," Carver called to him.

Septimus grunted and shook himself, then forced his eyes away as he stepped up to the rope. He couldn't have been wrong about Adam, could he? Every sign had been there, and they had been quite clear. Overt, even. He was dead certain the man had been flirting with him at the lake that morning, displaying himself like a strumpet. Now, however, as Septimus peeked over his shoulder at the sound of Adam's laughter, he questioned everything.

"Gentlemen, you may pick up your rope," Carver announced.

Septimus swallowed, then bent to grasp the thick rope. Even if he had been right, Adam was the son of a baron. Chances were that it was incumbent upon him to marry and produce an heir. Although Septimus could not remember whether Adam was, in fact, his father's heir. Had he not said something about being a younger son and—

"Haul!" Carver shouted, cracking through Septimus's thoughts as though he'd fired a canon.

Septimus pulled on the rope as hard as he could, as though he'd been issued orders by his captain in the heat of battle. Carver was the very devil himself. Whatever load rested under the surface of the water, it was far heavier than Septimus—or any of the other competitors, by the look of things—had anticipated. Determination took over Septimus's mind, and he tugged on the rope for all he was worth. Damn noblemen and their deceptive ways. His muscles burned with his efforts to haul on the rope. He'd had enough of being treated like a friend by men whose only qualification was the womb they had emerged from. Adam was just like Captain Wallace, for all he knew. He refused to be overshadowed again. He'd made his way up in the world by the sweat of his own brow once before, and he could do it again. His breath came in shorter and shorter gasps as the heat of exertion blasted through him. Damn Adam for tempting him into thinking he could have something sweet and refined. The man had goaded him into making a fool of himself in the competition, and he likely wasn't even watching now.

He doubled his efforts as the net full of rubbish emerged from the water. Carver had secured everything from old barrels to broken anchors in both Septimus's and the others' nets. A few of the competitors gave up when they realized what they were up against, but not Septimus, and not Malcolm either.

"Huzzah, Mr. Bolton!" Lady Eliza called from somewhere behind Septimus.

"Hurrah!" Adam's voice echoed as well.

Septimus nearly lost his grip on the rope. He failed to resist the temptation to check over his shoulder to see if Adam was watching. Sure enough, he was. Not only watching, but he had stepped away from the ladies and had his eyes fixed on Septimus.

"He's getting ahead of you," Adam called.

Something that felt very much like a burst of pride shot through Septimus, and he hauled his line harder, muscles burning. The crowd that had gathered to watch the competition cheered louder and louder as both he and Malcolm brought their loads closer to the shore. Septimus forgot all about his decision to allow Malcolm to win. He forgot about everything but being Adam's champion, about winning him as well as the prize. Above the shouts and cries of dozens of other spectators, he only heard Adam's voice, spurring him on.

Somewhere in the back of his mind, he knew he was a damn fool for shifting like a boat tossed on stormy seas from resenting Adam to wanting only to win for him within the space of a few quickened heartbeats. And then he told himself he would ponder the whole thing later as the load in his net emerged fully from the water. Malcolm was only a few feet behind him, so he worked with as much concentration as he could muster to drag the load over the line, then to lift it to his back and shoulders so he could carry it. Malcolm stayed only a few feet behind him as He growled and staggered up the beach to the finish rope.

At one point, Septimus caught sight of Adam breaking fully away from his lady friends to rush to the finish. He nearly tripped over himself then. Only through sheer will and determination did he push on, dropping his load with a grunt moments before Malcolm did the same. The crowd burst into cheers for all of them.

"We have a winner," Carver declared. "Congratulations, Mr. Bolton."

The crowd applauded. Malcolm smiled through his disappointment, panting and sweating, as he reached for Septimus's hand. Along the road, the three ladies caught up to Adam as he beamed across at Septimus. The lady in blue grabbed his arm, and Adam didn't shake her off. Septimus's spirits sank as fast as they'd risen.

"You should take the prize," he panted, facing Malcolm. "You've a family to care for."

Carver marched up to join them in time to hear the conversation.

"And you do not?" Malcolm asked, still winded and definitely surprised.

Septimus shook his head. "I am a guest at Wodehouse Abbey for the summer. I served with Lord Beverley aboard the *Majesty*."

"I... I thank you for your generosity and your service," Malcolm said, sending a quick smile to his wife near the road.

"Go on and take her your prize." Septimus waved for Malcolm to collect the keg.

As soon as he stepped away, Carver faced Septimus fully and smiled. "That was extraordinarily generous of you," he said with a calculated look. "And I'm impressed with your strength and technique."

Septimus nodded in thanks and said, "I was raised as the son of a fisherman in Cornwall and have served in His Majesty's Navy since I was a lad."

"But not now that the war is over," Carver guessed.

Septimus could only nod in response. His attention was already being pulled away from the conversation as Red, Barrett, and the children joined the ladies crowding around Adam. They all made a perfect picture together—fine clothes, clear complexions, smiles that hinted not one of them had ever known hardship.

"You say you're staying near Hull for the summer?" Carver asked.

Septimus turned his attention back to the man. "I am."

Carver shifted his stance, fixing Septimus with another thoughtful look. "I own a fishing operation here in Hull. I could always use men with your strength and skill. If you find yourself in need of employment, do seek me out."

Septimus didn't know what to think. The offer of employment was generous, and it did tempt him a bit. But working as a fisherman again after serving as sailing master on the *Majesty* was a large step backwards for him. After his rejection from the Admiralty, he'd sent a letter of appeal, as well as a few others begging for help in his endeavors from men he believed would speak for him. Accepting defeat and a position as a fisherman was out of the question.

"You are too kind," he said, nodding to Carver with what he hoped came off as a friendly smile and not a grimace. "I will let you know."

They parted ways, and Septimus made his way gingerly over to the group of his friends. He prayed that the tumult he was experiencing didn't show on his face, and especially that Adam didn't notice it.

"Do you not win the mackerel for winning the competition?" Lord Francis asked him, his lower lip thrust out in a pout.

"I chose to give it to Mr. Malcolm," Septimus said. "I believe he and his family need it more than we do at Wodehouse Abbey."

"But I wanted mackerel for supper," Lord Francis sighed.

His sister swatted his arm. "Uncle Redmond can buy you mackerel for supper," she hissed.

"How extraordinarily generous of you," Adam said, drawing Septimus's attention once again. Septimus gulped at the admiring smile Adam wore, the warmth in his eyes, and the heated approval that he did nothing to hide. All while the lady in blue continued to cling to his arm and grin at him as though he were the prize she'd won.

The entire thing was close to doing Septimus's head in. "If you will excuse me," he said in a deep grumble, "I think it would be wise for me to find a pint or even water, if there is any to be found."

"Oh, yes," the lady in blue said. "We must treat your champion to tea and cakes, since he has given up his prize. Do you not agree, Mr. Seymour?" She batted her eyelashes at Adam.

Septimus rethought the idea of putting anything in his stomach. He wasn't sure he could keep it down as their group headed back toward the center of Hull. The two other ladies rushed to have Red and Barrett escort them, which left Septimus walking behind them, Lady Eliza and Lord Francis on either side. At least Lord Francis took his hand, making him feel as though someone still thought highly of him.

All the while, though, even once the flighty ladies located a booth selling tea back in the square where the heart of the festival was set up, Septimus could hardly take his eyes off of Adam, even though he wanted to. He simply could not shake the feeling that, once again, he was being played for a fool by a nobleman. He kept his distance from the rest of the group, pretending to be interested in a series of pamphlets about Luddism and the necessity of destroying the machinery of industrialization, as Adam engaged in a lively conversation with the lady in blue and one of her friends.

"Lady Helena could do much better for herself, if you ask me," a man spoke nearby where Septimus loitered, shocking him out of what he'd thought were clandestine observations. Septimus turned to find Martin Goddard, Adam's rival, leaning out of the booth beside him. He hadn't realized he'd wandered close to Goddard's booth. "All of them could," Goddard went on. "I've been trying to tell Lady Helena for months that she could have a far more comfortable life with a businessman such as myself than with a fool who thinks all the world's problems could be solved by educating urchins." He snorted.

Septimus's brow went up as he glanced from Adam and the lady in blue, Lady Helena, to Goddard. He was in no mood to pretend civility, so he bluntly said, "You fancy the woman yourself?"

Goddard straightened, looking offended. "Of course, I do. Half of Hull fancies her. Her father is a merchant and on the town council."

"But she has designs on Mr. Seymour?" Septimus asked. It was, perhaps, beneath him and made him feel like one of the gossiping fishwives he'd grown up around, but his bruised pride needed to know just how big of an arse he'd made of himself.

"She fancies him," Goddard growled, crossing his arms. "All the ladies do. None of them are going to win him, though."

Sudden worry on Adam's behalf gripped Septimus. "Why not?" he asked.

Goddard sniffed and shrugged. "No well-born lady's father will allow his daughter to marry a man with no greater prospects than a fantasy of some sort of *charity* school. His esteemed family is poor, despite their title. He has nothing to offer other than a smile. I, on the other hand, am well on my way to making a fortune. Every one of those ladies will be fawning over me by the end of the year, just you wait." His smile was smug and off-putting.

Septimus wasn't sure whether to grin or frown. Goddard had answered more questions than he knew. The man was a petty, small-minded boor who was jealous of Adam, and likely anyone else who worked for the things he wanted to be given in life. And yet, he'd also given Septimus the impression that Adam wasn't in immediate danger of engaging himself to a woman, either for love or material gain.

At the same time, as Septimus made his way back to the group, his heart wasn't content. The only thing the day had proved so far was that Septimus had fallen back into his old, tired patterns of wanting pretty, lofty things that he couldn't have. Some things in life were for him and others weren't. It was a tale as old as the titles that men like Red, Barrett, and Captain Wallace had inherited through the generations of their blue-blooded families. Septimus could admire Adam from afar all he wanted, he could even lust after the man in secret, but he was more certain than ever that anything more was utterly impossible. The sooner he got back to the sea where he belonged, the better.

6

Surely Septimus couldn't be jealous of Lady Helena, Lady Margaret, and Lady Anne, could he? Adam contemplated the question through the rest of the afternoon, as their merry group had tea together, then took in the rest of the sights, sounds, and flavors of the festival. There were plenty of performances, games, and diversions for the lot of them to partake in, even competitions for the children. Adam considered for all of two minutes that he should keep Lord Francis and Lady Eliza busy with the assignments he'd created for them that morning. before allowing them to simply partake in the fun of the festival.

If only he could truly embrace that fun as well.

"Are you not enjoying yourself, Bolton?" he asked Septimus later in the afternoon, when the two of them veered off from the rest of the group for a moment as Lord Beverley and Lord Copeland stood with the ladies and the children, watching a troupe of Morris dancers that had come all the way from York for the occasion.

Septimus grunted, as if surprised, and dragged his gaze from the dancers to Adam. "I am enjoying myself," he answered in a tone that would be better suited to sitting through a particularly dull sermon.

"Only, you seem a bit put out about something," Adam went on. He shouldn't have goaded Septimus, considering he had a fair idea what had taken the smile off the man's face, but he couldn't help himself.

"The competition earlier tired me," Septimus mumbled, then did a terrible job of pretending he was fascinated by the dancers.

Adam hid his grin by pretending interest in the dancers as well. Septimus was jealous, which was ridiculous. Lady Helena had been a friend of his since childhood, before her family moved to Hull. It was pure coincidence that their acquaintance had renewed when he, too, moved near to Hull. He was aware that a part of her hoped he would someday take more of an interest in her, but that would certainly never happen. Adam could have come right out and said as much to Septimus, but he found the gruff man's struggle against feelings he was clearly trying to push aside to be far too endearing to bring it to an end. If he even had that within his power. In Adam's experience, if someone was determined to feel a certain way about someone or something, removing one of their reasons for those emotions would only create other excuses to hold onto the same feelings.

The rest of the day continued to be pleasant in spite of the undercurrent of tension between Adam and Septimus. Whether Lord Malton would approve of the lessons Adam had planned for his children or not, Adam was deeply satisfied to see Lord Francis and Lady Eliza so deeply engaged throughout the day. In his experience, children who were engaged in the world around them, asking questions about the novelties they saw and experiencing new and different things—be they Morris dancing or fried squid—became companionate and con-scientious adults. That was more valuable than creating an adult whose head was filled with figures and verses.

Engaged children also meant exhausted children, as they all discovered after enjoying a seaside supper of fish pie and mead for the adults, while sitting on a stretch of rocks overlooking the quiet end of the beach. After the day they'd had, Lord Francis and Lady Eliza could barely keep their eyes open long enough to walk back to the street where Lord Beverley had arranged for Wodehouse Abbey's carriage to pick them up.

The children were dead asleep by the time they reached the house just after dark.

"Do you need help disposing of them?" Lord Bev-erley asked with a teasing light in his eyes as Adam stepped down from the carriage, turning to receive a sleeping Lord Francis from the arms of Lord Copeland.

"I don't think that will be necessary, my lord," Adam said with a grateful smile. "If Mr. Bolton will just help by carrying Lady Eliza up to the nursery, we'll be able to hand them off to Ivy, and the lot of you will be free to enjoy your evening as you see fit."

"I don't think there's a single part of me left that has the energy to enjoy anything," Lord Copeland laughed as he, too, stepped down from the carriage. "As dull as it sounds, I think I'll make an early night of it."

"That is dull," Lord Beverley teased him. "And I intend to do the same thing."

"An early night tonight so that we might all stay out until dawn on Thursday, menacing half the pubs in Hull with our presence," Lord Beverley laughed, thumping Lord Copeland's shoulder. "You do plan to join us, do you not, Septimus?" he called back into the carriage, using Septimus's given name, now that they were in the private sphere of home.

Adam was impressed by the informality the three men showed to each other. He assumed it came from spending so many years in such close quarters aboard ship. He'd only known the three a short time, but they seemed more like brothers than mere gentlemanly acquaintances to him. In fact, they were far closer than he was with his own brothers.

Septimus was slow to answer the question. He stepped carefully out of the carriage, Lady Eliza's sleeping form flopped over him like a particularly sprawling shawl. She was too big to be carried, and yet Septimus managed her as though she were a sack of feathers. For the second time that day, a show of Septimus's strength had Adam's insides trembling. He forced himself to turn away and calm down. At least until he was able to hand Lord Francis over to the care of Ivy, the nursemaid.

"I will go out with you," Septimus finally answered, as they started up the front steps into the house, "as long as the carousing does not get out of hand."

"Does your carousing tend to get out of hand?" Adam asked, flashing an eager grin at Septimus before glancing questioningly at the others.

Lord Beverley and Lord Copeland exchanged a look, then laughed.

"We would not be living up to our reputations as officers of the Royal Navy if it didn't," Lord Beverley answered.

"Though we cause far more trouble when our

mates from the *Hawk* are with us," Lord Copeland said with an intriguing wink for Lord Beverley.

"Yes, well, Lucas, Spencer, and Clarence will be joining us as soon as their business in London is concluded," Lord Beverley said, "and then you'll see."

"God help us all," Septimus mumbled.

Adam's lips twitched into a grin. He didn't think Septimus intended his words to be overheard, and when he noticed Adam's reaction, his face colored and he stepped ahead of the rest of them, taking the grand staircase two steps at a time, even with a ten-year-old girl in his arms.

"When are the others expected?" Adam asked as the rest of them followed Septimus and Lady Eliza up the stairs.

Lord Beverley shrugged. "It could be a fortnight or it could be a month. There's no telling when it comes to Admiralty business."

"And I know how much you are looking forward to seeing Lucas once more," Lord Copeland said with a wry, sideways grin, nudging Lord Beverley's arm.

"Only because he still owes me three guineas after losing that bet," Lord Beverly said in return.

Even a dolt could see that there were more reasons than that. Adam hid his grin by turning his head to check on Lord Francis as he stirred, then settled back into sleep against his shoulder. He was curious to see what would happen when this Lucas, whoever he was, arrived at Wodehouse Abbey.

At present, however, Adam had his own intricate friendships to work out. Septimus had paused at the first landing with a confused look on his face, clearly not certain where the nursery was. When Lord Beverley and Lord Copeland headed down the hall into the wing of the house where their bedrooms were located, chatting as they went, Adam nodded for Septimus to continue up to the second floor with Lady Eliza.

"Are you looking forward to your friends from the *Hawk* joining the party here at Wodehouse Abbey?" Adam asked as they fell into step.

"It will be good to see them again," Septimus said without looking at him. His tone wasn't precisely off-putting, but Adam had the impression Septimus wasn't in the mood for conversation. Or perhaps simply not conversation with *him*.

"I trust these friends are officers from the *Hawk*?" he asked on, regardless of the wall Septimus had tried to put up between them.

Septimus hesitated—as Adam had learned he had a tendency to do—before answering, "Lord Lucas Salterford, Lord Spencer Brightling, and Mr. Clarence Bond."

"More nefarious nobs?" Adam asked.

He shouldn't have teased Septimus for his prejudices, he absolutely should not have. Septimus scowled at him in response, seeming to prove it even more. But in the short time that they'd known each other Adam had discovered that few things were more delightful than getting under Septimus's skin, like a burr under a saddle, and irritating him until the man couldn't stand still.

"They are my friends because they have proved themselves to me," Septimus said, raising his voice a bit, then lowering it when Lady Eliza sucked in a breath, waking up. She tensed for a moment before sagging against Septimus and tightening her grip around his neck.

Adam had never found himself jealous of a ten-year-old girl before, but the way Lady Eliza had wrapped herself around Septimus's strong form showed him that there was a first time for everything.

"I wonder," he said, "what it takes for a man to prove himself to you."

Septimus glanced sideways at him, but was spared having to answer as they reached the nursery.

"I was wondering what became of the lot of you," Ivy said, sliding Lord Francis out of Adam's arms and into her surprisingly strong ones. Ivy was solid and stocky, and Adam suspected she could have given Septimus and Mr. Malcolm stiff competition that morning.

"I trust you enjoyed your surprise off-day?" Adam teased her in return. "Did you polish off that gothic novel I know you've been reading?"

"Oh!" Ivy exclaimed, then burst into giggles as she carried Lord Francis to his bed and settled him so that she could undress him for the night. "Listen to you."

"Where should I put Lady Eliza?" Septimus asked in a grumble, frowning.

It was all Adam could do not to laugh. First Lady Helena and her friends, and now Ivy? It was strangely flattering to have the man so jealous over him for so many reasons.

"I can put myself to bed," Lady Eliza murmured, still half asleep, attempting to wriggle out of Septimus's arms.

She stayed where she was, though, until Adam gestured for Septimus to follow him out of Lord Francis's room in the nursery, across the playroom, and on to Lady Eliza's bedroom. Lady Eliza did fumble her way out of Septimus's arms then, though instead of putting herself to bed as she declared she would, she merely slumped over to her bed and crawled atop the covers.

"Should we..." Septimus began, gesturing to her, his cheeks going pink.

"Most certainly not." Adam grinned. "That job belongs firmly to Ivy."

They walked back out to the playroom. Adam told Ivy they were leaving, and she bid them goodnight. Once they were in the hall, heading back to the wing of the house where Septimus had his guestroom, Adam deliberately slowed his steps.

"You are good with children," Septimus said, as they neared the stairs at the end of the hall.

That opening salvo of conversation surprised Adam. "Thank you," he said. "I've always liked them. In spite of being a baron's son, I always enjoyed helping the other children at school."

Septimus frowned at him. "You did not have a private tutor, such as yourself?"

"No," Adam laughed. "My father could barely afford to keep a butler and a maid. I'm still not certain how he managed the tuition for my brothers and me to attend a local grammar school near Whitby. I suspect, though I have no proof, that my very willingness to help out with the younger children, to teach a few of their lessons when I got older, meant I was able to attend tuition-free."

Septimus's face relaxed a bit and his brow inched up, but he said nothing. Not until they reached the stairs and started down. "I am sorry that I assumed your father's title meant you were well-off."

"We were never poor," Adam told him. "It was just that there were quite a few of us, and the estate's income never quite covered expenses. And before you ask, no, Father's estate was nothing at all like Wodehouse Abbey. It was little more than a crumbling country house in constant need of repairs, with a few baronial fields around it that yielded less and less with each passing year."

They reached the first floor and the hallway containing the guest rooms that were currently in use. If he found it odd that Adam continued to follow him as he walked slowly down the dark hall, even though Adam's own bedchamber was on the same floor as the nursery, Septimus didn't say anything. Adam had learned earlier that Septimus's guest room was at the far end of the hall.

"I suppose, with an estate in that sort of condition," Septimus said with painful slowness, "it is incumbent upon all of your father's sons to marry money."

The implied question was so sweet and so sheepishly not-asked that Adam had a hard time keeping his grin in check. "My eldest brother Andrew married a viscount's daughter last year," he said. "My other brother Ansel married an industrialist's daughter just three months ago. And my sister Anne is engaged to a rather prosperous farmer with whom she is deeply in love. Therefore, I believe my family's situation is improving quite a bit." Which was another, frustrating reason potential patrons of his school were constantly telling him to impose on his family connections for funding.

They paused at the end of the hall, just outside of Septimus's guestroom door. Light from the nearly full moon shown down through the window at the end of the hall, making it brighter than would have been there otherwise. Septimus eyed Adam warily, as if he'd received the answer to the question he hadn't asked, but had developed more questions because of it. Adam decided to put the man out of his misery.

"Lady Helena is a friend of mine from childhood,"

he said. "Her mother and mine were close before Lady Helena's family moved to Hull. We renewed our acquaintance when I joined Lord Malton's household, and I became acquainted with Lady Margaret and Lady Anne through her, but there is no greater attachment, nor any sort of understanding between any of us, beyond casual friendship." He took a step closer to Septimus. "And I believe you understand why."

He glanced up at Septimus as he moved close enough to feel the heat radiating from the large man's body. Adam made no effort whatsoever to hide the desire he felt pulsing through every inch of him. He wasn't usually as bold or aggressive as all that, but something about Septimus Bolton made him challenge himself, and Septimus.

"You're the one that I want," he said impetuously, resting a hand on Septimus's chest. The man's heart raced like the wind over the moors under his touch. "I wanted you from the first moment I saw you, which I will admit, is not something I experience with any regularity. In fact, I don't believe I've ever felt such a deep and gripping desire at the first sight of a man." He brushed his hand up to Septimus's shoulder, teasing his fingers against the warm skin above the man's collar.

"You shouldn't..." Septimus tried, his voice coming out rough and ragged.

That was as far as he got. Adam clasped his hands on either side of Septimus's face, loving the rasp of a day's stubble against his palms, and slanted his mouth over his. He thrilled at Septimus's sharp intake of breath as their mouths met, and the way Septimus shuddered as Adam boldly drew his tongue along the seam of the man's barely parted lips. There was so much promise in the energy that throbbed between the two of them, and Adam was ready to explore all of it.

But as he attempted to deepen their kiss, Septimus pulled away, rolling to the side before planting his back against the door to his room and grasping the handle. "We cannot do this," he said in a harsh whisper.

Adam swallowed the burst of frustration that the rejection brought with it. "Please explain," he said, as though a student had given him an unclear answer to an exam question. "We cannot do this because you do not want to, or for some other reason?"

"I—" Septimus's mouth hung open for a moment before he found the power to continue with, "It is not because I do not wish to," he said, barely above a whisper. "I am not made of stone. I want to as much as —" He stopped himself, pursing his lips. "You are too young," he went on in clipped tones, standing straighter, as though he'd internally slapped himself into decent behavior. "Our stations in life are too different. Our temperaments and our lots in life are too different as well. We cannot."

Adam clenched his jaw for a moment, willing himself to patience. "You do not take me seriously," he said, wishing he didn't sound so hurt. Pouting was no way to seduce a man like Septimus. All the same, he found himself continuing on with, "No one takes me seriously. You see only my youth, my father's meager title, and my affable disposition, and you assume I am silly somehow."

"I never said that." Septimus's back stiffened, as though Adam had insulted him.

"You did not need to." Adam tilted his chin up. "Enough men have said it before you."

Internally, Adam winced, knowing he sounded

every bit the victim that he was claiming not to be.

"I am not those men," Septimus said, a hint of fire in his eyes that reminded Adam of the possessiveness he'd seen when Septimus defended him against Goddard.

"Then prove it," Adam said.

For a second time, he threw caution to the wind and moved into Septimus. This time, with Septimus's back already against the door to his room, there was no way for the bigger man to get away. Adam clasped a hand around the back of Septimus's neck and drew him down for another kiss. He wasn't as circumspect this time, thrusting his tongue against Septimus's and taking what he wanted.

Septimus's response was immediate and clear. He made a sound of need deep in his throat, and his hands moved to Adam's hips. Adam arched into him, intending to show Septimus the evidence of what he did to him by grinding his erection against Septimus's hip, but found Septimus just as hard as he was when he did. That was like touching a match to gunpowder, as far as Adam was concerned. He moaned with need, plying his entire body against Septimus's and jerking against him. It was laughably crude of him, but after so long without so much as an object of fantasy to heat his blood, having Septimus there, in his arms, their tongues entwined as Adam sucked Septimus's into his mouth, was too much. He wanted the heat and the passion. He wanted to open himself to Septimus in every way. He wanted the man inside of him, brutishly, mercilessly, and he wanted to give him as much as he took.

But once again, Septimus wrenched away from him with a ripping gasp. "We cannot," he panted, emphasizing both words. "We..." He seemed to scramble for some clearer, more rational explanation, but could only shake his head and repeat, "cannot."

"But—"

Adam didn't have a chance to form his sentence before Septimus turned the handle of the door behind him and leapt back into the room. He didn't have time to think about charging after him before Septimus closed the door in his face. It wasn't a slam. In fact, he shut the door with surprising gentleness. But the click of the lock turning a moment later was as painful as if the door had smashed into Adam's nose.

He took a step back, suddenly remembering to breathe. Pain throbbed through him—both the pain of an erection denied and the ache of rejection in his heart. He rubbed a hand over his chest, biting his kiss-swollen lip. Part of him wanted to bang on Septimus's door and demand entrance, demand that the man let him into his life as well as into his bed. The part of him that knew better forced him to take another step back.

He drew in a shaking breath, forcing his nerves to steady and his thoughts to catch up to his emotions. Septimus wanted him. That was a victory. The pulse between them was real and potent. There was no need to rush into battle. They had the entire summer ahead of them. A siege was as good as an attack when it came to breaching an enemy's walls, and Septimus was far from being his enemy.

No, he thought as he took yet another step back, then turned to stride down the hall and back up to the nursery wing and his own room, he had no need to rush. Septimus wasn't going anywhere, and if he played the game right and proved that the two of them were a match for each other, he could win Septimus over in no time.

7

Try as he did, Septimus couldn't get the taste of Adam off his lips or the feel of his lithe body out of his skin. And they'd both been fully clothed for the two earth-shattering, time-stopping kisses. What had the young man been thinking, accosting him in the hall as he had? 'Accosting' wasn't even the right word. Reaching into his heart, and his cock, and turning his world inside out was more like it.

It was madness on every level, and even before Septimus's head hit his pillow that night, he'd made up his mind that the only solution to the throbbing, pulsing, all-consuming need that Adam's kisses had left him with was to avoid the young man entirely. His life was already adrift without a ship's wheel in his hand. He was already far too unsettled by the unasked-for changes in his life to add something as confusing as desire and attraction to the mix. He didn't need the heat that pulsed through him every time Adam smiled or his full-bodied reaction every time Adam leaned forward, pulling his breeches tight, or took the stairs with graceful steps. And he most certainly did not need to surrender the fate of his future into yet another fickle nobleman's hands.

Septimus was determined to go out of his way not to encounter Adam at all. It was why he woke before dawn every morning for the next week, making his way down to the lake for a swim without the distraction of the young man. He most certainly did not conceal himself in the small boathouse at the base of the dock, waiting and watching until Adam wandered down to the lakeside, stripped off his clothes and dove into the shimmering water, every morning. He refused to steal glances down the supper table at Adam during every interminable supper they all ate together. He did not linger outside of the nursery when Adam was conducting his lessons for Lord Francis and Lady Eliza, just to hear the sound of Adam's voice and his laughter. And under no circumstances did he linger by the open windows in the library to spy on Adam and Red discussing the children's progress as they walked in the garden, anxious that Adam would find Red more appealing than he was.

"You're worse than an aging spinster with her last potential beau at the end of the season." Barrett's laughing voice jerked Septimus out of his observations of Red and Adam in the library.

Septimus leapt away from the window, pacing to the other side of the room and pulling a dusty volume from the shelf. "I do not know what you mean," he growled, cracking the book's spine in his haste to open it. He'd picked up a tome entitled *Heaven and Hell*, by Emanuel Swedenborg. As soon as he saw as much, he let out a wry huff of a laugh. That described the situation perfectly.

Barrett craned his neck as he peeked out the window, then strolled across the room to Septimus, chuckling. "They didn't hear or see you, if that makes a difference."

Inwardly, Septimus let out a sigh of relief. If enough time passed with Adam believing he wasn't interested, perhaps the young man would spare him the misery of tangled emotions and unrequited lust by forgetting about him.

Which would bring with it an entirely different sort of misery.

"You are imagining things," he told Barrett, knowing full well his friend wouldn't be fooled. "I am merely restless. This is the longest I've ever gone without any sort of occupation. I can barely think without a ship's deck under my feet."

"Or perhaps you can barely think without a nubile young tutor's body under yours," Barrett teased him with a rake's grin.

Septimus snapped his book shut. "I cannot imagine what you are talking about." He shoved the book back onto the shelf—or at least tried. He missed, nicked the bottom corner of the book, and dropped it to the floor with a thud.

Barrett's grin twitched and his eyes flashed as though he were having the time of his life. "I think you can imagine it all too clearly, which is why you're so discomposed."

"I can assure you, you are mistaken," Septimus said, raising his voice and marching away from Barrett.

He didn't know where he was going, though, and only ended up stranded on the other side of the library with nothing to do and nothing to look at but the curtains billowing in the breeze. Somewhere on the other side of those curtains, Adam was engaged in cheerful conversation with Red. Not him.

"I am desperate for word from the Admiralty, Barrett," he confided in his friend. "They must answer my appeal in response to their denial of a commission. I have no purpose, no use on dry land. I do not know what to do with myself."

Barrett shrugged, walking to a small table crowded with decanters of spirits. "You could always drink yourself into a stupor," he suggested, uncorking one decanter, sniffing its contents, then replacing the stopper.

Septimus shook his head. "I was never one to overindulge in alcohol, like the rest of you."

"True," Barrett chuckled. He moved on to one of the bookshelves, running his fingers along the spines of the books. "You could read, take up a study of a particular subject."

"I've tried," Septimus said, sighing and shoving a hand through his hair. "Nothing holds my interest."

Barrett grinned at him as he glanced away from the books, as if he already knew which subject had thoroughly captivated Septimus's interest. He nodded to the window. "You could borrow one of Lord Malton's fine horses and go for a ride."

"I do not know how," Septimus confessed, feeling horrible for an entirely different reason. Gentlemen knew how to ride. He was certainly not one of them.

"You could learn?" Barrett suggested.

Septimus shook his head. "I have no wish to torture a horse in that manner."

That earned him a hearty laugh from Barrett, which spurred him on to say, "Or you could seek out Mr. Seymour's company and acquaint yourself better with him." He paused before adding, "Perhaps while he's bent double over the arm of an obliging chair with his breeches around his ankles while you pound—"

"I will be doing no such thing," Septimus interrupted the lewd picture Barrett painted—a picture that had him hardening at the very thought. "You mistake my character entirely if you think I would importune Mr. Seymour in such a manner."

He attempted to march across the room, intending to leave, but Barrett caught his arm, holding him to his place. "Firstly, have I ever told you how impressed I am at the way you speak like a gentleman when you become agitated."

Septimus shook out of Barrett's grip. "I do not."

Barrett ignored him. "Secondly, you're so randy for Mr. Seymour that it's driving Red and me to distraction." He didn't seem able to control the grin that twitched at the corner of his mouth. "Lord Malton's footmen are all in danger of being inappropriately propositioned, thanks to the cloud of lust following you wherever you go. Hell, at this rate, Red and I might be forced to resort to buggering each other." He shuddered comically at the thought. Even though there had been times in the past when their group of friends had been desperate enough to turn to each other for relief, Red and Barrett were like brothers. Septimus couldn't even conceive of them together.

"Do what you want with whomever you want," Septimus growled all the same. "You've never had trouble finding a friend like that before."

"I haven't, but this discussion is not about me." Before Septimus could protest, Barrett went on with, "Thirdly, Mr. Seymour is quite obviously game for whatever you have in mind. You're not the only one in heat."

Septimus's face burned. It occurred to him that a week of attempted avoidance was only making the problem worse. But that was no reason for him to go back on his principles. Even if he did, what guarantee did he have that Adam wouldn't use him for what he needed, then throw him over for a more suitable liaison?

"I just want to go back to sea," he told Barrett, letting out a heavy breath and dropping his arms to his sides. The gesture made him feel helpless and unmanly. "It's all I know and all I want to know."

Barrett made a sound of sympathy for him. "Damnably inconvenient for Bonaparte to lose his little war so that the Navy needed to be reduced."

"I would take anything," Septimus said. "As well as my appeal to the Admiralty, I've made inquiries of a few merchant captains I know in addition to asking them to support my request for a naval commission, but..." He let the words trail away and made a helpless gesture.

"My friend," Barrett said, clapping a hand on his shoulder, "you may not want to hear it, but there are more things in the world than the Navy and the sea. What you have before you is a chance to build a whole new life for yourself. You also have a handsome and clever young man who seems interested in providing you with a delicious diversion until you form that new life, at the very least. And who knows? Perhaps Mr. Seymour will provide the key to discovering your new self. You won't know unless you give it a go."

"And put myself at the mercy of another nobleman? After the way Wallace betrayed me?" Septimus huffed. "I do not think so. I am not a big enough fool to travel that route a second time." He headed for the library door.

"Seymour is barely a nobleman and you know it," Barrett called after him. "He is as far in temperament from Wallace as possible, and I'd wager he has ten times the scruples Wallace has. Do not let the betrayals of your past prevent you from pleasure in your future."

Septimus raised a hand to make a rude gesture without turning around to look Barrett in the eye as he did. He marched out of the room, no idea what he could do to ease the gnawing restlessness within him. The idea that Barrett was right about him letting the sting of Captain Wallace's betrayal and other misadventures of his past prevent him from enjoying something right in front of him that could be good was as irritating as salt spray in his eyes. At the same time, his friend didn't know. He didn't know what it felt like to be held back for no reason other than his birth. He didn't know what it was like to have a weak man take credit for his actions, and to have the entire Admiralty believe that bastard simply because of his birth. Barrett might not have believed his pain was real, but Septimus knew it was. It might not have mattered to men like Barrett and Red that his ambition had been thwarted for unjust reasons, but nothing mattered more to Septimus. He couldn't simply release those resentments for a pretty pair of eyes, an eager mouth, and an arse that he would give his right arm to be able to bury himself in.

Those frustrations stayed with him for the rest of the morning. They were so acute that he didn't bother spying on Adam once the young man returned from his conversation with Red. Septimus couldn't bear to stay where he was, shiftless and purposeless, for another moment. He might not have been able to ride, but he could walk. He set out down the lane leading away from Wodehouse Abbey shortly after luncheon, intending at least to walk into Hull to inquire at the post office if there were any letters for him that had yet to be delivered.

He calmed a bit when he reached the last stretch of land before a series of cliffs and coves that bordered the sea. The salt air reminded him of home, and the steady roar of the waves against the rocks was like a lullaby. The birds circling above, calling out to each other, were like friends from his past. At the same time, they only exacerbated the feeling that he was out of place and out of his depth on land, with nothing to anchor him and make him whole. There had to be something he could do, some employment he was suited to that would fit his ambitions. Something he could—

His thought was cut abruptly short at the sound of Adam's laughter from the beach below the cliff whose edge Septimus walked along. He froze, his insides clenching with longing at the sound, so much that he thought he must simply be imagining it in his emotional distress. Moments later, Adam's laughter rang out again, this time accompanied by that of Lord Francis and Lady Eliza.

Knowing the children were there made Septimus feel safe for some paradoxical reason. He walked to the edge of the cliff, glancing over to see the trio climbing among the rocks and tidal pools below. Adam had his shoes off, his breeches rolled up his shapely calves, and wore nothing but his waistcoat and shirtsleeves as they splashed around in the tidal pools. The children were as free and disheveled as any of Septimus's childhood companions in Cornwall—Lady Eliza with her skirt tied up around her waist and Lord Francis with his breeches rolled to above his knees—which immediately made Septimus wonder if Lord Malton knew or approved of the sort of mad-capped lessons his tutor was dolling out.

"Look, it's Mr. Bolton," Lord Francis called from below, pointing up to where Septimus stood.

Septimus felt as though he'd been caught stealing extra food from the galley. He forced himself to put on a smile and wave down at Lord Francis all the same. Of course, Adam glanced up with a look of surprise, raising a hand to shield his eyes, the sea breeze tousling his sun-kissed hair and making him look like some sort of demigod bathed in sunlight. When he waved, Septimus thought his heart might take wing.

"Mr. Bolton," Adam called up to him. "You must come down and join us."

"We're cataloging sea life," Lady Eliza informed him, as though she were counting her jewels before her presentation to the king.

"There are stairs about fifty yards that way," Adam said, pointing farther down the beach.

There was no getting out of it now. After a week of successfully avoiding Adam—reasonably successfully —Septimus had been caught. He strode along the cliff's edge as it sloped closer to the beach, located the weathered, wooden stairs, and descended the rest of the way to the sand and rocks. The sea birds above seemed to be mocking him for his thumping heart with their shrill cries. As uneasy as Septimus felt about the situation he was walking into, the give of the sand under his feet and the sharp scent of decaying sea life in the cove greeted him like old, happy memories.

"You have to remove your shoes," Lord Francis ordered as Septimus approached, as though he were already the duke he would someday become. "Otherwise, they become salty and Ivy has to clean them."

"We wouldn't want to give Ivy more work," Sep-

timus said, veering off to a cluster of large rocks that
held a collection of shoes, stockings, jackets, and other
items of clothing that had been discarded. He told
himself he would only remove his shoes and stockings
because a future duke had asked him to, but he would
retain the rest of his clothing.

Half a minute later, he had his shoes and stockings
off, his breeches rolled up, and his jacket discarded as
well. His heart pounded as though he were manning
the cannons and facing a broadside that could smash
his ship to bits.

"What is this one called?" Lady Eliza asked Adam
as the two of them stood ankle-deep in one of the tidal
pools. She held up a starfish that was about the size of
her palm.

"Ah," Adam said in his wise, teaching voice. "That
is a *Asterias rubens*, also known as the common sea
star."

"It's quite pretty," Lady Eliza said, tilting her head
to the side to smile at the creature in her hand.

"Yes, it is," Adam said.

Septimus glanced from Lady Eliza and the starfish
to Adam, only to find Adam staring at him and not his
pupil. His heart lurched in his chest, but he frowned.
"It's quite common-looking," he grumbled.

"I wouldn't say that." Adam straightened from
where he'd been crouched closer to Lady Eliza. He
shrugged. "Perhaps it's a bit rough around the edges,
but some people find that an aesthetically pleasing
quality."

Septimus's pulse sped up. "Some people are de-
luding themselves."

He marched past Adam and Lady Eliza, following
Lord Francis as the lad ventured into slightly deeper
water, making Septimus nervous. The tide was on its

way out, and even though they were close to shore, there was no telling what sort of currents lurked under the water that they couldn't see. Besides which, the entire area seemed to be dotted with caves—which was likely quite useful for smugglers, come to think of it.

"Would you like to record this one in your journal, Lady Eliza?" Adam asked, returning to teaching. Septimus greeted the question with relief.

"Yes, I would," Lady Eliza answered. She tiptoed out of the pool and over to the rocks where their clothes rested. She had a journal waiting for her there, and once she deposited the starfish on a flat part of the rock and dried her hands on her skirts, she began writing or sketching in her journal.

"You have an unusual method of teaching the children of a duke," Septimus said, telling himself he was capable of having a perfectly normal conversation with Adam, and that he would not spend the duration of it captivated by the way Adam's mouth moved as he talked or remembering what it tasted like. "It seems unusual that Lady Eliza is a part of her brother's lessons as well."

"Lord Malton hired me specifically because I was willing to include Lady Eliza in the lessons when several of the other tutors he interviewed refused to," Adam said. "He believes, as I do, that education should be well-rounded and available to all, even women."

"How surprisingly unusual," Septimus said, opening his hand to receive a rock that Lord Francis had picked out of the tide pool and gave him for safekeeping. What the lad saw in the rock was a mystery to Septimus. As fast as the boy had run up to him to hand the rock over, he rushed back to whatever he'd been looking at. Septimus went on with, "I have been given to understand that the nobility cares more for displays of wealth and privilege than displays of knowledge."

"You have evidently been in the company of the wrong noblemen," Adam said, a touch of harshness to his comment.

That harshness had the hair on the back of Septimus's neck standing up. "I have been in the company of both right and wrong noblemen, Mr. Seymour," he said, pivoting away from watching Lord Francis to frown at Adam. "I've found that both sorts behave the same way when their backs are against the wall. They look out for their own kind and leave the rest of us to sink or swim."

"Noblemen do that amongst themselves as well, not just to the lower classes," Adam said, wading closer, then resting his hands on his hips. "Men of deficient character have a tendency to look out for their own interests first, regardless of birth. Which leads one to conclude that it is not the condition of nobility that has caused the wrong sort of behavior, but the quality of the character of the noblemen that you have known that is in question."

Septimus frowned, baffled at how quickly their conversation had turned into a battle. At least, he believed it was a battle. It certainly felt like one. He itched to defend himself, to prove that his assessment of the world was right, and that Adam was the same as the rest of them. Adam merely stared at him, the intensity of his gaze making the strongest argument that he was as different from the rest of them as could be.

"The moment a nobleman has to choose between a course of action that will increase his own prestige and power, or support what a man without the benefit of a lofty birth deserves, he will always choose his own self-interest," Septimus said, determined to prove his point.

"I wouldn't," Adam said.

His words were so simple and so beautiful, but whether Adam knew it or not, they were a lie.

"You're telling me that, as the son of a baron, if you found yourself in a situation where the school you wish to open would simply fall into your lap, through inheritance or royal decree or some such, but in doing so, you would, perhaps, be displacing a family like Mr. Malcolm's from the festival, you wouldn't take what you wanted because it was your right?" Septimus challenged him.

Adam blinked, lowering his head slightly, his already wind-pinkened face flushing a deeper shade of red. A moment later, he glanced up at Septimus and said, "I would like to think that, if such a *wildly unlikely* situation were to occur, I would be able to find a compromise that benefited all parties."

Septimus shook his head. "I don't believe you." He stepped away, following Lord Francis, who had moved to the edge of the tidal pools. "In my experience, anyone of noble birth will always put themselves first."

"In your experience," Adam repeated, chasing after him. "I'm beginning to think your experience has jaded you."

Septimus laughed out loud at that. "Naturally, it has jaded me. As any man would be jaded by the things I've experienced."

"But it doesn't have to be that way, Septimus." Adam stepped closer to him, resting his hand on Septimus's arm. That touch, with nothing but the cotton of his shirt covering his skin, combined with the sweetness in Adam's voice, represented a temptation far more potent than a kiss stolen in the night. The poor man was so innocent in the ways of the world. He was unspoiled, and Septimus was loath to be the one to spoil him.

"It *does* have to be that way," Septimus said, plucking Adam's hand off his arm and setting it deliberately aside. "There are barriers in this world, boundaries. There are lines that cannot be crossed. Believe me, I know."

"I do not believe that," Adam said tilting his chin up. "Every boundary is crossed eventually by someone. Every line is put in place so that it might be stepped over. And just because you've encountered one thing in the past does not mean it will always be so in the future."

The man was irritatingly persistent. If Septimus wasn't careful, that persistence would be irresistible. He couldn't tangle himself in a situation where he would be hurt again, and he didn't want Adam to land in one where he would only be disappointed.

"Adam," he said, facing him squarely. "I am not ignorant of the true intent of this conversation. You might find my arguments against... you might find them silly, but I do not. You cannot imagine the distress I've been caused by—"

That was as far as he got before a sharp yelp from Lord Francis snagged both of their attention. An unexpectedly large wave had washed in just as the boy bent to reach for something under the water, knocking him off balance. Lord Francis was knocked off his feet and disappeared under the sea foam.

Septimus leapt into action without a second thought. The boy hadn't gone far, so it took only a few steps for Septimus to reach him. He scooped the boy up, hoisting him to his shoulder as Lord Francis coughed and sputtered in surprise.

"That was unexpected," the boy gasped as soon as he caught his breath.

"Are you well, Lord Francis?" Adam asked, alarmed, as he splashed over to Septimus's side.

Lord Francis nodded and blinked, eyes wide. "I believe so. The sea is dangerous."

The lad was perfectly well. Septimus let out a breath of relief. He even found it in himself to grin and pat the boy's back as he shuddered and clung tightly to Septimus's neck.

"Perhaps it's time to return home," Adam said, letting out a nervous laugh. "It strikes me that doing our sums for the rest of the afternoon might be safer than studying marine life."

"I should say so," Lord Francis gasped.

Septimus had to admit that he liked the lad, even if he would be a duke someday. Lord Francis continued to cling to him as they returned to the rocks, where Lady Eliza was still drawing her starfish. She kicked up a fuss when she was told to throw the creature back so that they could return home.

"Brothers ruin everything," she sighed in disappointment as they all wiped sand from their feet so they could don their stockings and shoes.

"Yes, they do," Adam answered her with a bit more bitterness than Septimus would have expected. "Are you coming back with us, Mr. Bolton?" he asked, tucking Lord Francis's dry jacket around his shoulders.

"No," Septimus said, fastening his shoes, then moving away from the domestic group.

"But you must," Lord Francis protested. "You are my hero."

Adam's mouth twitched, as though he shared Lord Francis's sentiments.

"I am no one's hero," Septimus said, staring straight at Adam. "I am not who you seem to think I am at all. I am merely a sailor without a ship."

"You're far more than that," Adam said softly.

"Yes, you are," Lady Eliza agreed, though she could have no idea what she was agreeing to. "You are Uncle Redmond's friend, and I like you."

"I like you too, Lady Eliza," Septimus said. "But, by your leave, I should like to continue my walk."

Lady Eliza sighed. "Very well, but you will be home for supper tonight?"

Septimus's mouth twitched into a smile over the way the girl asked the question, as though she were his beloved and she planned to cook the meal for him herself. Adam wore the same expression, but it filled Septimus with a far more potent feeling.

"We'll see," he told them both, then turned to stride off, needing to put as much space as he could between himself and the growing temptation that Adam represented.

8

The situation with Septimus was becoming clearer to Adam with each encounter they had. The man had been wronged, he was at a loss and longing for the sea, and he didn't know how to drag himself out of the morass he'd fallen into. All of that was understandable and ultimately forgivable, but it didn't ease the frustration Adam felt over Septimus's stubbornness.

"Come on," he said, helping Lady Eliza to pack her and Lord Francis's notebooks into the sack they'd brought to the beach for their lessons. "We'd best get Lord Francis home before the saltwater chills him to the bone."

"Did you see the way Mr. Bolton plucked me from the ocean like I was a starfish?" Lord Francis asked, all excitement and shivers, as they walked up to the top of the cliff, where the cart and pony they'd taken from the house waited. "He is quite strong."

"I can imagine," Adam said with a smile.

He could imagine quite a bit more than that. The moment of terror he'd felt at the possibility of harm coming to Lord Francis had immediately been eclipsed by the rush of admiration and arousal he'd felt at the speed with which Septimus had leapt into action. Strength was one thing, but as Septimus had swept Lord Francis out of the water, Adam had been filled with fantasies of Septimus in the heat of battle, muscles straining, sweat dripping, and every bit of his focus narrowed in on the fight. In spite of what Septimus had insisted, he was a hero, and Adam was filled with the urge to reward him as such.

The ride back to Wodehouse Abbey wasn't as comfortable as it could have been. Once the initial shock and excitement of his rescue wore off and the cold set in, Lord Francis did more complaining than singing Septimus's praises. That complaining set Lady Eliza off, and by the time they reached the house, both children were exhausted and frustrated, bickering and near tears.

Adam felt guilty for handing them off to Ivy with only a short explanation of what had happened so that he could head back downstairs in the hope that Septimus had returned. Their business wasn't finished. Adam was certain he'd come close to arguing Septimus out of his reticence, and that if the two of them could just spend some time alone together, something more than awkward conversations laced with inuendo might blossom between them. Septimus had been stalking him all week, after all. Adam was well aware of it, but had let the aggravating man believe his interest had gone unnoted because he'd found the spying endearing.

Septimus was nowhere downstairs, though, so Adam returned to his room so that he could change out of his salty, sticky clothes, rinse the sand from his legs, and don something clean. The process took longer than he anticipated it would, considering the amount of sand and salt he'd accumulated, but once he was satisfied with his state of cleanliness, he marched back downstairs in search of Septimus once more. The man had to have returned from his walk by now. It was nearly time for supper, and Adam hoped to draw Septimus aside for a frank talk before they joined the others.

"You have a letter, Mr. Seymour," Worthington informed him as he reached the front hall, before he could dash off to the back of the house to search for Septimus.

"I do?" Adam changed directions, crossing the hall to take the letter from Worthington.

He didn't recognize the hand the letter was addressed in. Rather than reading it where he stood, he took it into one of the nearby parlors, where lamps where lit. He was glad he'd chosen a room with chairs that he could sink into once he opened and read the letter, because disappointment pressed heavily down on him after the first few lines.

"*Dear Mr. Seymour. We are in receipt of your request to become patrons of your school, but we regret to inform you that our offices will be unable to fulfill this request.*"

Adam didn't even bother to do more than skim the rest of the letter. Another rejection. Another suggestion he rely on the generosity of his titled family to fund his sweet and unimportant endeavor. If felt like his second dismissal that day, and even though being denied funding for his school yet again paled in comparison to Septimus's rejection of his affections that afternoon, it was the last feather that broke the horse's back.

He stood, even though he'd only just sunk into the chair beside the fireplace, and ripped the letter to shreds, tossing the pieces into the fire. He was tired of being shunted aside as unimportant and unworthy of serious attention. He was sick of being belittled, as though a man's desire to work for the improvement of children made him childlike himself. He knew his own worth, and it was damn well time that others saw and appreciated his worth as well. He wouldn't be ignored anymore, simply because he was young and inexperienced, and just happened to be the son of a minor baron.

He charged out of the parlor, striding down the hall in search of Septimus. It was usual for Lord Beverley and his friends to gather in the billiard room so close to supper, but when Adam rounded the corner, a scowl on his face, he only found Lord Beverley and Lord Copeland.

"Has Septimus returned from his walk yet?" he asked, heedless of the way he addressed the two noblemen, or of the way he tipped his cards by referring to Septimus by his Christian name.

Lord Beverley and Lord Copeland exchanged knowing looks as they straightened from the billiard table and rested against their cues, grins spreading across their faces.

"He returned to the house briefly about half an hour ago," Lord Beverley said. "Then he muttered something about wanting to be alone."

"I believe he intended to ask Cook for a parcel of supper to take down to the lake," Lord Copeland revealed, his expression full of mischief, as if revealing to Adam where Septimus had gone was tantamount to playing a joke on the man.

"Thank you," Adam said, giving the gentlemen a quick nod before rushing out of the room.

So Septimus intended to keep avoiding him, did he? Adam would just see about that. He was not some loathsome neighbor who always came to call at the least convenient moment. He was a man with feelings and ambitions, a man with desires, and Septimus was the object of those desires. He refused to be belittled by anyone, least of all the man he desired, for another moment.

The fire of frustration Adam had fanned in himself had cooled a little along with the evening air as he strode through the grass on his way to the lake. Septimus hadn't snubbed him on purpose. At least, not the way every potential patron and institution of investment to whom he'd appealed about his school had snubbed him. Septimus was only trying to protect himself. If only he could prove to the man that he needn't worry about being hurt by him.

He spotted Septimus sitting at the end of the jetty, his jacket tossed aside, his feet dangling in the lake, as he ate whatever Wodehouse Abbey's cook had prepared for his supper. The sight of Septimus's hunched shoulders sent a pang of longing through Adam, and he slowed his steps as he reached the jetty. Septimus was clearly troubled, and all Adam wanted to do was help.

He'd barely set foot on the jetty when Septimus jerked straight and twisted in alarm, as if he were about to be attacked. As soon as he spotted Adam, he swallowed the bite he'd been chewing, then asked, "What are you doing here? Shouldn't you be at supper?"

The way he frowned, as if Adam were a child caught out where he shouldn't be, ignited all of Adam's frustrations anew. "Why have you been avoiding me?" he asked, marching onto the jetty.

Septimus put down the bowl he'd been eating from and scrambled to his feet. The evening sun cast him in hues of red and gold, making him seem larger than life and more handsome than ever. "Because you want things from me that I'm not able to give," he answered with a contrasting scowl.

"Not able, or not willing?" Adam asked, marching up to stand only a few feet from him and squaring his shoulders in challenge. Septimus might have been a larger-than-life representation of masculine perfection, but Adam had worth as well, and he would not let it be denied.

"They amount to one and the same," Septimus growled, heat and indignation in his eyes.

Adam pursed his lips before bursting out with, "You claim prejudice against noblemen because you have been prevented from achieving your ambitions by one unscrupulous captain."

Septimus's brow shot up. "How did you know about that?"

"Lord Beverley told me," Adam said.

Septimus scowled. "It was not just Captain Wallace. I was routinely passed over for promotion because I was not a nob and could not afford to buy my way into the sort of captaincy I deserved."

"Nonetheless," Adam insisted, "You were denied what you wanted because of your birth, and now you are guilty of treating me in the same underhanded manner."

Septimus balked. "I have done no such thing."

"You have," Adam insisted. "I want you, Septimus, and it is as clear as day that you want me as well. And as far as I can tell, the only barrier you've put in place to prevent the two of us from being together is some fabricated argument about class and birth."

"It is more than that," Septimus growled. He glanced around and must have felt as though he were physically trapped. He abandoned his jacket and the remaining parcel of food that lay on the end of the jetty and walked past Adam, heading for the grassy slope by the side of the lake.

"You dare walk away from me when I am trying to speak frankly with you?" Adam shouted, storming after him. "I thought you were a hero, but those are the actions of a coward."

"I am not a hero," Septimus snapped, whipping to face Adam at the base of the jetty, causing Adam to flinch, "as your class is always telling me. I'm nothing more than a means to an end for a nobleman who will take credit for my work while keeping me in my place."

"I have never treated you as such, and I never will," Adam protested.

"Because I refuse to give you that chance," Septimus growled, attempting to march on, as if he would return to the house.

Adam caught him and prevented him from going farther. "Everyone refuses to give me a chance," he roared, his frustration getting the better of him. Septimus's arm went slack, and he stared at Adam in shock. "Every authority I encounter, every potential patron I attempt to convince, every man I take a fancy to." He gestured to Septimus. "Every one of you refuses to see me as more than a silly schoolmaster, too delicate because of his birth to have any serious desires, and too unimportant among the ranks of the aristocracy to be taken seriously."

Septimus's expression dropped into a scowl. "Has something happened?" he asked.

Adam blew out a breath, feeling foolish for his overly emotional reaction. He rubbed his forehead, staring at the grass under Septimus's feet. "I received another refusal to fund my school in the post when the children and I returned to the house." He glanced warily up at Septimus. "That was the sixth refusal of patronage I've received."

"I am sorry," Septimus said. He didn't seem to know what to do with his hands or to know whether he should stand where he was, continuing to have the conversation, or leave Adam to his troubles. For a moment, Adam almost had the impression Septimus would embrace him.

The fact that he didn't only twisted the knot in Adam's gut tighter. He stared hard at Septimus and said, "It was not the most frustrating rejection I received today."

Septimus's face colored. "I never intended to make you feel rejected," he said, unable to meet Adam's eyes.

"But you did," Adam said, swaying toward him, his body vibrating with locked up passion. "The way you shrank away from me when I kissed you, the way you have eschewed my company all week when I have offered friendship and more—" He shook his head. "You make me feel as though you do not see me as worthy of your attentions."

"That isn't true," Septimus said, looking shocked. "If anything, you are the one who might deem me unworthy because I am not your equal."

"Have I ever given you cause to think I would see you as anything less than wonderful?" Adam asked, feeling as though he were a hair's breadth away from saying or doing something wild that he couldn't take back. "I am not some officer aboard a ship who purchased his way to a rank above you, taking credit for your actions. I am a man no different from you, struggling to achieve my own ambitions and being blocked at every turn. Why can you not see that?"

"I can see it," Septimus said, then did the very last thing Adam expected.

He took a large step forward, reaching for Adam and clasping his hands on either side of his face. With a breath that sounded almost like a gasp of disbelief, Septimus brought his mouth crashing down over Adam's, causing Adam's whole world to career to a stop as desire blasted through him. Everything he'd wanted from the moment he'd first seen Septimus was there before him, encompassing him and firing his blood with promise.

He wasted no time in grabbing hold of it, embracing Septimus and digging his fingertips into the firm muscles of his back. As fiercely as Septimus kissed him, Adam kissed him back. Their tongues tangled as each sought to gain the advantage over the other, and their lips pressed and slid in concert with bruising force. It was raw and powerful, heating Adam to impossible levels and sending his blood pumping. His cock leapt to attention, straining painfully against his breeches. He leaned into Septimus, grinding his erection against Septimus's hip and feeling just how aroused Septimus was in turn.

"I have wanted you from the moment I first saw you," Adam panted, shifting to work through the buttons of Septimus's waistcoat. "Think of me what you will for admitting as much. Call me a rogue or a wanton, but do not cast me aside because of it." He stared fiercely up into Septimus's eyes, daring him to back away now.

Septimus stayed right where he was. He allowed Adam to push the halves of his waistcoat aside as he finished, then tug his shirt from his breeches. Adam's whole body shuddered with longing as he spread his hands across the bare skin of Septimus's stomach and sides. The man was fit and solid from his life on the sea, but the way his muscles tensed under Adam's touch hinted at a sort of vulnerability Adam wanted much more of.

"We shouldn't do this," Septimus said, his voice thick and rumbling, as Adam stroked his way up to his chest, circling Septimus's nipples with his thumbs until they were hard. "Not here. We're in the open. Anyone could see us."

He followed his warning by cupping a hand under Adam's chin and tilting it up for another kiss. Adam adored the power in Septimus's grip, shivered at the hint of mastery it brought with it. He imagined Septimus dominating him in a dozen different ways, all within the space of seconds, to the point where his fantasies blended into pure emotion. That emotion spurred Adam on, making his breath come in ragged gasps as Septimus nipped at his lower lip before slanting his mouth over his for a kiss.

It was too much and not enough all at the same time. The cool evening air was a heady contrast to the heat rippling from Septimus's half-exposed torso. And still, Adam wanted more. He broke away from Septimus's mouth, sinking to his knees and bunching Septimus's shirt in his fists as he licked the expanse of skin beneath Septimus's naval. Adam tasted salt and musk, groaning deep in his throat at the way Septimus tightened with pleasure. The wiry hair forming a trail pointing below Septimus's breeches tickled him as he rubbed his cheek against the plane of Septimus's belly. He moved lower, nuzzling the bulge in Septimus's breeches and breathing in his scent. Even though the fabric, Adam could feel the heat and hardness of Septimus's cock. His own prick throbbed in response.

He acted before he let himself think, unfastening

the falls of his own breeches first to relieve the ache of constriction, then fumbling with the front of Septimus's breeches. Septimus seemed stunned with arousal, which worked in Adam's favor as he tugged Septimus's breeches down to his thighs. Septimus's cock leapt to freedom, thick and hot and already moist at the tip. Adam had never seen anything so beautiful, even though the deepening twilight cast shadows, obscuring what they were doing. He didn't need to see, he only needed to feel, and he felt everything.

Hands shaking with arousal, Adam reached for Septimus's shaft. He closed his hand lightly around it, breathing shallowly as he stroked slowly, learning the shape. Septimus tilted his head back and let out a sigh of pleasure, though he continued to radiate tension, and Adam felt there was a fair chance the man would pull away from him at any moment. He wouldn't allow it. He leaned in, brushing his lips against the flared tip of Septimus's cock to wet them with the moisture he found there, then licking across his slit.

"God help me," Septimus gulped, burying his hands in Adam's hair.

It was a sign of victory. Septimus wouldn't pull away after all. Adam continued to kiss and lick his head, then drew him in with a deep, impassioned sigh. He took his time, pulling back only to plunge down again, over and over as he became accustomed to the invasion of Septimus's cock in his mouth. He wanted more, wanted to take all of Septimus, no matter how uncomfortable it might turn for him, but he paced himself. His reward was the way Septimus's breath hitched and the uncontrolled way he fisted his hands in Adam's hair, tugging until it was almost painful.

Adam adored every bit of it and redoubled his efforts to take Septimus all the way. The unfettered sounds Septimus made were beautiful and feral, spiking Adam's desire to dizzying heights. He reached down to grasp his own prick as he continued to move on Septimus, moaning at the storm of pleasure they were creating together. It was even better when something within Septimus seemed to snap, and instead of merely accepting Adam's gift of pleasure, he held Adam's head firmly and thrust hard and fast into his mouth.

The shift in power sent Adam soaring. Perhaps it was some quirk in him, but he loved being used for pleasure by a man larger than him. His eyes might have watered involuntarily and he may have sputtered a bit, but he loved it. He groaned and worked his tongue eagerly as Septimus thrust hard and deep enough to choke him. It was carnal and sloppy as spit escaped his mouth, but the taste of Septimus and the almost impossible fullness of Adam's mouth being filled until his jaw hurt was heaven. Adam stroked himself furiously as he swallowed convulsively to give Septimus even more sensation, and within moments, the white-hot flash of orgasm blasted through him, and he spilled copiously into his hand, crying out around Septimus's cock.

Whether Septimus was aware of Adam's overwhelming pleasure or not, he came himself a few moments later, causing Adam to swallow and draw him even deeper down his throat. It was pure, sensual madness, but it was also the single most erotic experience Adam had ever had. He sagged back, gasping for breath, when Septimus stumbled away from him. Septimus's passion-hazed eyes went wide as he stared down at Adam, seeing how transported he was, and likely seeing the evidence of how hard Adam had come as well. As wicked as it all was, Adam had never been happier.

Until Septimus panted, "What have we done?"

His terrified question hit like an arrow in Adam's heart. He spread his arms to the side, doing nothing to hide his softening cock from Septimus's view, and said, "Nothing that we both didn't want to do."

"We shouldn't have," Septimus said, wiping the back of his hand across his mouth. He blinked at Adam—though with a great deal of desire still in his eyes, along with alarm—then scrambled to tuck himself back into his breeches. "You're a nobleman," he growled. "And too young, and—"

"And utterly and completely yours, if you want me," Adam finished for him.

For a moment, Septimus was still, eyes wide as he watched Adam, rather like he was a wild creature that might attack. Adam burned for him, in spite of being spent. He could see the confusion in Septimus's eyes, see the agony of being lost. And he knew that, if Septimus would just give him a chance, he could help him to find—

"No," Septimus said, taking another step back and shaking his head as he tucked his shirt into his breeches. "We cannot do this. I cannot—" He didn't finish. Instead, he started to turn away.

"What is so wrong with me?" Adam called after him, putting too much of his heart and his pain into the question. "Why can you not see me as anything more than a silly little nobleman?"

Septimus froze, glancing over his shoulder at Adam. "It isn't you," he insisted.

Adam pushed to his feet, straightening his clothes. "It isn't because I'm a baron's son," he shouted, in spite of warning himself not to be hurt. How could he not be hurt with Septimus continuing to reject him after what they'd shared? "It isn't because I'm too young either." He balled his hands into fists as Septimus lowered his head. "It's something else, isn't it? Something not even you can name, otherwise you'd name it instead of flailing me with excuses."

Septimus lifted his head and appealed to him with a look. "Adam, you are a treasure, but..." He didn't complete his thought.

Adam stood straighter, squaring his shoulders, anger pushing in to replace every wonderful feeling he had just embraced. "You would do well to ask yourself what is really holding you back," he said. "What is the true reason you refuse to let yourself embrace what is standing right in front of you, asking for your friendship and your trust, asking for more?"

"I... I don't know," Septimus admitted, his expression pinching.

"Then find out," Adam said, heart breaking with frustration. He marched forward, heading past Septimus and up the hill. All he wanted was the solitude of his own room, the cool sheets of his bed, and the end of what had been a torturesome day. But he turned to call over his shoulder, "Find out before you drive us both to madness."

9

What was truly holding him back from entertaining the idea of a tryst with Adam? Septimus asked himself that question over and over for the next few days. He insisted to himself that he knew the answer full well, as he tramped through the moors at one end of Wodehouse Abbey the day after his explosive encounter with Adam at the lake, and as he clomped through the small woods at the other end of the property the following day. What was he so frightened of?

Septimus rejected the idea that he was afraid of anything as he swiped at a low-hanging branch along the wooded path. He'd braved the heat of battle without flinching. He'd strapped himself to a ship's wheel for the duration of a wild storm to bring his crewmates through to safety. He'd chased down privateers, and perhaps most courageous of all, he'd endured nights carousing with Red and Barrett—as well as Lucas, Spencer, and Clarence from the *Hawk*—where rum had run more freely than good sense. He'd had more than his fair allotment of lovers to share those times with as well, though none that were intended to be serious or last longer than the night. So why shy away from a man as open and willing—and devilishly talented with his mouth, as it happened—as Adam?

The woods did nothing to solve his problems. Every path he walked through its shady depths left him feeling as though he were being watched. The moors only reminded him of the sea when the wind blew the grass and heather in ripples like waves. The sound of the wind in the grass even reminded him of the fizz of sea foam in the sunlight. Walking the beach was perhaps most painful of all. The sea was right there, and yet it was as far away as if he'd been deposited in the center of a vast desert.

In the end, all of his walking and contemplating did nothing more for him than ruining his boots and requiring him to make a sojourn into Hull for a new pair—which drained the last of the ready money he had. Worse still, the post office didn't have so much as a scrap of paper with Septimus's name on it sent by the Admiralty, or anyone else. He was forced to return home with new boots that he was certain would leave blisters on his feet, a heavy heart that was caught between thoughts of Adam and a yearning to return to the sea, an aching head, and nothing else to show for his troubles.

"Septimus, there you are," Red called out to him as he trudged up the final slope to Wodehouse Abbey's back gardens. "We've been looking everywhere for you."

Neither Red nor Barrett looked as though they'd been doing anything other than getting into trouble. They stood among a large spread of balls, pall mall wickets and mallets, cricket stumps and bats, and even several tennis racquets. The way they were laid out made no sense to Septimus at all and resembled none of the games any of the implements were intended for, but the scene was curious enough that he veered off of his intended path, old boots slung over his shoulder, to see what his friends were doing. With any luck, whatever it was would take his mind off of his troubles.

"We are attempting to invent a new game," Barrett explained with an impish grin as Septimus came to a stop on the lawn near the mess. "We do not have enough men for cricket, we've no interest in pall mall, and neither of us are certain of the rules of lawn bowling."

Septimus nodded. That must have been what the collection of solid-looking balls and thin pins was all about. "I'm of no help to you on that score. I barely know lawns, let alone lawn bowling."

"That is why we intend to invent a game," Red said, marching over to Septimus and slapping him on the shoulder. "What do you think? We set up the pins at either end of the lawn, the stumps in the center, and the wickets in a configuration throughout the playing field. The game is played with teams of two. One attempts to roll a bowling ball from one end of the field to the other, through the wickets without knocking over the stumps, and on to knock over as many pins as possible. The other uses a pall mall mallet and ball to knock the bowler off course and to attempt to knock down the stumps."

Septimus blinked at him. "That sounds unnecessarily complicated and utterly mad."

"Of course it is," Red said with a broad smile. "That is why we've invented it."

"And you've an odd number of players," Septimus pointed out.

"Do we?" Barrett asked, nodding toward the house.

Dread swooped in Septimus's stomach even before he turned to find Adam striding down through the summer garden to the cleared lawn. Adam paused when he spotted Septimus, looking as though he'd forgotten how to put one foot in front of the other for a moment. His brow furrowed tightly before he smoothed his expression, as though nothing at all were amiss between the two of them, then continued on.

"Just in time," Barrett said, marching over to meet Adam, a pall mall mallet over one shoulder.

"When Worthington said you required my presence, this is not what I thought I would find," Adam said, attempting to smile at Barrett and Red while sending Septimus a fierce look that communicated he hadn't forgotten a single second of the evening a few days before.

"This is always what you must expect to find when Red has time on his hands and no calls to pay," Barrett laughed, moving behind Adam to squeeze his shoulders and propel him forward.

Septimus worked to swallow the burst of possessiveness that knotted in his gut over the way Barrett touched Adam. The man had no right to put his hands where they weren't wanted.

And Septimus had no right to view Adam as someone he could claim or feel jealous over. He'd given up that right when he'd pushed Adam away the other night. That didn't stop him from feeling as though the young man should belong to him or to no one, Barrett included. It was *his* cock Adam had wrapped his mouth around the other night, *his* pleasure that had concerned them both. And yet...

Septimus sighed inwardly. Why couldn't he surrender himself to the desire he had for the young man? What was truly holding him back?

Septimus shook himself out of his thoughts when he realized Red was partially speaking to him as well as Adam as he explained the rules of the invented game once more.

"Teams of two," Red said, counting off the rules on his fingers. "One man bowling across the lawn, one hitting a ball with a pall mall mallet."

Barrett brought one of the heavy lawn bowling balls over to Septimus and dropped it into his hands. Septimus nearly fumbled the thing, its weight was so unexpected. Barrett then handed a pall mall mallet and ball to Adam, who took them, but held them as though he didn't have a clue what he was doing.

"Work from one end of the field to the other, bowling through the wickets and on to knock down the pins. Meanwhile, the other team member tries to interfere with the bowler and knock over the stumps."

"At the same time?" Adam asked. "Or are there turns?"

Red and Barrett exchanged a glance, as though they hadn't thought that through.

"I think if all of the action takes place at once, the game will be more exciting," Red said.

"I think you're right," Barrett said, then faced Septimus and Adam. "Your team starts at that end and ours at this."

A jolt of sizzling awkwardness shot down Septimus's spine. It doubled in intensity when he turned his head to stare at Adam, only to find the gorgeous young man staring fiercely back at him, blue eyes luminous with indignation. He snapped his gaze to Red and Barrett as he felt his face heat. "You want the two of us to be a team?"

"Most assuredly, we do," Barrett said, his smirk far too mischievous for Septimus's comfort.

Septimus sighed heavily, scowled, and turned away from them, stomping to the end of the field where five of the bowling pins were set up. He shed his jacket, tossing it aside, debated for a moment, then unbuttoned his waistcoat and cast that aside as well. Adam followed suit, stripping down to his shirtsleeves several yards away and throwing his clothes beyond the boundary line. It all felt calculated. If Septimus had to wager, he'd say the entire game had been invented as a ploy to thrust him and Adam together. Well, if that were the case, he would teach Red and Barrett a lesson by winning the game instead of losing his mind and his heart, and other organs, to Adam.

"We'll shout when it's time to start," Red called in delight, as he and Barrett headed to the opposite end of the field, their heads together like gossiping fishwives.

Septimus reached the pins, then turned to face the field. Adam was only a few yards from him, his mallet over one shoulder and his ball in his hand.

"Shouldn't you be tutoring Lord Malton's children?" Septimus asked. He considered himself kind for giving Adam a reason to abandon the game and go about his own business.

"They're having a dancing lesson," Adam said, his frown deepening. "Lord Malton's aunt, Lady Grosmont, pays for a dancing instructor to come once a fortnight."

"Aren't Lord Francis and Lady Eliza too young to learn to dance?" Septimus grumbled as Red and Barrett debated something on the other side of the field.

"One is never too young to dance," Adam said. He continued to frown, but an almost irresistible aura of good humor seemed to radiate from him, as if joviality were his natural state and everything that had come between them recently was an aberration to his true character.

It was the last thing Septimus needed to feel. He was far more comfortable with Adam being frustrated with him than he would be if the young man forgave him for his callousness. Forgiveness meant he would be right back in the stew of difficult emotions where he'd found himself the evening before. What was his real problem?

"I have no intention of losing this or any other game to those two jackanapeses," Septimus growled. "So you had better put your all into this monstrosity."

Adam dropped his ball onto the grass and lined up behind it with his mallet. "If you will remember, Mr. Bolton, I put my all into everything I do."

Septimus's whole body went hot and his cock stirred to life. He remembered a little too well. It was a blessing when Red called, "Now!" from the other side of the field.

The game was a wild, disorganized, ungainly mess. As manicured as the lawn was, the grass was still too high for any of the balls to roll easily. Septimus was barely able to bowl his halfway to the placement of the first wicket, or what he thought was the first wicket. They'd never discussed the pattern he was supposed to employ when bowling through the wickets. Red and Barrett didn't seem to have much of a clue either as they approached the hodgepodge in the middle of the field. Septimus figured he'd roll his ball through a few wickets, then charge to the pins at the other side, simply to get the game over with faster.

"Bowl it through the center," Adam called from one side as he slapped his ball with the mallet, then dashed ahead to hit it again in the direction of the stumps at the center of the field. "I'll stop you from hitting the stumps."

Septimus figured that was as good an idea as any, but before he got halfway there, Barrett's pall mall ball sailed across the grass and knocked his ball off course.

"What in blazes are you doing?" Septimus shouted at the man.

"Winning," Barrett laughed at him.

"But you cannot do that," Septimus argued, lunging to retrieve his ball, then yanking his hand out of the way when Barrett's ball came perilously close to smashing his fingers.

"I invented the rules," Barrett said. "I can do whatever I'd like."

"This is preposterous," Septimus grumbled. "Adam, smash this fool's ball away."

Adam nodded, then turned to hit his ball toward Barrett's. The resulting melee reminded Septimus of an old game he'd played as a child where players attempted to bash a ball and each other with sticks in an attempt to score points. For a moment, he was so genuinely concerned for the integrity of Adam's toes and shins that he stood and contemplated intervening.

That idea was dropped when Barrett broke away from the melee and hit his ball toward Septimus's. Or rather, toward the stumps in the middle of the field.

"If I knock them down, you lose," Barrett called gleefully.

Septimus lunged for his ball, intending to hurl it toward the pins at the far end of the field. "I thought the purpose was *not* to knock down the stumps."

"Oh, perhaps you're right," Barrett said, aiming for Septimus's ball, once he'd released it across the grass.

"Twat," Septimus grumbled, chasing after his ball.

He glanced over his shoulder in time to see Adam smashing his ball forward, as if to chase Barrett off. "Hurry," Septimus called to him. "As much nonsense as this game is, I refuse to lose it. I've lost too much already."

It hit him as he reached to scoop his ball up and hurl it toward the pins, which finally seemed within reach. He hated to lose. He'd lost too much of late. He couldn't bear to lose one more thing. Especially if that thing was a lover.

As soon as the notion cracked over him, he pushed it aside, focusing on the daft game. He grabbed his ball one more time, then hurled it toward the pins, knocking all five over.

"Ha!" he shouted, standing and whipping around to face the rest of the field. "I won!"

Barrett and Adam immediately abandoned whatever scuffle they'd gotten into and straightened to see what was going on. The look of hope that Adam wore was enough to make Septimus feel like the hero he knew he wasn't.

That look collapsed a moment later when he glanced all the way across the field to find Red sitting next to a pile of pins, tossing his ball up and catching it repeatedly. "I knocked these pins over five minutes ago, and none of you noticed," he called to the rest of them.

Septimus kicked one of the pins at his feet. "This whole thing is balderdash. I do not have time for games."

He started to march off toward where he'd left his old boots by the side of the lawn, but Barrett followed him, and Red jumped up to chase after him as well. Adam stood where he was, eyes narrowed at Septimus, until he swung his mallet in what appeared to be pure frustration. His ball sailed over the grass and crashed into the stumps, knocking the bails off. Septimus would have been impressed by his aim if he weren't so busy wrestling with the conclusion he'd just come to about his fear of loss.

"Let's play a different game," Red insisted, reaching Septimus in time to grab his arm and steer him back to the center of the lawn.

"Another game you made up?" Septimus growled.

"If you'd like." Red had far too much mischief in his eyes for Septimus's liking. He pushed Septimus forward—forward toward Adam—then ducked aside to have a word with Barrett. The two of them put their heads together, speaking low and rapidly, as Septimus crossed his arms, rested his weight on one hip, and glared at them.

He also peeked at Adam. Whether he'd intended to or not, Adam had struck a jaunty, rakish pose, his pall mall mallet slung over one shoulder, his golden hair tousled, his blue-green eyes bright with energy, not all of it spritely. Adam watched Septimus as though he had more than a few things to say. Septimus couldn't drag his eyes away from Adam's mouth once he'd focused on it. How dangerous would it be, truly, for him to indulge in all the things that mouth could do?

He shook his head and turned away. Too dangerous. He refused to risk having his heart broken by a man when it was already broken by the sea. He'd lost one love, and he didn't know if he could withstand losing another. It was safer not to take the risk.

"New game," Barrett said, stepping away from his consultation with Red. "And it's a simple one. You'll like it. Grab a mallet."

Septimus let out a heavy sigh, rubbed a hand over

his face, and marched to the side of the lawn to select a mallet from those remaining. Whatever new madness his friends had in store, he would have to endure it or he'd never hear the end of it. The two had been forever making up games and pastimes for the other officers during long stretches of boredom aboard ship, and anyone who had refused to participate always found themselves on the wrong end of pranks later. Though Septimus felt rather like he was part of a prank now.

"This one is simple," Red explained once Septimus made it back to the center of the field with a mallet. Red and Barrett had removed the stumps from the center of the field and set the pins again. The wickets remained in place, but Septimus wasn't certain why. "Teams of two," Red went on. "One ball." He dropped the yellow pall mall ball in his hand to the grass. "First team to knock the other side's pins down wins."

"Knock them with the ball?" Adam asked.

"By hitting it with the mallet, yes," Barrett said.

"Fine." Septimus sighed. He pointed to a spot a few yards away from the ball and told Adam, "Start there and block Barrett from smashing my feet."

"Oh, no," Barrett said. "We're changing teams. You're on my side now."

"And Mr. Seymour is on mine," Red said.

Septimus tamped down the pinch of jealousy that hit him as Adam blinked, then shifted to the opposite side of the ball from him. It was maddening that he could see full well what Red and Barrett's aim was, but he was powerless to simply throw down his mallet and walk away. Like he'd walked away the other evening. Perhaps that had been a grievous mistake.

"Ready?" Barrett asked, nudging Septimus toward

the ball—which also nudged him toward Adam. Septimus set his mallet-head on the grass, no idea how he could best hit the ball to get it to do what he wanted, but highly aware of Adam squaring off opposite him. "Go!" Barrett called.

Septimus pushed forward, surging toward the ball. As he'd predicted—and likely as Barrett and Red had intended—in the process of trying to smack the ball, he bashed straight into Adam. The two of them grappled for a moment, attempting to get their mallet around the ball enough to hit it out of the way, but also mashing their shoulders together and shoving against each other. Septimus had no idea that the sport of full-contact pall mall could be so invigorating, though perhaps not in the right ways.

Much to his frustration, Adam ended up getting the better of him and smacking the ball off toward what he presumed was his end of the field. They hadn't set those boundaries before play began. Not that it mattered. It was as clear as day that the purpose of the game wasn't to knock any pins over, but to pummel him and Adam against each other until something cracked.

Unfortunately for Septimus, the game succeeded in its aim. He dashed ahead of Adam, lunging into his way and causing another bruising round of vertical wrestling as each of them tried to maneuver the ball away from the other. Elbows were thrown, hips checked, and, at one point, Septimus let go of his mallet with one hand to grab Adam's shirt. He ripped the seam near Adam's shoulder, exposing a tempting expanse of skin and surprisingly firm muscle.

Sweat drenched them both in no time, but Adam didn't seem to mind. In fact, the otherwise refined young man didn't seem bothered by a bit of rough play at all. The implications of that nearly did Septimus's head in. He ended up so aroused by Adam's determined ferocity that he lost the ball. Adam stole it right out from under him, smacking it across the field and knocking the pins over with one powerful stroke.

"You've won!" Red called as he and Barrett jogged down the field to join Septimus and Adam.

"And where were you through this whole game?" Septimus demanded of Barrett.

"Watching," Barrett replied with a smug grin, confirming in Septimus's mind what the purpose of the whole thing was.

"Congratulations." Red marched over to Adam, clapping a hand on his shoulder.

Septimus narrowed his eyes at Red, and at Adam as well. The way Adam stood there, victorious and proud—not to mention dripping sweat and red-faced with exertion—ignited Septimus's imagination. The images of other ways he could make the young man sweat that assailed him were more of a defeat than losing the ridiculous game. He couldn't keep the wall up between the two of them indefinitely. Because Adam was right. It wasn't who he was or how he'd been born that had kept Septimus at bay. It wasn't his age or his experience. In fact, Septimus's reasons for caution had nothing to do with Adam at all, and everything to do with his own cowardly heart.

No more. Adam was right. He was through being a coward, through with letting other men determine the course of his life and his love. Fear was the worst possible reason to hold back from pleasure, and even if it destroyed him, he couldn't deny himself anymore.

"You win," he said, sending Adam a look he hoped the young man would interpret as what it was. "You win everything." And the sooner they could celebrate horizontally the better, as far as Septimus was concerned. Who knew? Perhaps if he had a nice tumble with Adam, he'd move past the crippling fear of yet another loss. Perhaps turning his heart and body over to Adam would help him find the peace he so desperately needed. Swallowing his pride and admitting Adam was right wouldn't matter in the long run if he ended up happy for a moment. He could do what he had to do, get Adam out of his blood, and move on.

He recognized the lie for what it was even before he finished thinking it. Adam was not the sort of man one got past after one fuck. But if it was safer for him to think that...

"Perhaps we should continue our conversation from the other night," Septimus said, taking a step toward Adam.

Adam gaped at him, still panting from exertion, and brushed his damp hair away from his forehead. "As easy as that?" he asked, incredulous. "As if it's just another mad game where you make the rules up as you go along?" He shook his head and threw his mallet down. "I think not." He turned to Red and Barrett. "Excuse me, my lords."

He nodded, then marched off to collect his clothes, then head up to the house, leaving Septimus wondering what had just happened and how he had managed to fail to get what he wanted yet again.

10

Adam knew he was walking into a trap from the moment Worthington informed him that his presence was required on the lawn. He's seen the way Lord Beverley and Lord Copeland had been watching the manner in which he and Septimus interacted—or rather, failed to interact—for the past few days. For a change, Adam shared Septimus's prejudices against noblemen, for Lord Beverly and Lord Copeland were clearly two gentlemen with high opinions of themselves and their ability to steer the course of lives around them, and too much time on their hands.

Yes, the trap had been set, and he'd walked right into it. What he hadn't expected was to be treated to the sight of Septimus pushing himself athletically, using his magnificent and powerful body in sport. It was all Adam could do to resist tackling the man, instead of simply tussling with him over a silly ball, and riding him like a ravenous beast. The fact that he was so consumed with the idea had made him terse with Septimus, when perhaps he should have been more understanding. Unless he was mistaken, something had caused Septimus to rethink his rejection and to make what might be considered the beginnings of an advance toward him.

Which Adam was thoroughly not in the mood to accept. He'd put his heart on the line with Septimus the other evening. He'd given far more than he ever had with a man he'd known for such a short period of time. And with the taste of Septimus still in his mouth, the bastard had walked away from him yet again. The sting of rejection wasn't simply going to melt away because a couple of mischievous noblemen maneuvered him and Septimus into a situation where their passions were purposely inflamed. He wasn't so wool-headed that he would fall for a ploy simply because it was now convenient for Septimus to accept his advances, likely to improve his standing in the eyes of his friends.

Or perhaps he was merely exhausted from the last few sleepless nights. He'd spent too much time lying awake, staring at the ceiling in his small room, wondering if he could have approached Septimus differently and if their interactions could have ended with a different result.

Either way, he refused to be a pawn in someone else's game now, even if those someones were lords who ranked far above him.

"Mr. Seymour, a letter has come from you," Worthington greeted him as he entered the house through a side door at the end of the main hallway.

Adam snapped his head up from where he'd been scowling at the marble floor in front of him while he walked. A pulse of hope shot through him, but he let it go a moment later. What was the point of hoping that someone might finally be willing to finance his idea for a school when he had received so many rejections already? It was better not to hope at all than to keep dashing his heart against the rocks of disappointment.

"Thank you, Worthington." He managed a smile as he took the offered letter from the butler and turned it over. He vaguely recognized the hand it was addressed in.

Worthington followed a few steps behind as Adam strode toward the stairs. "I see you have damaged your shirt, sir," he said. "If you would like, I could have one of the maids mend it for you."

"That would be lovely, thank you," Adam said.

He hesitated for a moment, then threw caution to the wind and put all the things he was carrying on the stairs so that he could pull his shirt straight off and hand it to Worthington. Worthington looked shocked at the impulsive gesture, but rather than make a comment about how Adam could have waited until he'd reached his room and sent the shirt down later, he schooled his expression to neutrality and carried the shirt away, as if such things happened on a daily basis at Wodehouse Abbey.

With that done, Adam gathered up his waistcoat, jacket, and the letter, and continued up the stairs, the cool air of the hall causing his bare chest and back to prickle as his sweat dried. He turned the letter over a few times, then decided to go ahead and get the worst over with by opening it.

Its contents weren't at all what he expected.

"*Dear Adam. I trust you are well and that you have been enjoying your employment with Lord Malton. I still think it surprising that you took a position as a private tutor when we all know how much promise you've always shown as an educator. And that is precisely the purpose of my missive.*

"*I am not certain if you remember, but I currently*

teach at Archbishop Holgate's School here in York. As it happens, there will soon be an opening for an instructor, and I have given the headmaster your name. If you have any interest at all in forgoing your quest for a school of your own in favor of teaching at this august institution, I can all but guarantee a position for you. I can assure you that the compensation you would receive would be more than adequate, perhaps even enough to set aside for the future and your own school. Do let me know at your earliest convenience."

The letter was from Adam's old university friend, Jeremy Fulbright. It went on for another page with details about some of their mutual acquaintances, plans for Jeremy's upcoming wedding to the young lady from York that he'd been walking out with since before graduation, and other tidbits that Adam wasn't interested in at the moment. It was kind of Jeremy to write, even kinder that the man would think of him for a position at a school that had been in operation for over two hundred years already, but teaching in York wasn't what Adam wanted, even if it paid well.

What Adam wanted had apparently chased after him without Adam knowing it.

"Adam, wait," Septimus called from several stairs down behind him.

With a frown, Adam turned to see what Septimus wanted. The sight of Septimus's strong form and ruggedly-handsome face always arrested Adam, but seeing the man still slick with sweat, his shirt plastered to his broad chest, sent a wave of lust through him that was at odds with everything he had just promised himself about not allowing himself to be used in a game for someone else's amusement.

The way Septimus glanced up at him, his gaze raking him with fingers of fire and resting particularly on his naked chest, tested Adam's resolve even more. There was something about having Septimus several steps down from him, looking up, that was as arousing as it had been the other evening, when he'd been on his knees in front of the man. He'd never felt the need to be fixed into one role in pleasure, and even the hint of Septimus deferring to him that way had Adam hard so swiftly that the only thing he could do to save himself embarrassment was to turn and continue up the stairs.

"What do you want from me, Septimus?" he asked wearily as he turned the corner at the landing to head up to the second floor. "Is it to drive me wild with promise and passion, only to dash my hopes again?"

Septimus didn't answer immediately. Instead, he took the stairs two at a time until he walked beside Adam the rest of the way up.

"I realized quickly that I did not deport myself as honorably as I should have that night," he mumbled.

"You're speaking like a gentleman," Adam told him in return, sending him a sideways glance. "Is that because you feel you must, since I am so far above you?" Sarcasm was thick in his tone.

"I am trying to apologize," Septimus said with more force. When they reached the top of the stairs and started down the hall, he blinked, then said, "You're not going into the nursery in your current state of undress, are you?"

Adam almost laughed. "My bedchamber is right here," he said, stopping at the first door on the right.

Septimus blinked. "You're lodged on the same floor as the nursery?"

"It is the customary room in this house for the tutor, yes," Adam said. He gripped the door handle, turned it, cracked his door open, then looked straight into Septimus's eyes and asked, "Are you coming in or do you wish to have this conversation in the hall, where the children and the servants might happen upon it?"

Septimus's face pinched into a frown that said he wasn't amused with Adam's flippant manner. "We both know the answer to that." He planted his hand on the door and pushed it open, walking into the room ahead of Adam.

Septimus stopped only a few steps into the room to glance around. The room wasn't as elaborate as the guest rooms. It was only slightly finer than the servant's rooms. A single, narrow bed rested with its head against one wall. A plain cabinet beside it that held a lamp and a jar containing a certain type of salve that had proved useful during his sleepless nights. Adam rather wished he'd returned the jar to the drawer in the morning, as Septimus would certainly know it's purpose, and therefore guess at Adam's recent activities. Across the room was a simple wardrobe, and under the window was a washstand, where Adam headed as Septimus looked around. Adam set his letter from Jeremy on the mantel above the fireplace, threw his jacket and waistcoat over the chair beside the washstand, then dipped the cloth hanging from the side of the stand into the water left in the bowl from that morning so that he could wipe the dried sweat from his face.

"Is there a reason you followed me to the privacy of my bedchamber, other than to gape at my accommodations?" he asked, finishing with his face and wiping off his shoulders and chest.

Completely expectedly, Septimus shifted from taking in the room to watching Adam, hunger in his eyes. "I wanted to apologize," he said in a gruff voice, seemingly unable to pry his gaze away from Adam's chest.

"You've no need to apologize," Adam said. "The game was a rough one. We both played a bit too hard."

Septimus dragged his eyes up to meet Adam's. "I was not referring to Red and Barrett's mad game just now."

"Neither was I," Adam said in a quiet voice, staring unflinchingly back at Septimus.

Septimus's face colored, and he snapped his gaze away. Unfortunately, it landed on Adam's bedside table. His eyes widened slightly before narrowing, and he swallowed uncomfortably. "I behaved callously the other night," he mumbled, appearing to force himself to look away from the jar on the table, but not knowing where else to look.

Adam didn't know what to say to that. He hadn't expected an apology, not truly. He would have been lying to himself if he said there wasn't something undeniably arousing about having the object of his desire alone in his room with him while both of them were in varying stages of undress. It was the reason he'd subtly locked the door while Septimus was looking around, before he'd moved to the washstand. At the same time, he was loath to be toyed with, the way Lord Beverley and Lord Copeland had toyed with him and Septimus both. He still wanted Septimus, but not if the man came at the expense of pride and self-respect.

"Do you have more to add?" he asked, setting his cloth on the washstand, then crossing his arms. "Or have you simply come to gape at the impoverished surroundings of the son of a baron, a man you cannot trust because his station is so high above yours?"

Septimus found it in him to meet Adam's eyes

again. "I do not distrust you because you are a gentleman," he insisted. Adam's expression shifted to mild surprise. Septimus took in a breath, then let it out and said, "I have come to that conclusion after days of contemplating the question you put to me."

Adam let a beat of silence pass before saying, "So your prejudice against noblemen for the way they've betrayed you and passed you over within the ranks of the Navy is not the reason you're behaving like a prudish spinster faced with a suggestive sausage on her supper plate?"

For a moment, Adam thought Septimus might choke in his effort not to laugh at the image he'd painted. "I should think that, as a man who had my cock down his throat the other day, you'd know full well there is nothing prudish about me or my desires."

It was Adam's turn to fight the urge to grin and forget every bit of the tension that crackled between them. Everything would be so much better if they could both set aside the things that had hurt or rankled them in favor of simply falling into each other's arms and enjoying themselves. But as short a time as the two of them had known each other, Adam was certain they'd already gone too far for anything between them to simply be casual fucking that ended once they were both sated.

He shifted his stance, uncrossing his arms and planting his hands on his hips instead, aware of how his breeches had dipped low without a tucked-in shirt to keep them up. "If it is not your prejudice against noblemen that stopped you from accepting my offer the other night, can I presume that you have given some thought to the question I asked?"

Septimus blew out a breath and rubbed a hand over his face, then paced to the side. One sort of tension drained away from him, but another rose up to take its place. "It only just dawned on me now," he said, then gestured to the garden outside the window. "When I found myself desperate not to lose some stupid game my friends invented for the sole purpose of throwing the two of us together." He glanced back to Adam with a wary look.

"I am well aware of the purpose of the game." Adam nodded in confirmation, waiting for him to go on.

Septimus stared out the window for a moment longer. The look of wistfulness that came into his eyes and took over his entire expression tugged at Adam's heart. A moment later, he realized Septimus must have been looking at the extraordinary view of the sea available from that window.

"I've lost too much already," Septimus said, so quiet that it made him vulnerable. "Forgive the metaphor, but I am all at sea now. I don't want to lose anything more." Another short stretch of silence passed before Septimus forced his gaze away from the window and onto Adam. "Call me a coward if you must, but I dread the idea of taking something else, *someone* else, into my heart only to have it ripped from me, as so many other things have been of late."

"Who is to say I would be ripped from you?" Adam asked with a shrug. All things considered, it was a bold question for him to ask—one that implied more than a quick tumble or two for both of their satisfaction. It implied time, a future.

Septimus seemed to know it. He stepped away from the window with a serious look. "It may not seem like such a big thing to you, but it is for me. As silly as you might find it to hold oneself back from enjoyment simply because of the possibility that enjoyment might end, I've seen too many endings to recklessly set myself up for another one."

Adam nodded slowly. He sensed that he had Septimus in the palm of his hand, that the man was ready to relent, but he didn't want to crush something that felt so fragile. "Could you not simply live for today and let tomorrow worry about itself?"

He stepped carefully up to Septimus, resting his hands on the man's damp shirt, feeling the heat of his chest and the beat of his heart. His own heart raced as if to catch up to Septimus's.

"You make it all sound so simple," Septimus said, lifting one hand to rest on the side of Adam's face. He traced his thumb over Adam's lower lip, sending shockwaves of pleasure through him. "But what if it all hits the rocks and splinters into nothing?"

Adam shrugged, feeling an inner pull that likely trumped any undertow Septimus had ever experienced at sea. "Then at least you would be able to say you tried," he said.

He didn't give Septimus a chance to answer. He slipped his hands up to his shoulders, leaning into him, and burying his hands in Septimus's still-damp hair. He didn't care that they were both messy from their earlier activity. The scent of sweat and skin was masculine and alluring. It made Adam want to do mad things, to taste Septimus and savor him, and to offer himself up for the man's pleasure.

And yet, he waited—waited for Septimus to be the one to make the first move. Adam's mind was made up. He would have done anything for Septimus, let himself be used in any way Septimus wanted him, even if it meant the two of them would part at some point and Septimus would be nothing but a delicious memory he could savor for the rest of his life. Not that

he would be in a hurry to banish Septimus from his
bed or his arms or his life. Quite the contrary. But
every risk came with a possibility of failure as well as
of success. Adam was willing to take his chances, but
was Septimus?

The answer came a heartbeat later as the tension
that had wrapped itself around Septimus softened
and his arms closed around Adam. He leaned in,
tilting Adam's head up and stealing a kiss. It was deep
and sweet at first, its own form of surrender to what he
could no longer avoid, no matter what the cause of his
fears. Septimus brushed his tongue along Adam's
lower lip, coaxing him to open for him, although
Adam would have opened in every way without the
prompting.

With a growl of need, Septimus kissed him harder.
His fingertips pressed possessively into the flesh of
Adam's sides as he slipped their tongues together, then
drew Adam's into his mouth. Adam let out a sound of
pleasure and acceptance, tightening his hands in Septimus's hair, as their mouths explored each other more
deeply. Inch by inch, moment by moment, Septimus
let go of the anchor that had held him back from truly
giving himself to Adam. Every deepening of their kiss,
ever stroke of his hands against Adam's body was the
sweetest reward any man could ever have hoped for.

"You are too much for me," Septimus murmured
against Adam's mouth, then slid his lips across Adam's
cheek to his neck and shoulder. "You are beautiful and
warm and..." He lost the train of his thought as he nib-
bled on the spot where Adam's neck met his shoulder.
His hands circled Adam's hips, one coming around to
press against the hardening outline of Adam's cock as
it strained against his breeches.

Adam moaned shamelessly at the intimate touch,

arching into it and wordlessly begging for more. His hands roved Septimus's body, bunching up his shirt and pulling it free of his breeches as he did. He wanted to feel his skin hot against Septimus's, feel their bodies writhing together as they sought out pleasure and release.

At last, Septimus wanted the same thing. He palmed Adam's cock for a few more moments through his breeches, then shook himself and leaned back. Instead of retreating fully, however, it was as if a match had been lit. He moved away from Adam enough to pull his shirt up over his head and to toss it aside, then swayed back toward Adam, his hands going for the falls of Adam's breeches.

Adam let out a cry of triumph as Septimus pushed the constricting fabric aside and drew his throbbing prick out. His tip was already slick with moisture, which Septimus spread as his thumb circled Adam's head. Simply touching didn't seem to be enough for Septimus, and before Adam could do more than gasp in surprise, the large man was on his knees in front of him, gripping the base of his cock so that he could close his mouth around the tip and draw Adam in to the wet heat of his mouth.

Adam nearly yelped at the intensity of the pleasure that shot through him. He fisted his hands in Septimus's hair, feeling as though he was in serious danger of coming far too quickly. He didn't have it in him to ask Septimus to stop, though. Along with the fierce pleasure of Septimus's mouth and hand on him came the sweet realization that Septimus couldn't take him very far, and that perhaps this wasn't something he did often. Wondering that had the paradoxical reaction of bringing Adam right up to the edge in no time.

"Wait," he panted, pulling away from Septimus. "That's lovely, but I want more." He stroked a hand from Septimus's hair, across his cheek, to cradle his jaw and lift his head so he could look into Septimus's eyes. "I want you in me," he said, so breathless with need he could barely get the words out. "All of you."

Septimus made a sound of desire that went straight to Adam's soul and leapt to his feet so fast Adam was surprised he didn't keep going through the ceiling. They scrambled toward Adam's tiny bed, then were waylaid by the grating necessity of removing boots and peeling off breeches. The interruption was blessedly short, and the result was that both of them ended up gloriously naked.

"You are everything I adore," Adam sighed, surprising Septimus by pushing him to his back, straddling his hips, and stroking his hands up and down the defined muscles of Septimus's chest and the firm planes of his stomach. He loved the way Septimus's wiry hair felt against his palms, the way the man's nipples hardened under his touch, and the way both of their cocks leaked in anticipation of everything that was to come between them. Adam bent down to lick the saltiness of Septimus's chest as he balanced with one hand on the bed and grasped Septimus's cock with the other. "If you let me," he panted, kissing his way up to Septimus's mouth, "I will put you through your paces until you cannot remember your own name."

Septimus growled at the prospect and bucked against Adam, thrusting into his hand. He clasped his hands on either side of Adam's head and kissed him with punishing force. As reticent as he'd been before, now that the dam had been broke, Septimus was as eager as Adam had ever known a man to be. His body flexed and moved with power under Adam, and the intensity of the energy poring off of him was nearly frightening, but Adam loved every moment of it. He craved the veiled sense of danger that Septimus presented.

That tingling sense of excitement at possible danger flared to an inferno of need when Septimus used his considerable strength to reverse their positions. Better still, he manhandled Adam to his stomach, pressing him down with the full weight of his massive body as he reached for the jar of salve on the table. Adam made a wild sound that encompassed excitement, fear, desire, and pure, giddy joy as the lid— which he'd neglected to secure on the jar the night before—popped off and rolled right off the bed.

"If I didn't know better, I'd say you planned for this," Septimus rumbled, with a combination of passion and humor against Adam's ear.

"I can assure you, that salve was for my own personal use, up until now," Adam replied, wriggling under Septimus in a way that brought his arse into intimate, suggestive contact with Septimus's iron-hard prick. It felt bigger than it looked pressed against the cleft of his arse as it was, and Adam was desperate to feel just how much it would burn and stretch once Septimus was inside of him.

"And have you made frequent use of this salve?" Septimus asked, pulling his hips back.

Adam would have felt bereft without the heat and weight of Septimus against him, except that he knew full well the reason for its temporary absence, and what he was in for once it returned. "Practically every night," he said, half laughing, half groaning, tilting his hips up in blatant, wanton invitation. "Every night since you arrived at Wodehouse Abbey."

"Minx," Septimus scolded him, then grabbed his thighs—one hand slick and cool with salve—and pushed them open wide.

Adam whimpered shamelessly, nearly laughing as he did. There was no point in being coy or pretending like he was some fainting violet with no idea what was going on. He loved being fucked—though he hadn't been nearly enough in his life, as far as he was concerned—particularly by a man bigger than him. Particularly by a man whom he admired and adored, who made him smile with his reluctant vulnerability, and who made his heart ache and sing with the depth of feeling in his eyes. There was no point whatsoever in pretending to be anything but ridiculously, hungrily wanton as Septimus spread a dollop of the salve across his hole, then slipped a finger into him to test his readiness.

"God, yes," Adam groaned raggedly into his bedcovers, pushing back on Septimus to take him deeper.

Septimus had the nerve to laugh. "You could make a small fortune catering to sailors on shore leave in any corner of the Empire," he growled, adding a second finger to stretch Adam farther. "You want it so desperately that you're hardly making me work at all."

"I want *you*," Adam insisted, "not a passel of sailors with ready money. Only you, ever since the first moment I saw—oh!"

Adam was rendered utterly speechless as Septimus lifted his hips, held Adam open, and pushed inside. The surprise of invasion brought with it a burn that reminded Adam it'd been a while since his last time, but as soon as he adjusted and gave himself over to the pleasure, to Septimus, it was glorious. Septimus let out a deep groan of enjoyment, moving slowly at first, as if learning Adam from the inside out, then pulled out, adjusted, and sank deep again.

"My God, you are magnificent," Adam cried as the pulse of Septimus hitting his stride and moving faster within him increased. "It feels so good, so—"

His mindless babbling was cut off as Septimus found exactly the right spot inside of him to send blinding pleasure all through Adam's body. Between the arrogant sound from Septimus that followed proved he knew exactly what he was doing, and the way he thrust harder and faster, Adam thought he might come apart completely, body and soul.

It was better than anything he'd ever experienced before. His body was Septimus's, fully and completely, and Septimus used it with skill. The pleasure that soared through Adam was so potent that there was no need for him to reach for his cock. He burst into an orgasm that had his head spinning and his balls emptying every last drop in a fountain that Adam didn't think would ever end. It could only have lasted a few moments, but it was so powerful that time seemed to stop as Septimus had him completely.

Just as Adam began to slam back into himself, Septimus cried out and jerked against him, filling him with a sense of warm fullness that went far beyond mere physical sensation. The shattering pleasure was beautiful, but perhaps even more so was the ebbing of that intensity as they collapsed into a spent pile on the bed.

They were every bit as sweaty as they'd been while playing games on the lawn, and at first Septimus didn't appear to have the energy even to pull out of him, but Adam didn't mind one bit. He felt accepted and embraced at last. Better still, as he faded into a stupor of exhaustion, he knew deep in his soul that the connection between him and Septimus would last far longer than one wild moment of passion. The thread that bound them together was much stronger than that, and he thrilled at the thought of days and weeks and more ahead of them.

11

There had been times at sea when Septimus had felt as though he'd never see land again—when they'd been blown off course or storm currents had pushed them back from the shore, in spite of his best navigational efforts. The deep-seated worry he had felt during those times—anxiety that had curled through his gut and squeezed his lungs so that every breath felt as though it could be his last—was of the same sort that he'd felt since being forced out of the Navy. But as he awoke from a deep slumber the next morning to a heavy weight on his chest, he realized that the metaphorical weight he'd been carrying since the *Majesty* had been decommissioned was gone. He'd spotted land at last, the storm was over as suddenly as it had started, and he could see home on the horizon.

The *actual* weight covering him was much heavier than a mere blanket, and much warmer as well. That sleep-confused thought was replaced by the realization that it wasn't a blanket at all, it was a body. Adam's body. Adam was splayed and naked above him, apparently sound asleep, with his head resting on Septimus's shoulder and his morning wood wedged tightly against Septimus's own.

Everything rushed back to Septimus from there—the ridiculous game Red and Barrett had invented the day before, the intense conversation he and Adam had had in which he'd bared his soul, and the descent into absolute carnal bliss that the two of them had engaged in afterward. Several times. Septimus had behaved as, well, as a boy Adam's age again in his eagerness to tangle up with Adam in every way they could imagine. Not that Adam was a boy. Far from it. Septimus felt foolish for assuming that Adam's youthful appearance made him somehow green and innocent. The truth was far from that, although Adam had laughingly insisted that he wasn't as experienced as all that... right before he'd swallowed Septimus with all the enthusiasm and talent of an Italian.

The thought brought a smile to Septimus's face. He let out a contented sigh and shifted to stretch his back as much as he could without waking Adam, throwing one arm behind his head as he did. He lazily stroked Adam's back with his other hand, wondering what divine madness had happened to bring him to where he was.

On the surface, he was in Adam's bed with the indomitable man draped over him because there was barely room for one of them to lie comfortably in the damnably small thing, let alone for the two of them to lie side by side. Septimus had suggested at one point that they relocate to his guest room and the much larger bed there, but their efforts to get up and dress so that they could creep through the halls long after dark somehow ended with them undressing again so that Septimus could fold Adam over the end of the bed and pound him into a moaning, sighing puddle of satisfaction. That memory had Septimus laughing even harder.

"Have I thrown my lot in with a madman?" Adam mumbled, writhing and shifting over Septimus as he awoke.

"It seems that you have," Septimus told him, stroking the length of Adam's spine.

Adam purred like a cat and arched into the touch. "If this is madness, I will abandon myself to it freely."

He continued to stretch and wriggle over Septimus, driving Septimus's senses wild as Adam placed a series of mischievous kisses across his chest and shoulders. Adam seemed eager to pick up where they'd left off the night before, and brushed his hands over Septimus's sides with touches that were both light and demanding. Septimus might have been the one to take the aggressive role so far in their lovemaking, but the way Adam handled him and pressed down on him left no doubt in Septimus's mind who controlled the rudder of their liaison.

"Are you still afraid of losing me?" Adam asked softly, once he'd kissed and licked his way up Septimus's neck to his lips.

The question squeezed Septimus's chest, causing him to suck in a breath. He planted his hands firmly on Adam's arse. "Oh, yes," he said gravely. "Now more than ever."

Adam's expression seemed to twitch between a frown and a smile, as if he couldn't discern whether Septimus was serious or teasing him. "You won't, you know," he said, raising a hand to brush the hair back from Septimus's forehead. "Not anytime soon, at least. I am quite content right where I am."

He smiled in a way that felt brighter than the early-morning sunlight peeking through the curtains on one side of the room. Septimus echoed Adam's gesture by sweeping the hair away from his forehead, then stroking a hand over the side of Adam's beautiful face, and then rubbing his thumb across Adam's kiss-reddened lower lip. Adam hummed in approval, then captured Septimus's thumb between his lips, sucking it deep into his mouth. The sensual gesture made Septimus iron-hard and restless, but it also anchored him in a way he never would have expected. Adam was like the sea in the way he'd surged steadily into his life, as relentless as the tide, and as all-consuming. He could see now that it had been futile for him to resist the pull between the two of them from the start.

"What are you thinking?" Adam asked, letting Septimus's thumb go and resting his chin atop his hands as he folded them on Septimus's chest.

"I'm thinking that my life is not my own, and any efforts I've made to steer its course have been in vain," Septimus said, unnerved by his own honesty. Adam inspired him to be honest about everything, even the things that had him tied in knots of confusion.

"A wise conclusion to reach," Adam said with an impish grin.

"I'm thinking that I haven't a clue what to do with my life," Septimus went on, "but perhaps I know with whom I wish to do it."

A pink flush painted Adam's face. "Truly?" he asked, lifting so that he could gaze down at Septimus. "I've wrestled you out of your stubborn insistence that you could not possibly take a gentleman lover because the nobility are devils who cannot be trusted so easily?"

"One glance at this room and I could see you're hardly a gentleman," Septimus laughed.

"As I've been telling you all along," Adam commented, with an overly serious look.

"And one look at that sweet, eager arse of yours

and I decided I didn't care," Septimus laughed even harder.

"Never underestimate the persuasive power of a fine arse willingly presented," Adam laughed with him.

It was surreal. The entire situation was so far outside of the bounds of anything Septimus had ever experienced before that he had no idea what to do with it. All he knew was that the terrifying, endless stretch of uncertainty that was his future suddenly didn't seem to matter. He was no longer concerned about when he might be offered a commission or focused on that elusive day when he could return to the sea. All he wanted to experience was the moment he was in right then and there, with Adam growing increasingly restless atop him, their bodies primed and heated, and their hearts beating as one.

"I do not know if this is the answer to the riddle of what happens next in my life," Septimus said, stroking Adam's tangled hair, voice rough with emotion. "But you are correct to say that you have broken down my defenses with your charm—and your exquisite body," he added in a moment of humor. "As you said yesterday, I am willing to try."

"Good," Adam said, leaning down to treat Septimus to a deep kiss.

It was a kiss of promise, a kiss that attempted to reassure Septimus that all would be well. There was no possible way that Adam could know as much, but the certainty with which Adam kissed him, the confidence with which Adam's hands roved his body, eventually sliding between them to grip both of their cocks together, was enough for Septimus in that moment. He relaxed into Adam's ministrations, giving himself over to whatever the younger man wanted from him.

Adam wanted everything, and he made no secret of it. The man made the most arousing sounds of enjoyment as he stroked the two of them together, jerking his hips for added friction. When that didn't seem to be enough, Adam bent over him, biting Septimus's shoulder with a groan as he moved more insistently against him.

Whether it was the love bite that Septimus was certain would leave a mark, the fact that he'd been aroused since waking, or Adam's energetic movements, Septimus came apart in no time, spilling himself into Adam's hand and across his belly as he did. Adam made a sound of wonder and joy, and a moment later, added his own warm seed to the erotic mess on Septimus's belly.

The young tease had the nerve to straighten, crouching back on his haunches over Septimus's thighs, and smirk down at the result of their passion while still trying to catch his breath. "That's a beautiful sight to greet the day with," he said, arching one eyebrow lasciviously.

"So I've put my trust and my happiness into the hands of a shameless strumpet, have I?" Septimus asked.

Adam responded by biting his lip and gazing down at him with a look that was so blatantly wicked that Septimus's balls twitched, as though looking for a few more drops to spill.

The erotic moment was broken by the nearly comical growl of Adam's stomach, which reminded them they'd skipped supper the night before so that they could dine on each other. That was enough to break the spell of the moment and to propel both of them out of bed.

"I need to go down to my room and bathe properly," Septimus said as he wiped the worst of the mess from his slightly sore body.

"I should do the same," Adam said, studying his naked body in a mirror propped in the corner of the room and grinning at the few bruises and red spots Septimus had left on it.

"You know we're going to be raked across the coals by Red and Barrett as soon as we appear downstairs," Septimus told him as he moved around the room, picking up various articles of his clothing that had been discarded in haste the night before.

"I suppose it's unavoidable." Adam gathered up his own clothes, draping them over a small stand by the cold fireplace. He paused to pick up a letter resting on the mantel—Septimus vaguely remembered Adam reading it on the stairs the day before—then put it down again and moved to the washstand. "The only thing for it is to smile in the face of teasing and be proud to be together."

Septimus arched one eyebrow at him as he pulled on his breeches. "Spoken as one who has never been teased before."

"On the contrary," Adam said, pouring fresh water from the pitcher on his washstand into the bowl, "I've been teased my whole life by everyone from family to schoolmates." He shrugged. "If you laugh with them instead of railing against them for it, the entire purpose of teasing is lost on them."

Septimus shook his head, not certain he agreed with Adam on that one. Once he was sufficiently dressed, he strode over to Adam's side, kissed him affectionately, then bid him adieu and crept out into the hall.

Septimus considered it a minor miracle that he was

able to get down to his room without being spotted by anyone, servant or master. He breathed a sigh of relief as he stripped out of his dirty clothes and set them aside to be laundered, selected new ones for the day, then set to work scrubbing himself thoroughly with soap and water in his washbasin. There was something wistful and sad about washing away Adam's scent on his skin and the evidence of their communion. It went against everything Septimus thought he knew about himself to be so deeply taken with a man, particularly when his life was in such a state of flux. And yet, he couldn't help but smile from ear to ear when he thought about Adam. Perhaps there was such a thing as a school at sea. Perhaps, when the time came and he had his commission and could return to life aboard a ship, he could bring Adam with him. Midshipmen needed someone to tutor them, after all, and even common seamen should be taught to read and write.

His mind was brimming with possibilities as he headed downstairs to break his fast, clean and brushed, without a trace of the night's activities to be found on him, except for the smile he couldn't wipe off his face. It was that smile that Red and Barrett noticed the moment Septimus stepped into the breakfast room.

"I told you," Barrett said, grinning like a fool. It was all he needed to say.

"I never had any doubt," Red said.

"Gentlemen," Septimus greeted them with an overly formal bow, his voice deliberately gruff, then headed to the sideboard. His stomach growled even louder than Adam's had, and he stacked a plate as high as he could to remedy the situation.

"Yes, I imagine you would be ravenous after the

night you had," Red commented, nodding to Septimus's plate as he took a seat at the table.

"Exercise can be exhausting," Barrett added with a mock-sage hum.

"So can fucking," Septimus mumbled before shoveling a forkful of eggs into his mouth.

Red and Barrett burst into laughter, Red nearly spilling the cup of coffee he'd just picked up to sip.

"Good for you," Barrett congratulated Septimus with a salute. "It's about time you took matters into your own hand and began to enjoy this holiday."

"We are here to convalesce and recover our strength following years of war, after all," Red pointed out, drinking his coffee, then putting the cup down.

"I dare say that with a man of Mr. Seymour's youthful exuberance, Septimus's strength will be completely sapped rather than recovered," Barrett laughed.

"Yes, thank you both for your well-wishes," Septimus said, sending them both leveling looks. "Any further opinions on the matter should be addressed to Captain Shut-Your-Gobs of the HMS Wankers." He made a rude gesture at them with his free hand before continuing to eat.

Inwardly, though Septimus couldn't remember the last time he'd been so pleased. He shouldn't have been, that much was certain. He stood to lose so much if everything went wrong. But for the moment, his joy eclipsed his worry. He could only pray that it would stay that way.

"I take it this means no more frequent trips into Hull to see if the Admiralty has answered your appeal and has a new ship for you," Red said, as he settled enough to continue with his meal.

"No," Septimus said, blinking across the table at

him. "Why would my association with Adam change anything with the Admiralty?"

Red exchanged a look with Barrett. "It doesn't," Barrett said. "But perhaps you'll have something more to occupy your mind with, aside from eating your heart out with longing to go back to sea."

"I still wish to go back to sea," Septimus said, cutting one of the five sausages on his plate into smaller pieces.

"But what about Mr. Seymour?" Red asked. "Aside from the fact that he is an excellent tutor for my nephew and niece, he has ambitions to open his own school. On land."

"Which would not preclude me from returning to sea," Septimus said.

Although as soon as the words passed his lips, he wondered. Half the men in the Royal Navy or more had wives on shore. Adam wasn't exactly a wife, but Septimus could imagine that sort of arrangement between the two of them. He liked the idea of having a sweetheart to come home to at the end of each mission. Even so, there was no telling how long it would be until the matter came up. Perhaps Red and Barrett were right to hint that he could find something else to occupy himself in the interim, that would ease the frustration of waiting. Adam's charity school, for example. He believed heartily in Adam's aim for the school. Heaven only knew how aware he was of the necessity of an education for those who weren't born into privilege.

He was halfway through his meal and most of the way to deciding he would throw his support behind Adam's school until his hoped-for letter came from the Admiralty, when Adam himself surprised them all by striding into the room.

"My lords." Adam bowed gracefully to Red and Barrett. When he straightened, his gaze shot straight to Septimus, and his eyes shone with affection.

"Mr. Seymour, good morning," Red greeted him, barely able to keep his giddiness in check as he glanced between Adam and Septimus. "Do come in and join us for breakfast."

Adam looked as though he might refuse for a moment, but when his eyes landed on the sideboard and all of the food still contained there, Septimus could see his resolve break. Adam moved to fix himself a plate, then joined the rest of them at the table.

"We were just discussing you," Red went on, as Septimus reached for the coffee pot to pour a cup for Adam. Red's eyes fairly danced with glee to see the two of them interacting.

"I imagine you were, my lord," Adam said cheekily, peeking at Septimus. He then skillfully avoided all further comments by turning to Barrett as he speared a piece of ham and saying, "Lord Francis and Lady Eliza have informed me that they will not be doing lessons today because you promised to show them how to make and fly a kite?"

"I should have consulted you first," Barrett said with a conciliatory grin. "They were quite taken with the idea after a brief conversation about kites yesterday."

"They are quick-minded children who tend to be taken with anything of interest they're presented with," Red said, beaming with pride.

"They are," Adam agreed. "I consider them delightful models for everything I hope to accomplish with my pupils in the future."

"At your school?" Septimus asked.

"Precisely." Adam tossed Septimus a smile that sent happiness pouring through him.

In addition to that, the sheen of sausage grease that glossed Adam's lips as he ate sent blood and fire straight to Septimus's cock. That he even had the energy to be aroused after all of their activity since the evening before was a wonder.

"I have some questions about your school," Septimus said as he returned to his meal. "If you wouldn't mind me asking."

"I wouldn't at all," Adam said, even more delighted, if that was possible. "I would be more than happy to discuss it with you."

"Good." Septimus grinned at Adam. His heart felt as though it might expand beyond the capacity of his chest as Adam smiled back at them.

"Good lord," Barrett commented across the table. "It's worse than I thought."

"It is," Red agreed, shaking his head. "I don't suppose any of us will have a moment's peace now."

"Just wait until Lucas and the rest of them arrive," Barrett said, sending Red a teasing look.

"My brother will regret ever allowing us to spend the summer here," Red laughed.

Septimus smiled at the cheerful banter, though he had nothing to add. He was in over his head in so many ways, but unlike the gnawing frustration of the past fortnight, now, with Adam, he wasn't sure he minded drowning at all.

12

I t occurred to Adam that he should be alarmed that two lofty noblemen had conspired to throw him and Septimus together, and that they had apparently also arranged for the two of them to be able to spend the day together without the children in tow. He'd never exactly tried to hide who he was before, but the matter-of-fact attitude that had descended on Wodehouse Abbey with the arrival of Lord Beverley and his friends was so uncommon as to be surreal.

And Adam intended to take full advantage of the permissive atmosphere.

"You don't mind walking out with me?" he asked Septimus as they started away from the house and down the lane that would lead them to the shore.

It was a gorgeous, sunny, balmy day, and he had too much restless, happy energy swirling within him to idle away in one of the gardens. He absolutely could not countenance the thought of sipping tea and pretending he and Septimus were docile acquaintances enjoying a social call. Not when the sun was shining, the birds were singing, and everything was so very right with the world.

"That is to say," Adam caught the double meaning

in his words and blushed as he rushed on with, "you've been doing so much wandering over hills and dales these last few days. Might you need a rest?"

"No," Septimus answered, straightforward as always. "I like walking. It gives me something to do in a time when I feel particularly useless."

Adam's brow shot up at that. "You're far from useless, you know." A salacious grin pulled at the corners of his mouth before he could stop himself. His thoughts were forever traveling down libidinous paths when Septimus was around. It had only gotten worse since the evening before.

Septimus sent him a flat, sideways look. "I want to find a clever reply to your cheekiness, but I believe anything I say will only encourage you. And I know you understood what I meant."

"And what is so very wrong about encouraging me?" Adam asked, his grin broadening as he danced about, turning to walk backward for a few steps so that he could face Septimus for a moment and wink at him. He hadn't had that sort of energy since he was in the schoolroom, eager to impress the first boy he'd ever fancied. Not that anything had or could have come of that.

Septimus let out a wry laugh and shook his head. "Incorrigible," he muttered, but blushed and smiled as he did.

Adam bounced his way back into walking more sedately by Septimus's side. "I meant what I said, though. You are far more useful in more ways than you are, perhaps, imagining."

"Without the sea, I feel..." He frowned, staring at the coastline in the distance, and frowning. "I've no idea what to do with myself."

"What did you do before you went to sea?" Adam

asked with a shrug as they turned off the main road and started down a narrower path through a rolling meadow that would take them to the beach, about a mile on.

Septimus huffed a wry laugh. "I have always been at sea. Even as a lad. My father was a fisherman. A prosperous one, with friends in the Navy who were able to secure me a position as a cabin boy at the age of ten."

Adam's brow flew up. "So you really have no experience of life on land."

"Hardly any," Septimus said with another sideways look. This one was bashful, which Adam found utterly irresistible. Septimus might have been large and strong, with the seriousness of experience about him most of the time and a frown that could cause a lesser man to shake in his boots, but he had a strange sort of innocence about him as well, a vulnerability that deepened Adam's interest in him from the purely physical to something that squeezed his heart like a vise.

"What do you think of York?" Adam blurted the question before he could think about whether it was a wise or relevant one.

Septimus was so startled by the seemingly abrupt change of subject that he nearly missed a step. "I've never been," he answered.

"Do you think you'd like to?" Adam asked. "It's where I attended university."

It was also where employment as a teacher at an old and prestigious school was waiting for him, if he wanted it. Jeremy's offer had been the last thing on his mind, considering everything that had happened since he'd received the letter. As he'd thought the day before, teaching in York was far from being his first choice of a course for his life. He wanted his own school almost as much as he wanted Septimus in his arms for as long as he could have him. But there was a certain appeal in stability. Jeremy's letter had hinted Adam could earn enough money teaching in York to finance a school himself. Septimus could find employment of his own, perhaps as a boatman on the River Ouse. The two of them could find a house to let on the river, near the school. Their days could be filled with gainful employment, and their nights with pleasure.

"Why are you looking at me like that?" Septimus asked.

Adam blinked out of his beautiful, domestic thoughts. His face heated like the sun, and he shrugged, sending Septimus a sheepish smile. "I was off with the fairies for a moment," he said, wishing he could stay away with the fairies and take Septimus with him.

Septimus grunted, but the look in his eyes was pure, possessive fondness. "I wouldn't mind visiting York someday."

"Would you ever want to live there?" Adam asked softly.

Septimus shook his head. "It's too far from the sea." He paused after he answered, glancing to Adam with a somewhat suspicious look. "Why? Is there something in York?"

The sudden fear that if he revealed the truth, Septimus would break things off between the two of them then and there gripped Adam. He wasn't willing to risk damaging the perfect happiness that existed between the two of them in that moment for what amounted to a second-choice idea.

Instead, he said, "I still maintain that you would be a brilliant teacher yourself. Particularly if you were imparting lessons about navigation and seafaring to young men with a mind to make a living at sea."

Septimus glanced to him in surprise. "Are you intending to open a school for mariners now?"

Adam grinned at the idea. "That could be lovely," he said, letting himself daydream once more. "We would take in all children, of course, but we might gain a reputation for ourselves as an institution that takes in the sons of impoverished fishermen and educates them not only for business, but for a life in the Navy, or on commercial vessels."

They could build a cozy home for the school, perhaps on some promontory overlooking the sea, like the one they were approaching. There would be dormitories for the pupils, but also rooms for him and Septimus. They would be separate from the rest of the school so that the students never saw or heard anything they shouldn't, but it would be as cozy as a cottage by the sea for just the two of them. And the school could own several boats. Septimus would take the children out and teach them to sail, while he stayed home, teaching literature and maths, and whatever else young men needed to learn to make their way in the world. At night, Septimus would come home and Adam would serve him supper, which they would eat together before retiring to their bed for the night where they would—

"You have that odd look again," Septimus said, nearly laughing this time. "And do not even think of telling me your thoughts are innocent. Your breeches tell a different story."

Adam glanced down at himself and flushed even hotter. He cleared his throat and adjusted his stance, attempting to calm himself before they reached the beach, where there was a possibility they would encounter others.

"I am simply happy," he said, peeking at Septimus.

He went further than that, glancing around expectantly. When he was confident no one was near enough to see them, he reached for Septimus's hand and threaded their fingers together.

"You are a rascal, Adam Seymour," Septimus said, laughing and shaking his head, but keeping his hand in Adam's.

"And you must approve to some degree, Septimus Bolton," Adam fired back. "Otherwise, you would have told me to sod off, like you did for the first fortnight of our acquaintance, instead of compromising every one of your principles and succumbing to my wiles the moment I confronted you."

"I had no choice," Septimus argued with mock consternation. "You would have bludgeoned me into capitulation if I hadn't seen fit to give up the fight. Besides," he sent Adam a wry look. "It's not as though I have any better way to spend my summer."

"Oh, I see," Adam replied with equal wryness. "I am merely a preoccupation until something more engaging comes along."

"Precisely," Septimus said with a nod. He glanced ahead of them to the cliffs they were approaching that looked over the beach and the sea beyond, but sneaked in a teasing, sideways look, his eyes sparkling with mirth and affection.

The two of them broke into laughter. It was a perfect moment, as far as Adam was concerned, even if they did have to let go of each other's hands so that they could descend to the beach in order to continue their walk.

The shore closest to Wodehouse Abbey was not only overlooked by cliffs in many places, it was dotted with deep coves that contained caves. Over the years, particularly during the heart of the war, those caves had been used by smugglers attempting to bring French goods onto English soil.

"Smugglers were always a real problem in Cornwall," Septimus told Adam as they investigated one of the caves in particular. "Drove my father mad. They made it that much harder for him to make an honest trade. And they interfered with any young lady unfortunate enough to be caught out by one."

"How scandalous," Adam replied, peering around a dark corner to see if there were any smugglers or booty hiding there.

When he glanced back over his shoulder, he found Septimus regarding his backside rapaciously. Adam grinned, his pulse racing. He was bent over in rather a suggestive position as he searched for smuggled goods.

"It would be a terrible shame if an innocent young man, unfamiliar with the ways of smugglers and the sea, were caught unawares by a rough and wicked pirate," he told Septimus in a breathless voice.

"Would it?" Septimus asked, stalking closer to him. There was just enough light from the mouth of the cave for Adam to see the fiery look in Septimus's eyes. Not that he needed to see that look. The way Septimus reached to undo the falls of his breeches spoke volumes.

"Whatever shall I do?" Adam murmured, attempting to feign panic, but too giddy and aroused by the game they were playing to manage it. "My poor virtue," he lamented, then burst into laughter that echoed off the cave's walls.

That laughter stopped with a gasp as Septimus grabbed him around his waist and hauled his back up against him. The unmistakable spear of Septimus's cock pressed against Adam's backside, causing another gasp that turned into a moan. Adam wasn't even certain what sound he made as Septimus reached around to palm his prick through the fabric of his breeches. He was hard and aching for that touch and more in an instant.

"Did I not say that you would be the death of me?" Septimus rumbled in his ear, then brought his lips to Adam's neck above his collar.

Adam suddenly found himself wishing he hadn't dressed so formally, that he'd foregone a neckcloth, waistcoat, and jacket entirely. He wished he'd foregone clothes all together, though there was something sinful and erotic about the way Septimus raced through undoing the falls of his breeches, then pushing them down around his thighs, as Adam could do nothing but arch against him.

"Please don't hurt me, dread pirate," he groaned, wriggling his naked arse against Septimus's hot prick. Septimus made a sound that was something between a moan of pleasure and a laugh as he moved against Adam, nudging his legs as far apart as they could go with his breeches bunched just above his knees. When Adam felt the press of Septimus's cock against the cleft of his arse, he said in a more serious voice, "Honestly, please don't hurt me. I'm am truly not experienced enough to be able to take you dry."

Septimus responded with a chuckle, pressing kisses against the nape of Adam's neck. "I wouldn't dream of it. There are other ways we can enjoy ourselves."

Adam turned his head slightly to send Septimus a

curious look, but before he could say anything, Septimus nudged him forward a bit roughly, as though he truly were a pirate who had caught an innocent lad unawares. He tipped Adam off balance enough that he had to brace his hands against the cool, damp cave wall for purchase. A moment later, Adam heard the sound of Septimus spitting. He didn't have a chance to ask what that was about before Septimus surprised him into a gasp by sliding his now slightly slick cock through the gap at the top of his thighs.

"Oh!" he gulped as Septimus grabbed his hips to adjust him in a way that would provide the best friction for both of them. Septimus tested their position by thrusting a few times, rubbing against Adam's peritoneum and balls in a way that felt completely foreign, but surprisingly good. "I've never done this before."

"First time for everything," Septimus growled against Adam's shoulder, then started to jerk in earnest.

At first, Adam wanted to laugh at the sheer novelty of their coupling. He supposed it would do in a pinch when there was nothing on hand to smooth the usual sort of penetration. There was something sweet and intimate about it, as though he were giving himself over for Septimus's pleasure in a way that required real trust and closeness. It was wonderful to simply let himself be used that way.

His mind changed entirely once Septimus found his rhythm, then reached a hand around to fist Adam's cock as he did. Wild waves of pleasure shot through him, and it was all he could do not to tilt his head back and let out every wicked cry and moan that Septimus seemed determined to wring out of him. It was so much more than just two mates taking pleasure from each other where they could. It was fun and playful, joyful even. It was the kind of sensual, silly thing two long-time lovers did when they were feeling so randy that they couldn't wait until they were home to enjoy each other.

And yet, Adam did feel like he was home. He felt as though he had set foot in a new land and known the minute he saw it that it was where he wanted to spend the rest of his life. Perhaps it made him a lovesick fool, but whatever course his life took from there on out, he couldn't imagine it without Septimus.

Septimus's unrestrained grunts as he jerked hard against Adam seemed to echo the thoughts of Adam's heart. The crude but delicious way their bodies slapped together would live in Adam's imagination forever. As would the way Septimus came apart with a shuddering cry, painting the cave wall in front of them with his seed. Adam nearly laughed again at the wildness of the moment, and clenched his thighs so that Septimus wouldn't pull back from him before he was ready. Septimus seemed to know what he wanted and kept his body flush against Adam's, his spent cock tight between his thighs as he finished Adam off with a few more deft strokes. Adam cried out as he erupted, adding his own marks to the cave wall beside Septimus's.

A few heartbeats later, as the two of them slumped together, overheated and spent, Adam began to laugh in earnest.

"That was utterly mad," he said, his body relaxing as Septimus pulled away from him at last.

"You drive me to heights of madness I've never known," Septimus agreed, laughing himself. He slowly tucked himself back into his breeches and set himself to right. "I haven't been this randy since I was a lad just learning all the things a cock could do."

"Yes, I could see I have that effect on you," Adam laughed, stumbling away from the cave wall so that he could tidy up as well. He couldn't stop giggling for the life of him, though, and as soon as he had his breeches refastened, he wobbled over to Septimus and threw his arms around his shoulders. "But you have that effect on me as well. I think I could spend the rest of my life in your arms."

He leaned in for a kiss, but Septimus had gone stiff. For one terrifying moment, Adam thought he'd ruined everything by saying the wrong thing. He was daft to think Septimus was ready to talk about the rest of their lives yet. But he was determined not to be done in by his impetuousness. He pretended as though he hadn't said anything, kissing Septimus slowly, nibbling on his lower lip and, when Septimus relaxed enough to let him in, sliding his tongue along Septimus's.

The tension drained from Septimus, filling Adam with so much relief it made him dizzy. He rested his weight against Septimus, trusting that Septimus's strength would keep them upright. It felt so good to have Septimus's strong arms around him, his mouth playing with his, and to feel Septimus's heart thudding against his chest at they pressed together, that Adam closed his eyes and pushed everything else out of his mind but kissing Septimus.

At least, until the faint sound of raised voices somewhere outside of the cave and what sounded like hammering shook Adam out of his blissful revery. That must have been what had Septimus so tense before.

"What the devil is that?" he asked, leaning away from Septimus to glance out the cave's entrance.

"We should probably—" Septimus started, but

didn't finish his sentence. Instead, he stepped away from Adam—sweeping him with a glance as if to make certain he was put together right and wouldn't raise anyone's suspicions—then headed out of the cave.

On the other side of the cave from the section of beach they'd walked to get there, at the top of the cliff bordering the shore, a small crew of men had gathered at the front of what appeared to be a large, old house. A weathered wooden staircase led up from the cove Adam and Septimus crossed to the cliff and the house. By the time Adam and Septimus had climbed it, two of the three men who they'd spotted walking around the house had climbed back into a wagon that looked ready to depart. The third man was staring through the front door of the house. The hammering Adam had heard must have come from a fresh sign that had been erected beside the house's front door that read, "For Sale or Let."

An inexplicable thrill went through Adam at the sight of the building that came close to the pulsing excitement that he felt with Septimus's body wrapped up with his. He glanced up at the house, attempting to calculate on sight how many rooms it might have and how it could be converted. It was almost as if the Almighty had heard his earlier thoughts about a school by the sea and had set the house down on earth right then and there so that he could find it. He was amazed that he hadn't stumbled across the house before in his wanderings since coming to work at Wodehouse Abbey. In his heart of hearts, he knew that the house was destined to belong to him.

A moment later, the man standing at the doorway seemed to lose whatever patience he was attempting to hold onto as he called into the house, "Have you had enough of a look around, Mr. Goddard? Are these premises to your liking and are your clients ready to complete the purchase?"

A moment after that, none other than Martin Goddard stepped out of the house.

13

Septimus approached the old house with wariness buzzing in his gut. There was something so solid and so permanent about the massive thing. It wasn't large enough to be the manor house of some grand estate, but it was far larger than any house Septimus had ever seen. His first instinct was to wonder who would have built such a house and what impossibly high sum they were asking for the place.

His second thought came when he glanced across to Adam and saw hope gleaming in his eyes. His young lover was transfixed by the place. His face flushed, and Septimus could have sworn he saw Adam's heart beat faster. Adam wore the same look that Septimus had worn every time he'd approached a new ship that would be his home and his refuge for however long the winds were favorable. It sent twin jolts of emotion through him—joy on Adam's behalf and sheer, stark terror over how real Adam's plans for the future were. Adam's plans for a future *on land*.

All of that collapsed in a moment when the figure of Martin Goddard marched out the door, chin tilted up, imperious smile on his face, avarice in his eyes.

"Yes," Goddard said, looking down his nose at the

man who had been standing in the doorway but backed up as Goddard came through. "This will do. I'm certain my clients will take to the place the moment they see it."

A moment later, about the time that Adam's face started to fall into a mask of frustration and determination as he stared at Goddard, Goddard noticed him.

"Good heavens, what are you doing here, Seymour?" Goddard asked, sauntering down the house's front stairs to him. "Come to gawp at all the ways my career has advanced further than yours?"

Septimus narrowed his eyes at the arrogant prick, balling his hands into fists at his sides. He hadn't been impressed with Goddard at the festival the other day, and he was even less impressed with the man now.

"I'm interested in purchasing the house," Adam declared.

Septimus unclenched his hands and whipped to Adam in surprise. It wasn't as though he hadn't known from the moment he saw the look of dreams in Adam's eyes that Adam would want the place, but hearing him declare as much so immediately was like taking a cannonball in the gut.

"Are you certain?" he asked Adam cautiously.

Adam turned to him. "Can't you see it, Septimus? This house is perfect. The size is just right, the placement in relation to Hull is perfect, and it stands right here on the sea. I would be perfect for both of us," he added, lowering his voice, his eyes glimmering with excitement as he met Septimus's.

"I beg your pardon?" Goddard asked. When Adam and Septimus turned back to him, he shook his head and asked, "Perfect for what? For both of you?"

"For my school," Adam said, taking a step toward the front door. "Mr. Bolton will be teaching there," he lied smoothly. Or perhaps Adam didn't see it as a lie. He glanced up at the building's edifice, then stepped up the front stairs to peer into the hall. "Can we tour it?" he asked, turning to the man who had called for Goddard earlier.

The man gaped for a moment, glancing from Goddard to Adam, and then to Septimus, as if he were the final authority in the matter. Septimus found that amusing, or would have if he hadn't felt as though every nerve in his body had been pulled taut, as if his future hung in the balance. Adam, Goddard, and even the man showing the house were all young, which was one thing Septimus couldn't say.

"Is the house open to be toured, mister...?" Septimus asked the man.

"Reynolds." The man shook himself and jumped forward, as if he'd suddenly been called to action. "Nathaniel Reynolds. And yes, the house is available to be toured." He turned to the two men waiting in the wagon. "You might as well go back without me. I've another tour to give. Mr. Goddard." He turned to Goddard. "My associates would be more than happy to drive you back to Hull."

"Oh, no," Goddard said, crossing his arms and narrowing his eyes at Adam. "If you wish to attempt to swipe this house right out from under the auspicious investing eye of my clients, then I plan to stay and make certain you fail." He sniffed. "I doubt Mr. Seymour is in any sort of financial situation to be seriously considered for such a purchase, regardless."

Once again, Septimus felt the need to defend and protect Adam—mostly by pummeling Goddard into the ground. "You might be surprised at what Mr. Seymour is capable of," he told both Goddard and Reynolds.

Adam stood straight and tall, blushing with pleasure at the compliment, and glanced to Reynolds. "I should like to tour the house one way or another," he said, with strength and authority, but also the sort of kindness that Goddard lacked.

"Very well, sir." Reynolds waved to his companions, who drove the wagon off, then stepped into the house.

Their group made introductions before beginning a walk through the house's vast interior.

"As you can see," Reynolds said, walking ahead with Adam and pointing out various features of the downstairs hallway and parlors, "the house was designed for a large occupancy. Along with several parlors, a library, a study, a music room, and the usual dining rooms on the ground floor, there are seven bedrooms upstairs. The house also contains a large kitchen and rooms for various servant activities. There are four bedrooms for servants in the attic."

"Why is such a large house so far away from town, and yet not part of any estate?" Adam asked, as they wandered to the back of the house to see the kitchens.

"The house was constructed by a Mr. Henshaw for his rather large family, using the profits from a series of successful speculations he made on the cargo of trade ships journeying between England and the Orient," Mr. Reynolds explained.

"Is speculating on trading vessels truly so profitable?" Adam asked, glancing over his shoulder to Septimus.

"It depends," Septimus said with a shrug. "If the ships in question make it successfully to ports in the far East and are able to secure large cargos of luxury goods, and then if they are able to sail back to England successfully without losing cargo, crew, or the entire ship, fortunes can be made."

"If?" Adam asked, both curious and worried.

"Journeys of that sort could take over a year. The potential for disaster is high. Some men sink their entire fortune into speculation on ships that are lost at sea or captured by privateers." He nodded to Reynolds. "It would seem that this Mr. Henshaw was one of the lucky ones."

"Oh, he was," Reynolds said. "He became friends with a particular captain in whom he placed complete trust. The partnership made for half a dozen successful voyages over the course of a decade. Thus this magnificent house."

"It would make a perfect school," Adam said with a dreamy sigh.

It was the same sort of sigh with the same note of longing in it that would have fired Septimus's blood and prompted him to steal Adam back down to the smugglers' cave under any other circumstances. The way Goddard glared at Adam, as if he would pull out a knife and lodge it in Adam's back for even thinking about taking his prize, kept Septimus's arousal in check. It also fueled his desire to give Adam everything he wanted, even if those things made him feel as though heavy chains were being roped around his neck.

"A school, you say?" Reynolds asked Adam.

"Yes," Adam said. "It is my ambition to open a school for impoverished students."

Goddard snorted at the idea. "Sentimental nonsense," he said. "My clients wish to purchase the property in order to convert it into a convalescent home for the families of industrialists and successful men of business—such as Mr. Henshaw himself—and for

members of the nobility. The proximity to Wodehouse
Abbey and the prospect of invitations to balls and
such held by the Duke of Malton would be quite a
draw."

Septimus clenched his jaw and stared at Goddard
for a moment in disbelief before saying, "Your clients
wish to turn this house into a staging point for social-
climbers with more money than sense, who wish to
take advantage of Lord Malton's hospitality?"

"You make it sound like something wicked," Goddard said with a sniff.

It was wicked, as far as Septimus was concerned.
He hadn't yet met his host, Lord Malton, but he knew
Red like he knew his own brother. Anyone who
thought they could impose on a kind family in the
hope that it would increase their social standing was
exactly the sort of person that had caused his hatred
of the nobility in the first place. Goddard's scheme was
the epitome of using inborn social advantages to advance over more worthy souls. Perhaps it wasn't truly
the nobility themselves that he despised so much, but
those who used the advantages of birth, class, and
wealth to foist themselves into a position where they
didn't deserve to be.

"Perhaps you could show me the bedrooms?"
Adam suggested, sending Septimus a curious sideways look as he and Reynolds walked on ahead.

"Certainly," Reynolds said as the two of them pre-
ceded Septimus and Goddard back into the hall. "And
I must say, I am intrigued by your idea of a school,"
Reynolds went on. "As I understand it, this house has
always been filled with children."

Septimus let them get ahead, and as soon as he
could, he stepped in front of Goddard, blocking his
progress.

"If Mr. Seymour wishes to purchase or let this house for his school, you should know that I will do everything in my power to assist him," he said. "That includes preventing a bully with his own foolish social ambitions from getting in his way."

"I cannot imagine what you are suggesting," Goddard said, his voice anxious and wispy.

"I believe you can," Septimus said, narrowing his eyes.

"Is that a threat?" Goddard's voice rose an octave. "Are you threatening me, sir?"

"I am telling you that these clients of yours should search elsewhere for the property they wish to purchase," Septimus said. "Not only will I move heaven and earth to ensure Mr. Seymour fulfills his dream of a school, I will not allow my friends at Wodehouse Abbey to suffer the indignity of flocks of fortune-hunters darkening their doorstep, thanks to your efforts on behalf of your clients."

For a moment, Goddard stared at Septimus with wide, wary eyes. Then he burst into laughter, though it did nothing to ease the tension from his shoulders. "How very quaint of you, Mr. Bolton. And how very hypocritical." Septimus clenched his jaw and glared at Goddard, who went on with, "And what, pray tell, are you yourself doing by residing at Wodehouse Abbey for the summer? You cannot tell me that a man of your birth—and yes, I have listened to all of the gossip about Lord Malton's summer house guests and where they come from—is not counting the minutes until Lord Malton returns and hosts some sort of ball or house party. I would not be at all surprised if you snatched up the first industrial heiress or younger daughter of some earl with two or three hundred pounds a year to line your fishy coffers."

Septimus grinned in spite of the vicious insult. "Lord Beverley has been like a brother to me for years," he said, crossing his arms. "Serving together in a time of war forms those sorts of bonds. But I suppose you would know nothing of that, seeing as you are a trembling coward who kept both feet firmly planted on English soil, sniveling away on behalf of fortune-hunting clients, instead of serving in any capacity against Bonaparte."

"I have no... it wasn't like... you cannot insult me like..."

Septimus turned and marched away before Goddard could find words to justify his cowardice and greed.

He caught up with Adam and Reynolds as they made their way down the main staircase to the front hall.

"It is perfect, Septimus," Adam said, so filled with joy and dreams that he'd forgotten to address Septimus formally in front of the others. "I have to have it. Whatever it takes. This is the place."

"You are too late," Goddard said, marching up from the back of the hall, where Septimus had left him. "My clients want to purchase the place."

"Have they made an offer yet?" Septimus asked. He turned to Reynolds. "Have any offers been accepted?"

"No," Reynolds said, glancing cautiously between Septimus and Goddard. "Mrs. Henshaw has not received an offer yet."

"So the house belongs to Mrs. Henshaw?" Adam asked, the spark in his eyes taking on a competitive gleam as he peeked at Goddard.

Reynolds looked worried that he'd said something wrong. "The house is currently owned by the late Mr. Henshaw's widow, yes," he said. "She has resided with her sister, Mrs. Iverson, in Hull these last few years, since Mr. Henshaw's death. But she is old now, and none of her children have expressed an interest in taking over the responsibility and management of such a large house."

"I will speak to my clients about purchasing the place at once," Goddard said, marching past Septimus and Adam and straight out the door, as if a footrace would decide who earned the right to purchase the property.

Septimus waited until Goddard was gone before asking Reynolds, "You said Mrs. Henshaw lives in Hull with her sister?"

"That is right," the man said with a nod.

Septimus turned to Adam with a grin. "Then we should go speak to the woman at once."

Adam returned his grin. "I believe you're right. Thank you so much for showing us the house, Mr. Reynolds."

They parted ways with Reynolds, who stayed to lock up the house, and headed straight to Hull. Adam brimmed with excitement the entire way, telling Septimus everything he'd seen upstairs and how the house seemed destined to be filled with children.

"The parlors downstairs could easily be converted into classrooms," he said, nearly bouncing with each step he took along the road. "The music room and library could stay just as they are. Perhaps there is little practical purpose in giving music lessons to poor students, but music inspires the soul and could give them all the encouragement they need to achieve greatness."

"I'm certain your pupils would love music lessons," Septimus said, sending Adam an indulgent smile. The man was everything good and sweet in the world. It amazed Septimus that Adam could go from an erotic, sensual siren with no inhibitions whatsoever, rutting in a smugglers' cave with him one moment, and the next, to a teacher and prospective father of dozens of young men whose futures he wished to brighten. It certainly put to rest any unkind thoughts people might have had about the true character of men who enjoyed the sensual as much as Adam did. There was absolutely no correlation at all between the height of a man's character and his enjoyment of horizontal activities.

It was somehow comical to spend most of the walk into Hull close enough behind Goddard that they could see him hurrying along the road at a fast clip. Goddard truly did appear to view the whole situation as a race of some sort.

"Why does Goddard dislike you so?" Septimus asked Adam as they neared the edge of the town and finally lost sight of the odious man.

Adam laughed. "He dislikes me because nearly everyone else likes me."

"You are deliciously likeable," Septimus said, brushing his hand against Adam's in a way that any passerby would see as incidental.

Those same passersby would not have mistaken the cheekiness in Adam's return grin, though. "You are kind to say so." His grin widened for a moment before he went on with, "Goddard has always been jealous of what he sees as privileges that have been handed to me—higher test marks in school, the attention of the young ladies of our acquaintance, the favor of our elders. He believes he deserves those things over me, though only God knows why."

The explanation was obvious, but it sent a jolt of guilt through Septimus all the same. He was jealous of naval officers who received things that he could work and work for and never get. He'd stood by and watched others promoted over him for no reason other than wealth and status. He still boiled with anger at the way Captain Wallace had betrayed him—though that betrayal seemed somehow to be lessened over the past fortnight at Wodehouse Abbey. It came as a shock to Septimus that he had more in common with Goddard than he wanted to.

And yet, envy of what came easily to others hadn't made him into a peevish, angry ponce, had it?

The question still slithered through him as they reached Hull and asked around for Mrs. Henshaw's address. It was surprisingly easy to find, as it seemed most of Hull knew who the old woman and her sister were. Within half an hour, Septimus and Adam were knocking on the woman's door.

"What a pleasant surprise to receive a call from not one, but two handsome young men," Mrs. Henshaw greeted them, using a cane to rise from the chair where she sat in a cozy parlor, as the maid showed Septimus and Adam in.

"Please do not rise on our behalf, ma'am," Adam said, rushing to the woman's chair and helping her to sit comfortably again.

Septimus couldn't have been prouder of Adam or more touched by his kindness. He nodded to Mrs. Henshaw, then to the other old woman in the room, whom he assumed was Mrs. Iverson. "How do you do?" he greeted them.

"These old bones have known better days," Mrs. Henshaw laughed. She patted Adam's hand once she was seated. "Thank you, young man. And to what do we owe the pleasure of this visit?"

Adam glanced to Septimus, as though asking

him whether he should jump right into things. Septimus had no more experience calling on elderly ladies than he had in felling trees in the middle of a forest, but he nodded approvingly to Adam all the same.

"Well," Adam began cautiously, perching on the edge of the seat nearest to Mrs. Henshaw. "To be honest, I wish to inquire about the house you are selling. The one overlooking the cliff by the sea near Wodehouse Abbey."

Mrs. Henshaw chuckled. "As if I have more than one house to sell."

As she spoke, Mrs. Iverson gestured for Septimus to come sit on the small sofa under the window with her. The elderly woman's face shone with appreciation of Septimus's physique, and she raked him with a look as though she were a coquette at her first dance. Blushing, Septimus went to sit beside her. Mrs. Iverson said nothing, but gazed at him as though reliving episodes from her romantic past as Mrs. Henshaw went on. She grasped Septimus's hand in her two gnarled ones, and Septimus smiled.

"I raised twelve children in that house," Mrs. Henshaw sighed. "Eight of them my own, four of them George's from his first wife. Two were mine from my first marriage as well, God rest poor Robert's soul." For a moment, she looked wistfully out the window opposite her.

"How lovely," Adam said in a kind voice. "You see, I wish to purchase the house so that I might start a school. A school for boys who do not have the financial wherewithal to attend school otherwise. I wish to give those boys the start in the world that they deserve."

Mrs. Henshaw dragged her eyes away from the

window and her mind back from the past and smiled at Adam. "A school, you say? Do tell me more."

Adam rushed to explain everything to her, from his planned curriculum to the methods he would use to find or select boys for the school. Septimus hadn't heard everything himself, and was equally as enthralled as Mrs. Henshaw and her sister—who stroked Septimus's hand during the explanation as if it were a cat. Septimus didn't mind. He wondered when the woman had last had any sort of gentleman caller.

The more Adam spoke, the more Septimus could envision the school. Not only that, the more details Adam discussed, the more Septimus's imagination set about fitting himself into those plans and designs. His whole life had involved the sea. His heart was firmly in the sea. But the more Adam spoke, the more Septimus gazed at him and the life and light that seemed to surround him as he talked about his dreams, and the more Septimus could feel bits of his heart blending with those dreams, blending with Adam. He'd never imagined he could love anything as much as the sea, but now he heard the whisper of something else, like the gentle lapping of a calm sea against the hull of a ship, or the crackle and fizz of sea foam as it pushed and retreated over a rocky shore. The fact that his heart conjured up an image of the shore instead of the deepest part of the sea was new and telling.

"Your school sounds lovely," Mrs. Henshaw said with a smile, reaching across to pat Adam's hand as he finished his explanation.

Adam sat straighter, his blue-green eyes filling with expectation. "Will you consider selling it to me, then?" he asked. "It might take me some time to find a financier, but if I could approach men interested in becoming patrons of this sort of endeavor with premises for the school already secured, I'm certain that would go a long way toward convincing those would-be patrons."

Mrs. Henshaw's smile grew slightly wistful. "My son makes these sorts of decisions for me," she said. "I am drawn to your idea, but I must consult with him first. He is away at the moment."

Adam only looked disappointed for a moment. "I do not mind waiting," he said, glancing to Mrs. Henshaw as though she were a lifelong friend. "And if your son would like to call on me at Wodehouse Abbey to hear details of my plans once he returns, I would happily receive him."

"Wodehouse Abbey?" Mrs. Henshaw exclaimed, eyes bright. "My, but we are well-connected, aren't we?"

Septimus smiled at the easy manner between Adam and Mrs. Henshaw. He felt proud of Adam in a way that was as intimate as it was strong. If it were up to Mrs. Henshaw alone, he was certain Adam would have his school. But it remained to be seen what the son would say. And if the son also approved, Septimus had the feeling his entire world could be turned upside down.

14

Adam felt as though he were walking on clouds when he and Septimus left Mrs. Henshaw's house to head back to Wodehouse Abbey.

"I couldn't have asked for a more perfect house with a more perfect history for my school," he told Septimus as they sat side by side in the back of a farmer's cart, bumping along the road home. "I cannot help but think this is a sign that everything will work out just as it should."

Septimus smiled and laughed, bumping his shoulder against Adam's. Although that could just have been the rugged accommodations of the ride they'd managed to secure to spare their feet from more miles of walking. "I'm glad you're happy," he said, smiling fondly at Adam.

"This is good fortune for both of us," Adam told him, a bit bashful in spite of his happiness. "I was not merely joking earlier when I said you would make a good teacher, or that we could train future mariners in the school. I... I should like it exceedingly if you wanted to make the school your home."

He stopped just short of saying if Septimus would

like to make a home with him. On the one hand, their love affair was so new, so fresh. There was no telling what course it would take or whether Septimus would be interested in staying with him beyond the summer and his original plans. On the other, Adam had never felt such a deep and immediate connection with a man before. Everything about him and Septimus seemed to fit together, and in more ways than physically. Septimus had a calming, grounding presence to him that Adam had found invaluable in his confrontation with Goddard that afternoon. There was no telling what he would have done or what sort of trouble he would have caused with Goddard if Septimus hadn't been there to remind him of what was truly important.

By that same token, Adam felt deep within him that he was important to Septimus, though he had yet to enumerate all of those ways. Septimus had smiled more that afternoon than he had in the more than a fortnight of their acquaintance. He seemed more relaxed now than he had been since arriving at Wodehouse Abbey. Adam flattered himself to believe it was more than just the physical release that came with sexual satisfaction. Septimus liked him. He needed him. They simply worked together.

Now all he needed to do was to convince Septimus that a life together, operating a charity school, was a life Septimus should seriously consider.

"I never imagined myself as a teacher of any sort," Septimus confessed as the wagon neared the end of the lane that led up to Wodehouse Abbey.

Adam waited, heart beating faster with uncertainty, but Septimus didn't say more. He couldn't tell if that answer was agreement and a statement of intent to stay with Adam and work to build the school, or if it was a refutation of everything Adam felt so certain about in his soul.

"So," he went on slowly, sending Septimus a coy look, "you will consider throwing your lot in with me in this endeavor?"

Septimus's grin widened. "I'm not certain that anyone could resist anything you want."

Adam swallowed. Again, he'd received an answer that wasn't truly an answer and that could be highly favorable or terribly disappointing. He leaned into Septimus, willing himself to ask outright if Septimus would consider staying with him, being with him, even though everything between them was new. He'd never felt what he felt for Septimus for any other man, and he wanted desperately to think feelings like those only came along when one found one's other half.

"There are still a great many uncertainties, Adam," Septimus said in a serious, yet kind voice once they hopped off the back of the wagon, thanked the farmer for the ride, and started up the lane to Wodehouse Abbey's manor house. "Simply finding the perfect house is no guarantee that Mrs. Henshaw's son will agree to sell it to you. Goddard might be an arse, but he could very well have the right sort of financial backing behind him. I recall that letter you received when I first arrived, denying you the funds you'd asked for, and another one a few days later."

Adam let out a disappointed breath and frowned. He had forgotten he'd told Septimus about the rejections from potential patrons he'd received, even though that sixth rejection had been precisely the burr in his saddle that he'd needed to put his foot down where the embers growing between the two of them were concerned.

"I am certain we would be able to find the backing

we need," he said, determination putting energy in his
steps as he headed up to the house. "It is as if..." He
paused, glancing up to the sky and feeling the fire of
inspiration heating him from within. "It is as if God
himself wishes to see this through. I feel as though
this is my destiny, Septimus. I feel as though everything in my life has been leading and guiding me on
to this one thing, this one purpose. Haven't you ever
felt something that powerful before?"

Adam knew the answer the moment Septimus's
face clouded over with wistfulness. Of course he had.
Septimus didn't need to answer for Adam to know the
truth. Septimus felt that way about the sea, about the
call of the waves and the thrill of adventure. He could
see it in the lines that pinched around Septimus's eyes
and mouth as he glanced off to the side, at the vista of
the sea visible from Wodehouse Abbey's lawn.

"Yes, I know," Septimus said in a quiet voice.

It was beautiful and terrible—beautiful that Septimus loved something that much, and terrible that it
conflicted so desperately with everything Adam
wanted. He wanted Septimus as much as he wanted
his school, and he could see in the way Septimus
glanced back to him and smiled that Septimus longed
for him as much as he longed for the sea. But was it
truly possible?

Adam stilled the anxious quiver that sprouted in
his gut by reaching for Septimus's hand. Ships didn't
come along every day, and commissions in the Royal
Navy were even rarer, especially after the war. He
needn't tie himself up in knots, worrying that Septimus would leave him tomorrow. They had the whole
summer to contrive a solution to the problem neither
of them was willing to speak of. In the meantime,

Adam needed Septimus's help in figuring out how to make his school a reality.

"The two of you look as though you've had entirely too much sun," Lord Beverley said, stepping out of one of the afternoon parlors, once they returned to the house. It was clear he meant something entirely wickeder than too much sun, though heaven only knew where and how and how often they would have been able to have too much of what he was implying.

"It was actually quite an interesting day," Adam said, a stroke of inspiration hitting him. "Lord Beverley, are you aware of a certain house belonging to a Mrs. Henshaw that sits on a cliff not far from Wodehouse Abbey?"

Lord Beverley switched from sending Septimus cheeky winks to focusing on Adam with a degree of seriousness. "I am aware of it," he said. "We were all of an age with some of the Henshaw children, which made them perfect as occasional playmates growing up. My sisters were closer with the Henshaw girls than Anthony or Frederick or I were with the boys, though. Likely because Papa sent us all off to Harrow as soon as he could."

Septimus tensed just a bit. Adam wondered if it was because of the reminder of the difference in his status compared to that of his friends or if it could be something else. "Excuse me," he said, with a look that was just a bit alarmed. "You've reminded me that I haven't written to my sister since arriving here. And that I have a few other correspondences I need to take care of."

"You'd better run along and do that, then," Lord Beverley said with a grin. "One must never keep one's sister waiting for correspondence. They turn into perfect beasts." His eyes widened in teasing alarm as he glanced to Adam.

"I should write to my sisters at some point as well," Adam said, stepping over to Septimus's side. All things considered, he took the risk of kissing Septimus quickly, figuring the worst Lord Beverley would do was laugh.

Lord Beverley did laugh, which caused Septimus to blush brightly and hurry off down the hall as though his feet were on fire.

"That man is gloriously besotted," Lord Beverley kept laughing once he and Adam were alone. "I've never seen him so smitten."

Adam took that as a compliment. The very deepest of compliments. A compliment that gave him hope. But he had other matters of importance to discuss with Lord Beverley. "If I might have a word, my lord." He glanced toward the parlor Lord Beverley had just come out of, indicating a more formal conversation.

"Of course." Lord Beverley followed him into the parlor as if curious to hear what he had to say.

"It is about your niece and nephew," Adam began.

Lord Beverley's face registered surprise before he burst into a broad smile. "I thought you were going to ask me about Septimus, about the best way to his heart or some such."

Adam grinned mischievously in answer. "I believe I know the way to Septimus's heart," he said. "It is through an entirely different organ."

Lord Beverley laughed. "Perhaps you do know Septimus well, in spite of your short acquaintance. But I can assure you, Septimus is all heart. He has always been decidedly choosy about his bedmates, and rarely has he displayed open affection, as he just demonstrated."

Adam blinked into a look of mock confusion. "I do not know of what you speak, Lord Beverley. The organ I was referring to is his eyes, since he seems to love gazing out at the sea."

Lord Beverley narrowed his eyes at Adam while still grinning. "Oh, I can see that Septimus will have his hands full with you. The rest of us will never be able to coax him out on the town for the night now, not when he has something much more entertaining to occupy himself with in bed."

It was Adam's turn to laugh and blush hotly. "I only wish to make him happy," he said.

"And you do," Lord Beverley said with a nod, crossing to sit on one of the chairs near the fireplace. "But what is this about my niece and nephew?" he asked, steering the conversation back around to what Adam needed to talk about.

"If there is any possibility at all that I might be able to purchase or let Mrs. Henshaw's house, it will, of course, mean that I will no longer be able to continue in the capacity of tutor for your brother," he said.

"Obviously." Lord Beverley nodded.

"But..." Adam hesitated, not realizing how self-conscious he felt about things. "Do you think he would keep me on for the amount of time it might take for me to secure financing for the school? Knowing I would soon be leaving his employ? Many employers would give me the sack the moment they discovered I was even thinking of leaving."

Lord Beverley smiled. "I can assure you that Anthony is not like that. And I am certain that he could be advised of certain extenuating circumstances involving his guests that may be an even deeper reason you would not want to be dismissed out of hand." He winked at Adam.

Rather than taking it as a joke, Adam blanched. "I would think he would sack me even quicker if he knew of any of that."

Lord Beverley made a considering sound and tilted his head to the side. "Perhaps, but I doubt it. I would like to say it is because Anthony is of a liberal mindset, but in truth, Anthony is oblivious to nearly anything that is not running his estate, raising his children, and attending to Parliamentary business. If he had the slightest inkling about matters of the heart, I am certain he would have remarried by now."

"I see," Adam said, not certain whether that made him feel safer or not. "Then I shall proceed with my attempts to finance the purchase of Mrs. Henshaw's house without those worries."

He started to stand, but Lord Beverley stopped him with, "Do you really believe you can do it?"

Adam sat down again. "I must do it," he said, feeling it from the bottom of his heart. "I must find the money for the school. It is the only thing I truly wish to do with my life."

Lord Beverley grinned. "What is this? Tutoring my niece and nephew is not your life's ambition?"

Adam appreciated his easy manner and smiled in return. "In truth, no. Neither is teaching in York, no matter how prestigious the school."

Lord Beverley's brow inched up. "What is this about teaching in York?"

Adam regretted saying anything, but the cat was already out of the bag. "I received an offer from a friend of mine who works at Archbishop Holgate's School."

Lord Beverley seemed even more surprised. "I've heard of it. You've received an offer to teach there?"

"I have," Adam admitted slowly. "But as gracious

and flattering as the offer is, York would be a distant second best to opening my own school."

"Still," Lord Beverley said, tilting his head to one side, "it must be nice to know you have options."

"I suppose it is," Adam admitted, standing, "but my mind is quite firmly made up where my school is concerned."

"As it should be." Lord Beverley rose with him. "As I assume other things are firmly made up by our mutual friend." He winked as the two of them headed into the hall.

Adam shook his head. Lord Beverley had constantly surprised him since returning home with the easiness—and the crudeness—of his manner. On the one hand, it didn't seem at all like suitable behavior for the brother of a duke with a title in his own right. On the other, it confirmed everything Adam knew about sailors and the ways that young men behaved when left to their own devices. He counted himself fortunate to be considered Lord Beverley's friend.

That fortunate feeling continued through supper, when he was once again invited to dine with the guests, as were the children. Even though the man wasn't a member of the aristocracy himself, Adam could imagine Goddard blanching and probably calling for the intervention of the bishop if he could see not only the tutor, but the children as well, dining with lords. But that was just another oddity that Adam found endearing about Wodehouse Abbey and its noble occupants.

"And then Barrett took us out to play this exciting new game he and Uncle Red invented," Lord Francis babbled away during supper about the day he and Lady Eliza had spent with Lord Copeland.

"It was completely daft," Lady Eliza giggled,

spearing a stalk of asparagus on her plate. "But Barrett said playing it would help improve our character."

"Are you quite certain you should be referring to Lord Copeland by his Christian name?" Adam asked, sending a questioning look down the table to Lord Copeland, who seemed deeply amused by the children's retelling of their afternoon.

"Why not?" Lord Copeland said with a shrug and a wink for Lady Eliza. "We're all on holiday here. We might as well do all the naughty things we wouldn't dare to do otherwise." He sent a second wink to Septimus, who immediately blushed and seemed far more interested in his fish fillet than he should have been.

"When I accepted Red's invitation to stay with his brother the duke for the summer, I had no idea I'd be entering such a madhouse," Septimus confided in Adam later, after they'd escorted the children up to bed in the nursery.

"Be honest," Adam told him with a sly grin. "You enjoy it. You enjoy the madness and the informality of it all. And you never dreamed the nobility could be so lax."

"I never did," Septimus agreed. "I never dreamed they could be so fetching either."

The nursery hall was empty, so he pulled Adam into his arms and kissed him with searing passion. Adam didn't hesitate for even a moment. He slid his arms around Septimus, kissing him back with open invitation for more. He even went so far as to fumble his way under Septimus's waistcoat so that he could tug the hem of his shirt out from his breeches.

"How fortunate that my bedchamber is right here," he murmured in an inviting voice, nodding sideways at his bedroom door, only a few feet away.

"No," Septimus said, inching back and nearly letting Adam go. "I'm not going to do it."

Adam gulped, worried that his worst fears were about to come true and Septimus would cry off.

Relief washed through him a moment later when Septimus said, "I'm not going to spend another night sleeping in that torture chamber of a bed of yours. I've spent nights in hammocks swinging their way through a storm at sea that are more comfortable than that thing. You're coming with me to my room."

"Truly?" Adam lit up, feeling like a maiden at her first ball as Septimus took his hand and led him on down the hall. "Hold up one moment." He pulled his hand out of Septimus's, causing Septimus to be the one struck by doubt and worry. Adam leaned into him, kissed him quickly, then said, "Let me just gather a few things to take with me so that I won't have to run through the house in a state of undress in the morning."

Septimus grinned. "A wise idea. Though I would relish the sight of you running starkers through the halls of Wodehouse Abbey at dawn."

Adam laughed. The delicious thought that perhaps it would be a wise idea if he moved all of his things to Septimus's room flittered through his head as he gathered his dressing gown, clean clothes for the morrow, and the jar of salve from his bedside table, just in case Septimus didn't have such a thing in his room. Another part of his mind warned him it was far too early to consider such a thing, but fifteen minutes later, when he was naked and on his back in Septimus's wide, soft bed, his thighs hitched up over Septimus's hips, making scandalous sounds as Septimus circled his tongue over one of his nipples, it didn't seem too early at all.

"This is much nicer than a narrow bed and a thin mattress," he sighed, threading his fingers through Septimus's hair.

"I've wanted to see you splayed and hungry in my bed since the moment I first laid eyes on you," Septimus growled, kissing his way back up Adam's chest and neck to his lips. "And now I have what I wanted."

"And you can have it as long as you want," Adam panted, then lost whatever else he might have been tempted to say in the heat and wetness of Septimus's mouth against his.

The man truly was a kissing master, as well as a sailing master. He knew exactly how much pressure to use to make Adam feel wanted and wanton, exactly how to nip and suck at his lower lip, and just how to stroke and suck his tongue as though it were a precursor to stroking and sucking something else. He had Adam feeling like putty under him, drunk with passion and aching for more.

"You truly are a little strumpet," Septimus laughed as he balanced himself on his arms above Adam so that he could rake a gaze across his flushed body.

"I can't help it," Adam said, brushing his hands over the hard muscles of Septimus's chest and burying his fingers in the wiry hair there. "You bring out the trollop in me."

"I can see that." Septimus grinned, reaching a hand between them to fist Adam's cock.

The sensation was overwhelmingly good, and Adam jerked into it, giving both of them more. His tip was slick with moisture, and when Septimus repositioned himself to lick it and to suckle just his tip— giving him so much sensation, but not quite enough— Adam nearly arched off the bed in an attempt to push himself deeper into Septimus's mouth.

"You need to learn patience," Septimus chuckled, stroking him slowly and driving him mad. "You are too impulsive for your own good, and I fear it will lead you astray one day."

"You see?" Adam gasped. "You do make the perfect teacher. And you'll have years to teach me that lesson, a lifetime."

Only when Septimus stopped moving, his hand firmly around Adam's cock, his eyes as stormy as they were unreadable, did it dawn on Adam that he'd said too much. But a lifetime with Septimus was what he wanted. He was certain that was what Septimus wanted too, but perhaps it was too soon.

Fear shot through him when Septimus pulled up to his knees, gazing down at Adam with those stormy eyes. For a moment, Adam couldn't breathe. He was certain Septimus would banish him from his bed.

"You are impossibly beautiful," Septimus growled.

Adam might have disagreed. His legs were spread embarrassingly wide, and his overeager cock leaked onto his belly. On top of that, he still couldn't tell whether Septimus's words were a promise, or if they had a "but" coming after them.

Whatever the case, Septimus leaned forward, reaching past Adam to the jar resting right next to the pillow. Adam's breath caught in his throat, and he started to flip over.

"No." Septimus stopped him, using one hand to push Adam to his back again as he dipped his other hand into the jar. "I want to watch your face when you come."

Adam let out a shaky breath. That sort of intimacy went beyond just having a bit of fun in bed. Once again, he couldn't catch his breath, but for an entirely different reason, as Septimus slicked his cock, then lifted his legs up, spreading him wide and angling him just so. Adam felt he must have looked even more ridiculous, laid open for Septimus as he was, but he didn't care one bit as Septimus tested his hole with his fingers to make certain Adam was ready, then slid into him with a slow, strong push.

Adam groaned at the glorious sensations of pressure and burn, and then fullness and pleasure. He gave everything Septimus wanted and more in the cries he let out, the expressions of ecstasy that pinched his face, and the eagerness of his body to meet every one of Septimus's strokes. In turn, he watched the desire and the affection play across Septimus's face as he moved faster and harder within him, coming closer and closer to release. That look, the depth of passion in Septimus's eyes, said more than any ambiguous words could.

As last, when Adam took hold of his cock to bring himself over the edge that Septimus has brought him up to, he cried out with, "Oh, Septimus, I love you," as he spilled across his belly.

Septimus made a sound of beautiful, wordless desperation a moment later, then jerked hard into Adam, shuddering as he, too, climaxed. The moment was magnificent and made Adam feel like the most loved and treasured man on the planet. It was even better when Septimus let out a heavy breath and curled forward, covering Adam with his gorgeous body and kissing him soundly before laying his head on the pillow beside Adam's head so he could catch his breath.

Only then did Adam wonder if he'd gone too far, said too much, worn his heart too much on his sleeve. They were tangled up together, still joined, and limp with satiety now, but underneath it all, Adam worried that he'd let loose something he wouldn't be able to control.

15

Once, in Septimus's earlier days of sailing, the ship he'd been serving on hit a dead calm in the middle of the Atlantic. It was as rare a thing as St. Elmo's fire, and such a thing usually unnerved a crew until they feared for their very lives. But that particular calm had come after a horrendous storm, and the peace of it had been so welcome that his shipmates had treated it as a holiday, sunning themselves on the decks, indulging in extra rations of rum, inventing theatrical productions for each other, and playing music.

The week that followed Adam's surprise declaration of love when they were in bed felt like that calm —beautiful, peaceful, and potentially deadly if he didn't keep a sharp eye on things.

"The children have been diligent about their lessons of late," Adam insisted as the two of them lingered on the stairs after breakfast, as Septimus escorted Adam up to the nursery for the day's lessons. "They seem to do particularly well when the prospect of a walk or game with Lord Copeland is used to motivate them."

"Yes," Septimus said, rubbing his thumb over the side of Adam's hand as it was clasped in his, "I can see how the promise of time spent with a gentleman could make anyone accomplish their tasks for the day in a timely manner, though my reasons would be very, *very* different."

Adam laughed softly as they reached the top of the stairs, sending Septimus a look that was equal parts lust and bashfulness. Those looks from Adam drove him wild and made him want to drag the blessed man into the nearest unoccupied room to sod him within an inch of his life.

That was impossible, but when it was discovered that the hallway at the top of the stairs was empty, Septimus pivoted against Adam, pressing his back against the wall and stealing a kiss that left both of them breathless and overheated. Adam hooked one leg around Septimus's thigh and grabbed hold of the front of his waistcoat as their mouths mated in a dance that was becoming as familiar as it was arousing.

"We should stop," Adam sighed, pushing against Septimus with a reluctant show of strength. "I cannot very well walk into the nursery for lessons with a mast in my breeches."

Septimus rumbled with laughter deep in his throat, stealing one more kiss that wasn't exactly chaste, but wouldn't land either of them in hot water, then stepped back. The depth of affection in Adam's eyes as he gazed at Septimus, catching his breath and biting his kiss-reddened bottom lip was almost too much for Septimus. He'd never felt so deeply for any man before. He'd never found a simple, teasing look so charming. He'd never wanted to spend his days making someone happy. Lord, at the rate he was going, he'd be out on the moors, making daisy chains to drape over his beloved, and composing love ballads to

Adam. And not a soul on land or sea wanted to hear him sing.

"Come and find me when your lessons are over," he said, brushing the backs of his fingers over Adam's cheek. "We'll walk into Hull to see if there have been any answers to our requests for patronage for the school."

"Yes." Adam's eyes lit up. "I'm certain someone will respond soon with an offer to help."

"I'm certain," Septimus echoed.

He took a step back, feeling as though he were fighting some sort of incredible force that wanted to keep him as close to Adam as possible. They both had other occupations to attend to, however, and it was high time they attended to them.

With one last kiss, Septimus headed downstairs. As he descended, he shook his head in wonder over how drastically his life had changed in less than a month's time. The first part of his stay at Wodehouse Abbey had been marked by a deep sense of longing for something he could not have and the unnerving sense that he was in the wrong place. He'd missed the sea with every fiber of his body. Then came Adam, and everything changed. The longing within him transformed into the need to be one with another soul, to find love and purpose with him. He still wanted the sea. He always would. Just a whiff of salt air when the winds were blowing right clenched his gut and closed up his throat with longing. His dreams were still filled with voyages across the oceans, the feeling of a deck under his feet and a ship's wheel in his hands. He still felt the call of the sirens that led men to their fate in the briny deep. But he'd stopped checking the post several times a day for word from the Admiralty. Now, whenever the post came, he hoped it contained replies to the letters he'd sent to every sea captain of his acquaintance who had won a prize for capturing a ship to see if they would donate some of that prize money to the school. Now, everything within him wanted to help Adam reach his dream, even if his felt as far away as ever.

Septimus strode past the library, intending to walk down to the beach and along to Mrs. Henshaw's house to be certain Goddard hadn't stolen it out from under them yet, when Barrett's call of, "Septimus!" arrested his steps and caused him to change directions.

"What are you doing, skulking around the house, man?" Barrett asked when Septimus poked his head into the library. "Come in and have a coffee with me."

"If only I had time," Septimus said, though he took a step into the room all the same. "I was on my way to the Henshaw house to haunt it like a specter in case Goddard returned with his clients to interfere."

Barrett laughed at that characterization, but gestured for Septimus to join him rather than letting him go. "Goddard and these mysterious clients of his are still interested in the place?" he asked.

Septimus sighed—both over Goddard's antics and over the delay speaking with Barrett would cause him —but took a seat in one of the chairs opposite where Barrett sat, coffee in one hand, a book in the other. "In truth, I have my doubts about whether Goddard's clients are remotely interested in the house. Apparently, they received word of a potential property sale less than a mile from a marquess with three marriageable daughters and two sons, and quite suddenly they have decided that would be a far more suitable location for a seaside retreat."

Barrett laughed. "Lord help that poor marquess and his children. Fortune-hunters have grown decidedly bold these days." He closed his book and set it aside, took a sip of his coffee and put the cup on the table beside him, then went on with, "So does this mean your darling Adam will be able to secure the house for his school after all?"

Septimus's face pinched for a moment. "Not necessarily. There are complications on top of complications. Goddard is still pushing his clients, mostly, I believe, out of spite for Adam. Mrs. Henshaw adores Adam, of course, and wishes to sell the place to him, but the decision lies with her son, who is away on business at the moment."

"Damnably inconvenient," Barrett said.

"Yes, and equally inconvenient is Adam's lack of any sort of substantial funds to purchase the place," Septimus went on. "He has a surprising amount set aside already—so much that if he chose to abandon the idea of a school, he could live a comfortable life for the rest of his days."

"So you've nabbed yourself a gentleman of means, have you?" Barrett asked him with a wink.

The abrupt change in subject from the serious business of Adam's school to teasing about their attachment instantly had Septimus on the back foot. "It was never my intention to 'nab' anyone," he rushed to say, "least of all a gentleman of any sort."

"You have extraordinary luck then," Barrett continued to tease him.

"I doubt luck has anything to do with it," Septimus went on, flustered, heat rising up his neck. "Adam is lovely and beautiful and perfect, and for some mysterious reason, he adores me."

"That reason likely has to do with the fact that you're rather lovely yourself," Barrett told him.

"I am not," Septimus protested. When that only

caused Barrett to laugh, he let out an irritated sigh, then said, "That is to say, I'm nothing more than an old sailor, trapped on land with no prospects and nothing to give him."

"You're far from old," Barrett continued to laugh. "You're not even five-and-thirty yet. And you have a great deal to give." He paused, then said with a cheeky grin, "I happened to walk past your bedchamber late last night and heard you giving it. Young Adam seemed highly appreciative."

Septimus felt his face heat like a furnace. "We try to stay quiet," he mumbled.

"Yes, well." Barrett reached for his coffee again with a wry grin that said they'd failed in that attempt. "I'm glad, at least, to see your prejudice against the nobility has been reduced."

Septimus blew out a breath, sat back in his chair, rubbed a hand over his hot face, and said, "Adam has helped me to see that my prejudice is not against all noblemen, only those who use their birth and fortune to take what they do not deserve."

"A trait which is common to many a class, not simply the aristocracy," Barrett said.

Septimus hummed in agreement. He glanced to the door, wondering if Barrett would let him go or if he had further teasing he wished to engage in. He was surprised when Worthington stepped into the room with an envelope in his hand.

"Mr. Bolton," the butler said, "a letter has just arrived for you. I know how anxious you are for the post every morning, so I took the liberty of bringing it straight to you."

Septimus got up to cross the room and take the letter. "Thank you, Worthington," he said with a smile.

His pulse sped up at his stared at the letter in his

hands. It wasn't from the Admiralty, which caused a moment of disappointment, but that could only mean it was a response to one of the requests for patronage that he'd sent out on Adam's behalf.

"Well?" Barrett asked, sitting forward in his chair. "Who is it from? What does it say?"

"It must be an offer of patronage," Septimus said, tearing into the letter.

A moment later, as he read the opening lines of the correspondence, his jaw dropped, his gut tightened, his throat closed up, and his heartbeat soared. He was fairly certain he must have lost all color from his face as well, as Barrett stood and asked, "What has happened?"

Septimus read the letter in his hand twice to be certain he hadn't missed or misunderstood any of it. "I've been offered a position on a ship," he said, his voice strangely tight and thready.

Barrett's eyes widened in a match to Septimus's. "A ship? A position?" he asked excitedly. "What sort of position?"

"As captain," Septimus said, so stunned he could barely form the words.

Barrett gaped. "You've been offered a captaincy of a ship?" Happy disbelief caused the man to raise his voice. "Which one? Is the Admiralty recommissioning ships now? Where are they sending you?"

Septimus shook his head and swallowed, feeling a bit sick. "It's a merchant vessel," he explained, "owned by an acquaintance of Captain Seabold."

"I remember Seabold." Barrett nodded and began to pace in front of Septimus. "He was a good man to serve under. I wish we'd kept him instead of having Wallace foisted on us. Has Seabold turned to commerce now?"

"Apparently he has," Septimus said. "His friend has organized an expedition to Canton. He wants me to captain one of the ships. It would leave in just over a fortnight."

Barrett blinked. "Canton?" He paused in disbelief, then said, "So soon? And so far away?"

Septimus was so stunned that he resorted to sarcasm. "Yes, when last I checked, China was very far away."

Barrett's mouth quirked into a grin, and he took a step closer to Septimus. "What sort of incentive are they offering you to go that far, or have they not said? Would you even consider it? A journey like that could take a year or more, depending on whether the winds are favorable."

"As captain, they would offer me a percentage of the sale of the cargo," Septimus said, staring at the letter again, as if he'd imagined that bit. "The intention is to bring back tea, silks, spices, and things of that nature."

"Good God, man. You could make a small fortune all of your own." Barrett grinned from ear to ear, clapping Septimus's shoulder in congratulations. "Forget ferreting out patrons and investors for Adam's school. You could buy the Henshaw house and finance the school yourself for years to come." He brightened even more as he said, "I would be willing to wager that if you brought this cargo home safely, Captain Seabold's friend would let you lead another expedition, and another and another. You could have your life at sea and be a rich man in the process."

"It is possible," Septimus said, hoarse with disbelief. It was how Henshaw made his fortune, if what Reynolds had told them was correct.

There was only one problem. One deep, horrible

problem. He'd been handed everything he'd ever wanted in life, the sort of captaincy that men from his background could only dream of. Every bit of patience and hard work he'd ever employed to rise in the ranks of the British Navy had come to fruition. And if he took the offer, he would be parted from Adam. Parted for as much as a year. Potentially parted for life, if anything were to go wrong with the voyage.

"How can I accept this?" he said, his voice barely more than a shocked whisper, staring at the letter in his hands. "How can I just fly off and take up this offer? The timing would require me to leave almost immediately."

"How can you not?" Barrett said, gaping at him in surprise. "Septimus, this is everything you've wanted for years. It's everything you've talked all of our ears off about since we first came together on the *Majesty*. This is your dream, handed to you on a silver salver."

Septimus raised his eyes to stare forlornly at Barrett. "It would mean I would be forced to leave Adam, perhaps as soon as tomorrow."

Barrett's jubilant expression fell as he grasped the choice Septimus had to make. "It wouldn't be forever," he said in a subdued voice. "The entire point of the journey is that you return home in the end. You'd return home a wealthy man as well."

"*If* everything goes smoothly," Septimus said, beginning to pace. "And if the cargo fetches a good price. If disaster struck…" He didn't even want to contemplate the possibility.

"But you would be at sea again," Barrett argued. "Just as you've always wanted."

"It is what I want," Septimus said, taking that part of the argument into consideration. "The sea is all I know. It is my life and my soul. I am lost here on land. I have no place here, try though I have to find one."

"And what's to say that you could not come back here, call this place and Adam and his school your home? A home to which you would return after each journey?" Barrett shrugged.

"I could," Septimus said, unsure whether he was trying to convince himself of the possibility or talk himself out of it. "The school, if purchased, would be there whenever my voyages end. Having something and someone to return to would make me fly that much faster across the waves."

"Will Adam be able to establish his school without the payment you would receive from this offer?" Barrett asked gingerly.

Septimus winced. "Perhaps not. He has tried and tried to convince everyone, from nobles of his father's acquaintance to industrialists to speculators, to become patrons of his school and to provide him with the funds to open it, but all for naught. This may be the only chance for his ambition to be satisfied as well."

"Then it seems to me as though you have only one course of action," Barrett said, moving closer to rest a supportive hand on Septimus's shoulder. "It seems to me as though you must accept your friend's offer, even if it takes you away from your lover as soon as tomorrow."

Septimus glanced slowly and painfully toward Barrett. His heart's initial reaction was that he didn't want to part ways with Adam—not so soon and not ever. That surprised him down to his bones. His dreams had changed since meeting the dazzling young man, and the thought of months and months at

sea without him was too much to bear. It was something he never thought he would see happen.

At the same time, his gut told him nothing funda-
mental had changed, that the sea was where he belonged. It was a fantasy to think he could find
contentment teaching at Adam's school, even if he
were able to teach maritime business to Adam's
pupils. He needed the salt spray in his face and a
wheel in his hands. But he needed Adam as well.

He turned to Barrett, intending to argue both sides
of the issue until a miraculous solution presented itself that would enable him to have the sea and Adam
both, but before he could get a single word out, Adam
himself called from the doorway, "You would leave me
so soon?"

Septimus snapped his mouth shut so fast he
nearly bit his tongue, and turned to the library's doorway. "Adam. How long have you been standing there?"

"Long enough," Adam said, stepping into the room
with a hurt expression. "Long enough to hear that
everything between us means nothing to you and that
you plan to flee at the first opportunity you have." The
hurt in the young man's eyes shot straight to Septimus's heart.

"I think it would be wise for me to leave the two of
you to yourselves," Barrett whispered, clapping his
hand on Septimus's shoulder one last time before
heading out of the room.

Septimus watched his friend leave, dread sinking
in his heart, then turned to Adam, at a loss for how to
reconcile the two conflicting dreams that laid claim
to him.

16

A dam had only come downstairs to convey Lord Francis and Lady Eliza's request that Lord Copeland come up to the nursery to listen to them recite the poems that they'd learned in the last week. He could have sent Ivy down to fetch the man, but no. He'd wanted another glimpse of Septimus, if he could get it. He'd wanted more than that, if he were honest with himself.

He'd gotten far more than he'd bargained for.

"You're leaving," he said, both as a statement and an accusation, as Lord Copeland left the library. "A letter arrives, and without a second thought, you have plans to leave me." The pain that sliced through him was sharper than anything Adam had ever known, primarily because it was a manifestation of everything he'd most feared. He'd never staked so much of himself on another man before, never confessed love so deeply. It was as though he had been waiting for it to all be proven out of his reach, just like his plans for the school, and finally it had been. Now he was beginning to see the folly of planning a future when the present was merely a fantasy.

"I only just received the letter," Septimus said,

stepping closer to him and holding up the letter in question. "I've hardly had the time to make any sort of decision."

"But I heard you," Adam argued. "I heard you weighing the choice in front of you with Lord Copeland. This ship leaves in a fortnight, which means you must go immediately. It does not take a wise man to see what decision you will make." He was so hurt and furious that he turned to march out of the room.

"You do not know that," Septimus stopped him, grabbing hold of Adam's arm and anchoring him to the spot. "You cannot know what choice I will make when I do not even know myself."

"I believe you do know." Adam turned back to him. "Have you not felt the need to return to the sea within you since the moment you arrived at Wodehouse Abbey? Since the moment you set foot on dry land?"

"I have," Septimus said with a curt nod, his brow clouding with frustration. "I've made no secret of it. The sea has been my life for as long as I remember."

"Then why would you not return to it the moment she opens her arms to you?" Adam asked.

A warning voice within him urged calm. There was no reason to react so emotionally simply because the possibility that he could lose Septimus had sprung up. And yet, irrational as it was, Adam couldn't dismiss the burning disappointment of everything he'd ever wanted remaining forever out of his reach, only inches away from his fingertips. His school hung by a thread, dependent on men with money seeing him as a serious man of his word, and his heart was inches away from being broken, all because Septimus loved something more than he loved him.

Septimus took a deep, slow breath, closing his eyes

for a moment as if gathering his thoughts and his patience. "This is all very fresh," he said before opening his eyes.

"Yes, the two of us as one may be a bud that has only just blossomed," Adam told him, hands clenched in an attempt to help keep his emotions in check, "but that is no reason to discard it before it has a chance to fully bloom."

Septimus stared at him for a moment, then said, "I was referring to the offer for me to captain a ship. But if you assume that I am so fickle that I would completely disregard the bond that had formed between the two of us after receiving one letter, please do tell me more about that."

Adam rocked back a step, stunned by Septimus's burst of frustration with him. "Is that not what you were intending to do? Leave me as soon as the tide turns, perhaps without even saying goodbye?" he asked, sounding more belligerent than he felt. In fact, the anxious, heartbroken part of him fought not to feel like a green lad, barely out of the schoolroom, navigating his first serious romance. Wounded feelings had always been like a strong undertow for him though, and he wasn't certain how to fight them and behave rationally. Not when he feared losing the love he'd only just found.

"What I intend to do is what is best for both of us," Septimus said. He marched to the side, deposited the letter on a small table, then paced back to Adam. "Your difficulties in starting a school have not simply vanished because you've found the perfect premises for it. The aspects of the enterprise which have given pause to potential patrons are still in place. But if I were to accept this offer to captain a ship to Canton and back, I would be able to provide you with a great deal of what you need to proceed."

"At the expense of losing you." Adam flung out his fears along with the words, gesturing wildly with his arms, then bringing one hand back to clutch at his heart. "To do so this soon after finding you would be worse than giving up on the idea of a school."

Septimus's face pinched with emotion, and he rubbed a hand over his forehead. "You would not lose me entirely," he argued. "I would come home to you." He dropped his hand and took a step closer to Adam. "I will always come home to you, and this way, I may come home to you with a fortune that we can share."

"If you come home at all," Adam said. His heart soared at the way Septimus spoke of the two of them, as though their future together were a given, but even those glorious and beautiful thoughts would be for naught if one of the score of dangers seafarers risked caused a disaster. "Men are lost at sea all the time, Septimus. You, of all people should know this. The longer the journey, the greater the risk."

"Do you think so little of me as a seaman that you believe I would allow myself to come to harm?" Septimus said, his back going straight.

"Are you telling me you have never lost a competent friend or an acquaintance in a storm or a pirate attack, or simply to disease or starvation?" he asked in return.

Septimus pressed his lips shut and blew out a breath. He shifted his weight to one leg and planted his hands on his hips in a way that made him look more like a disgruntled pirate than the houseguest of a duke. "Yes, there will always be risk inherent in a life at sea," he said. Adam wondered if he recognized the sting in his use of the words 'life at sea'. Septimus's life, not his. A life he had nothing to do with. "I cannot guarantee the voyage will be perfectly smooth, with no storms or threats of any kind. But neither can I guarantee that I will not be thrown from a horse or crushed by an overturned carriage, or that I will not succumb to a fever on land. Life is inherently a risk, Adam, and love doubly so. Can you guarantee that you will not take a fancy to a younger, more comely man than me tomorrow?"

"How dare you assume that my feelings for you are less than all-consuming?" Adam nearly shouted, taking a step toward him. "I love you as I have never loved another, as I will never love another. I know this with as much certainty as I know that I will achieve my dream of a school one day."

"A dream that will be so much more within your reach if I am able to assist by taking this commission," Septimus argued, stepping close enough to grasp Adam's arms. "What is one year if it enables both of us to achieve our ambitions?"

"And what of next time?" Adam demanded. "What choice will you make when you return to me, only to long for the sea once more? Am I forever to be a sailor's wife, trapped on shore, waiting for the slightest word of my beloved for ten months out of a year? How would I be expected to openly mourn if you were lost at sea and I was left alone and bereft, without you?"

Septimus lowered his head, but did not release his grip on Adam's arms. He took in a deep breath, then said, "Would you rather I spend the rest of my life by your side, pining for the sea but never setting foot on a ship again? Would you be content with a man who never quite felt whole, a part of whose heart constantly longed for something else?"

Adam pulled away from him, miserable at the picture Septimus painted. And yet, there didn't seem to be a middle ground. Either he would forever feel as though a part of him were missing, in danger, possibly never to return, or a part of Septimus would be caged forever, never his, but never fulfilled either.

"Why does it have to be so difficult?" he whispered, his eyes stinging with the possibility of tears he was loath to shed.

"The ways of the world will always be difficult," Septimus said, resting his hand on the side of Adam's face. "There is little we mortals can do about it."

Adam glanced up at him, caught between finding those words poignant and hating them with every fiber of his being. "I cannot bear the thought of you leaving me so quickly," he whispered. Perhaps it wasn't fair of him, but it was what his heart truly felt. "I cannot bear the thought that I mean so little to you, that I am nothing more than a diversion and not worth the investment, just as everyone else has always told me I am not worth their consideration."

"Adam, that is not what I meant," Septimus said.

Adam wrenched away from him, taking several steps back. "I know that I do not have a serious bearing, that there is nothing manly or heroic in wishing to teach the poor, and that I am easy to dismiss because of my tender heart." He clutched a hand to his chest. "That does not mean this tender heart does not bleed."

"Adam, darling—" Septimus stepped forward.

Adam took another step away from him. "There are more things in this world than money," he went on. "We have only begun our efforts to find patronage for the school. That you would be so willing to abandon those efforts before they have borne fruit, that you would abandon me with them, makes me feel as though I am worthless to you."

"That is so far from the truth as to be absurd," Septimus said, coming after him again. "You are worth more than any treasure to me, Adam. Your dreams are fast becoming my dreams. But this commission could be a way for us both to fulfill those dreams. I am only trying to help."

"Then find a way to help that does not involve leaving me alone, wracked with fear for you, as helpless as a babe in a wood."

"I—"

Adam couldn't stay to hear more. His heart was too bruised and his head too jumbled. He knew he was not thinking clearly, but continuing to argue would be of no help whatsoever.

Instead of striding to the stairs and back up to the nursery, he marched straight on through the front door and out into the balmy June morning. It was a gross dereliction of his duty to Lord Malton and his children to leave the house in the middle of the day, when he should have been teaching lessons, but he was in no fit state to be around children, or anyone else, for that matter. He trusted that Ivy—or perhaps even Lord Copeland—would see to the children. In that moment, Adam could only see to himself.

He played through his conversation with Septimus over and over as his feet carried him down the lane to the road, then toward Hull, though with no real purpose other than that he was used to going that way. Every word Septimus had spoken and every expression that had pinched his face stood out in Adam's mind, but like bits of a puzzle he needed to sort. His life depended on sorting it and discovering the solution. Captaining a ship was Septimus's dream. It was

the ambition he'd never been able to fulfill in the
Navy, thanks to the unfair promotion of gentlemen
like Adam. Part of Adam thought it was cruel of him to
deny his lover the chance to have the one thing he'd
always wanted.

Another part of him felt it was cruel for Septimus
to deliberately set out on a voyage that would part
them so soon after they'd discovered each other.
While that parting could be temporary, it was true, it
could also be forever. And even if it wasn't, Adam's
own life and his ambitions had reached a crucial
point. He needed Septimus with him, needed his
lover's steadiness and experience to help him find the
patronage that his school required. The majority of
the requests for help that had been sent out in the last
week were sent to Septimus's friends and acquaintances. Adam couldn't help but feel as though the key
to achieving his dream lay in Septimus's capable
hands.

Those thoughts rolled over and over in his mind,
like waves beating upon the shore during a storm,
along the entire walk into Hull. When he realized he'd
reached the town without any purpose for being
there, he stopped in the middle of the road and let out
a heavy breath, his shoulders dropping. He was lost—
not physically, but at heart. He didn't know which way
to turn or what course of action would be right for
both him and Septimus.

He was on the verge of turning around and
walking straight back to Wodehouse Abbey when he
spotted Mrs. Henshaw's maid walking from the center
of town toward the old woman's house, a basket over
her arm. Without quite knowing why, Adam followed
her, and when he reached Mrs. Henshaw's door and

knocked, he told the maid he was there to pay a call on Mrs. Henshaw and Mrs. Iverson.

"We are so pleased that you would think to call on us." Mrs. Henshaw smiled as though Adam had brought the sun with him as the maid showed him into the parlor where Mrs. Henshaw and Mrs. Iverson sat. Right away, before Adam could even take a seat in one of their faded, old chairs, Mrs. Henshaw's expression turned worried. "But what has put that look of distress in your eyes, sweet boy?"

Adam fought not to sink into his chair at Mrs. Henshaw's perceptiveness. Mrs. Iverson sent him a sympathetic, knowing smile as well, but in all of his calls to the two elderly ladies, the dear thing had yet to speak a word to him.

"It seems I have a difficult decision in front of me," Adam said, weighing his words carefully. "I have a sweetheart, you see, and... she may have to go away." His face flared hot at the subtle lie, but there was no use alienating two dear women, whom he had come to consider as friends, with the truth.

"Oh, that is unfortunate," Mrs. Henshaw said. "Parting with a loved one is the tenderest sort of pain. I should know." Adam perked up a bit, curious about her story. "I lost my dear Robert, after all, my first husband."

"How did you manage?" Adam asked, leaning forward a bit.

Mrs. Henshaw shrugged. "It was not an easy thing," she said, her words slowed by age and by the cloud of emotion that descended over her. "He was my first love, the boy who knew me and loved me when I was but a girl. I thought I would never love again, and in truth, I never loved like that. Oh, I loved Henshaw, to be sure," she went on, raising a hand. "He was a good and a kind man. But he wasn't Robert."

"I would have loved to have met him," Adam said, pushing aside his own troubles so he could send the woman a kind smile.

"Our son is very like him," Mrs. Henshaw went on. "I was quite perceptive to name the boy after his father." She chuckled to herself over some memory that made her smile and glance hazily out through the window.

Adam waited for her to say more, but when he recognized that she'd slipped into the past, he was compelled to bring her back to the present. "I don't know what I will do without... my sweetheart," he said, tripping over the way he was forced to speak of Septimus. "She says this is for the best, that she may be able to help me finance my school by going away."

"Oh?" Mrs. Henshaw focused on Adam once more. "And how are your efforts to find patrons for your school progressing?"

Adam sighed, sitting back in his chair. "Not well, I'm afraid. We've sent out inquiries and requests for funds to purchase your house, but..." He let his words fade, taking his turn to lose himself in his thoughts. He shook himself, glancing to Mrs. Henshaw once more. "Your son hasn't said anything new about his plans to sell, has he?"

"He is due back from Scarborough today," Mrs. Henshaw said. "I promise you, I will discuss the matter with him the moment he calls."

Adam tried to smile at what could be viewed as a small advancement, but his heart was still heavy.

Once again, Mrs. Henshaw noticed. "You are more distressed about your sweetheart's absence than you are about the funds for your school, methinks," she said with a soft, knowing smile.

"All I've wanted for years was to build this school," Adam said with a sigh. "And I will build it, whether by purchasing your house or finding another property. I will raise the money for it through begging or borrowing, or working my fingers to the bone."

A stray thought struck him. He'd never replied to Jeremy to ask precisely what the wages he might be offered at Archbishop Holgate's School might be so that he could calculate how long he would need to save up enough to finance his school. If he were honest with himself, other than staying on as a tutor for Lord Marton—which would never allow him to save what he needed—Jeremy's offer was the only solid one he had.

He shook his head to banish the idea, but it refused to entirely leave him.

"And what does your sweetheart want?" Mrs. Henshaw asked.

"He wants to—" Adam began to answer before catching himself. He cleared his throat, regretting the heat radiating from his face, and started again. "She wants to... pursue her own interests... as a governess to a family in London," he lied, making his face heat even more. Within his lie, he sought out the truth and attempted to use it to explain. "All she has ever wanted is to be a governess to a fine family. She had that once, but it was taken away from her. Now she's been given an opportunity to have it again."

"But you would be very sorry indeed to see her go," Mrs. Henshaw finished for him, a bright spark in her eyes.

"So very sorry," Adam sighed. "I've never loved anyone as I love her."

"But you will lose her one way or another if you refuse to let her take up the position she's been offered," Mrs. Henshaw said, both as a statement of fact and as a warning.

"I fear so," Adam sighed.

Mrs. Henshaw nodded slowly.

"What do I do?" he blurted, suddenly hopeful that her decades of living might hold an answer to his current predicament.

"I cannot tell you that, dear boy," she laughed, reaching over to pat his hand. "But I can tell you that when you find yourself caught between two equally distasteful choices, quite often the answer lies in a third option you may not yet have considered."

"Such as?" Adam asked in a wry voice, even though he knew there was no way Mrs. Henshaw—or Mrs. Iverson, for that matter—could answer without knowing the full story.

Mrs. Henshaw laughed again. "I cannot tell you that either. I can only tell you that the true path of love is to put our loved ones first. I learned that lesson from Henshaw. He adored his ships and his speculation, even though I despised the sea. I lost a brother at sea, you see."

"Did you?" Adam found that fact interesting and terrifying, all things considered.

"I did. But Henshaw assured me that the chance of disaster, particularly on the ships whose cargo he speculated on, was minimal. I wanted to forbid him to throw away our money that way, but in the end, he was right. Not only did he make a fortune for all of us, his friend was able to employ my son, Robert, and now my son is a wealthy man himself with a veritable fleet of fishing boats."

Something about the story struck Adam right in

his gut. Several things, if he were honest. Too many for him to sort them all out at once. The story made him think of Septimus and of the longing Septimus had for the sea, and the possibility that Adam was overly anxious about letting Septimus go. And there could be a third path that neither of them had considered yet. There could be a solution, if only he was willing to look for it.

"Thank you, Mrs. Henshaw, for your wise counsel." Adam stood, boldly leaning down to kiss Mrs. Henshaw's cheek, then that of Mrs. Iverson. "You have given me quite a bit to think about."

"Thank you for visiting, Mr. Seymour," Mrs. Henshaw said with a smile. "You are welcome to call on us at any time. And do come back and tell us how you have resolved this conundrum with your sweetheart."

"I will, ma'am," Adam promised, stepping toward the door. "As soon as I sort things out for myself."

17

Septimus hated the fact that he and Adam had parted on bad terms that morning. It didn't sit well with him that his lover was deeply upset and that he was the cause of that distress. The pain in Adam's face as he had argued for the two of them to be together, no matter what the difficulties, had gone straight to his heart. When Adam had stormed out, that expression and the pain behind it continued to burn in Septimus's mind. He couldn't sit still, couldn't stay in the house that was beginning to feel like a beautiful torture chamber to him, so he left, marching down the drive.

When he made it to the beach, he broke into a run. Pushing his body to its limit seemed to be the only way to exorcise the demons of the choices that lay before him, like hidden rocks under the waves that could dash the ship to bits at any moment. He'd navigated those sorts of hazards and shoals before, and in his heart, he believed he should be able to steer himself and Adam through the dangerous waters they found themselves in now. Adam was young, he was impetuous, and he was likely just shocked by the unexpectedness of the day. They could find a way to make things right.

Septimus stopped running when he reached the cave where he and Adam had stolen those few, heated moments to commune with each other on the deepest levels. Septimus had never wanted a man so much that he was willing to misbehave anywhere that he might be caught. Not until Adam. He had half a mind to explore the cave, just to see whether the evidence of their mischief still painted the cave wall. Adam had coaxed him into doing other things that he never would have dreamed of either, such as considering a life on land. Nothing had come close to anchoring Septimus to shore for years, but now, as he walked past the cave to look up at the Henshaw house, his heart was torn in two.

The house rose up over the cliff like a lover looking out to sea and waiting for her beloved to come home. It had a certain hollowness to it, as if it were just waiting to be filled with activity and the sound of children's laughter once more. Adam would bring that to the house, if he could only find the patronage he needed for such an endeavor. There had to be a way, and Septimus could see himself, against all odds, helping to find that way.

To his other side, however, the sea moved and waved and beckoned to him. The scent of salt in the air and the sound of the tide lapping against the shore was as familiar to him as his own heartbeat. He couldn't simply abandon the sea after he had made it his entire life. He glanced up at the house again, sighed, then turned his gaze to the horizon. One journey. He could agree to one journey to the Orient as captain of a merchant vessel. He would make certain

Captain Seabold's friend had hired only the most experienced seamen and that they planned their journey down to the last detail to avoid the worst weather of the year. Distance might part him and Adam for a moment, but he would come home, and when he did, he would bring Adam everything he needed.

Septimus was confident that he'd made the right decision, but as he walked back to Wodehouse Abbey, doubt assailed him. There was no guarantee that they would be able to purchase Mrs. Henshaw's house. The decision would be made by her son. For all Septimus knew, the son might despise children or the idea of a charity school. He might be suspicious of two men intending to operate the school together, or he may be so enamored of the idea of selling to Goddard's client, provided that client was still interested, that he would accept whatever offer those people intended to make. Adam might never find the patronage his school needed. Everything might be for naught.

The only way to settle the matter, and the storm raging in his heart, was to find Adam and confront him over the matter once more. But Adam wasn't at the house when Septimus returned. Septimus checked the nursery just to be certain.

"He never came back after going downstairs to fetch Lord Copeland this morning," Ivy reported.

Septimus thanked her and went back downstairs to try the library again, then the music room, then outdoors. Adam wasn't at the lake or in the rose garden, or anywhere at all.

"I saw him with a parcel from the kitchens earlier this afternoon," Red reported when Septimus found him in his brother's study, writing letters. "It looked as though he'd planned a picnic for the both of you, but perhaps not?"

"Definitely not," Septimus said in a low growl.

He marched out to the woods, intending to give Adam a piece of his mind for deliberately avoiding him all day, but the woods were as empty as ever. The place had always unnerved Septimus. Trees were unnatural to him, but it was the constant feeling that he was being watched whenever he walked through it that bothered him.

That sense of suspicion manifested in the sudden appearance of a young man about Adam's age, with large, brown eyes and pale skin, who Septimus suddenly noticed standing among the trees a few feet back from the path. Of all things, the man had a hawk perched on his arm.

"Pardon me, but have you seen Mr. Seymour wandering the woods?" Septimus asked the young man, as if he were real instead of some sort of specter, as Septimus half thought he was.

The young man shook his head, then said, "He left here hours ago."

Septimus blew out a breath, then turned to backtrack the way he'd come, thanking the odd young man as he went. He and Adam must have been crossing paths over and over. That or the blasted man was deliberately avoiding him.

He decided Adam was, indeed, avoiding him when Adam did not appear for supper. Septimus waited, eating the first few courses of the unusually quiet meal without tasting them, then threw down his serviette and stood in a huff.

"Enough of this," he grumbled. "The blighter cannot avoid me forever."

He ignored whatever quip or word of advice Red and Barrett tried to offer him as he stormed out of the room and headed upstairs. There was only one way that he could think of to catch Adam and force him to discuss the matter, and that was to lie in wait in the one place he was certain Adam would return to at some point.

The upstairs hall was quiet but for the sound of the children talking in the nursery as they enjoyed their supper where they were supposed to, for a change. Septimus almost ignored them, but when he heard Adam's voice discussing whatever topic the children deemed appropriate for supper, he froze. His heart shot to his throat as anger and relief battled within him. He took a step toward the nursery, scolding frown in place, ready to take Adam to task for his behavior, then changed his mind. It would do no good to confront the blighter in front of the children. Instead, he held to his original plan and quietly stepped into Adam's bedchamber to wait.

He didn't have to wait long. Within half an hour, the door handle turned and a rumpled and dispirited Adam stepped into the room, his shoulders hunched and his face pinched with worry. The moment he spotted Septimus he started so hard that he nearly tripped over his own feet, and he gasped loud enough to be heard downstairs.

"What are you doing here?" he demanded as soon as he recovered, his anxious expression morphing into a frown.

"Forcing you to face me," Septimus told him, rising from Adam's tiny bed, where he'd been sitting. "We have unfinished business between us, and I am not letting either of us retreat into sleep for the night until the matter is at least discussed."

Adam glanced from Septimus to the door to the hallway beyond. "Not here," he said, sidestepping back into the hall and glancing toward the nursery. "The children have yet to go to bed."

"My room, then," Septimus said with a nod.

He stepped into the hall, intending to lead Adam downstairs, then changed his mind and grasped his hand instead. He didn't want to run any risk of letting the slippery man go.

The moment they reached Septimus's bedchamber and Septimus closed and locked the door, he rounded on Adam.

"You have been avoiding me since this morning," he said, wasting no time.

"I have had matters of great importance to think about," Adam shot back, unwilling to be intimidated. "Or do you not think they are very important?" He arched an eyebrow at Septimus in challenge.

Septimus let out a breath and rubbed a hand over his face. He loved Adam dearly, but at times, the darling let his age and impetuosity show. "Of course I find everything between us important," he said, willing himself to be patient, even though he wanted to shake sense into Adam. "You are the most important thing in my life at the moment."

"At the moment," Adam echoed with a wry laugh, pacing to the cold fireplace, then back to the table beside Septimus's bed. "I am certain that will change the moment you set foot on the deck of the ship that's been promised to you."

"Even if I do take up Captain Seabold's friend on his offer," Septimus said, crossing his arms and watching Adam as he paced, "that does not mean you will become less important. I would take the offer because of all the ways it could benefit us both."

"Yes, I understand that," Adam said. There was a strange combination of genuine understanding and bitterness in his tone. He wouldn't meet Septimus's eyes as he continued to pace the room. Septimus frowned, wondering what sort of arguments Adam had made within himself throughout the day.

"Then you understand that the risk of this journey is worth the reward?" Septimus asked, narrowing his eyes slightly. He wished he could see into Adam's thoughts, wished he could open the man up and study him like a chart.

Adam stopped and turned to face Septimus. He let out a heavy breath and pushed a hand through his hair in a way that made it stand up at odd, curiously arousing angles. "I understand that you love the sea, that it is your life. I understand that you would choose it over me."

"That is not entirely accurate," Septimus said, "nor is it entirely fair. You're welcome to join the crew of the ship and make the journey with me." The idea hadn't occurred to Septimus until he spoke it aloud. He wasn't certain whether it was a good one or not.

For a moment, Adam's eyes widened, and he blinked at Septimus as though he might consider it. All too soon his expression fell and he shook his head. "I cannot go to sea with you when my school is so close to becoming real." He resumed his pacing. "Aside from that, I have no experience on a ship at all, and I fear I would make a terrible seaman."

Septimus couldn't dispute that. The more he thought about it, the more he realized Adam was too refined and too delicate for the rough and rugged life of a sailor. His hands were too soft and supple, for one. Not that Septimus minded those hands. They were capable of magic that he had only dreamed of in his most ribald fantasies.

He shook himself out of those thoughts, setting them aside for later.

"As I told you this morning and am telling you again now, I would return to you," he said. "It would be a year at most."

"Barring disaster," Adam said, flinging a hand out to him. "Assuming there will be no storms or pirates, or... or attacks from angry Chinamen in Canton." He paused, peeked guiltily at Septimus, then continued with, "Or attractive sailors whom you would rather be with than some anxious, jealous, land-bound nobleman who is more trouble than he's worth."

Septimus's heart nearly melted in his chest at those few, brooding words. He stepped into the path of Adam's pacing, snatching the man into his arms and stealing a slow, deep kiss.

As soon as he felt Adam's body relax by a fraction, he rested his hands on either side of Adam's face and said, "You are the only man I want. You are the only man I will ever want for the rest of my days. Even though you are anxious and jealous—of the sea, no less—and impetuous."

"Impetuous?" Adam asked, one eyebrow raised.

"All young men are," Septimus reassured him with a smile.

Restless energy radiated from Adam all over again. "Now I am too young on top of the rest of it?" He tried to pull away.

Septimus stopped him, clamping an arm around his waist and brushing the side of his face with his other hand. It was evening, but Adam barely had any stubble on the lower half of his face. Whether that was his youth or he simply did not grow a beard as fast as Septimus did, it was just one more reason Septimus found the man devastatingly endearing.

"You are perfect, Adam. You are aggravating, but only because you want things so deeply, and you are willing to fight to achieve them," Septimus said.

Adam glanced doubtfully up at him. "I *will* open my school," he said in a voice of quiet determination. His expression softened to a degree of pleading that had Septimus's heart squeezing all over again. "But I need you beside me to do it," he added in a near whisper. "I've been trying for years, but only now, only with you in my life, have I been able to make any progress."

"I cannot cause miracles, my darling," Septimus said, leaning his forehead against Adam's.

"I have yet to be convinced of that," Adam said, impishness in his eyes.

Septimus grinned, and when that wasn't enough, he pulled Adam tighter and tilted his head up for a kiss. Adam responded eagerly, his tongue dancing against Septimus's, his body pressing into him. There was no mistaking the hard spear of his cock, even through the layers of clothing that separated them. Septimus wanted everything about Adam, every inch of his body, every open smile and laugh, every dream and aspiration.

He sighed, resting his forehead against Adam's once more. "I only have one offer of employment," he said with his eyes closed, speaking mostly to himself. "How can I be of any use to you if I am penniless and lacking any skills that will enable me to contribute to a household, let alone a school?"

"You could—" Adam began, but no words followed. The tension in his body changed as he held Septimus, brushing a hand up and down his spine.

"There's always—" Again, he stopped, tensing even more. "I want you to teach at the school."

"And I will," Septimus said with a sigh, nuzzling the side of Adam's face. His body urged him to end the conversation and take Adam to bed. If only he could be of more use to his lover than satisfying his bodily needs. "I'm not certain I could live with myself if I was more of a burden to you than a blessing." Adam opened his mouth to protest, but Septimus placed a finger on his lips. "The world does not revolve on love alone, my dear. We need money to survive, to build your school. I have only the one offer as a means to earn it, and it is an offer that could provide us with all we need for years to come."

"But—" Adam began.

This time, Septimus silenced him by pressing the finger over his lips into Adam's mouth. Adam's protest turned into a groan of pleasure as he sucked on Septimus's finger. He was so sensual in his enjoyment that Septimus's entire body heated in response. As far as Septimus was concerned, the conversation was over. They would pick up where they'd left off in the morning, debating their dreams and bashing their heads against the rocks of what was best for both of them, but for the moment, they needed each other in entirely different ways.

Septimus removed his finger from Adam's mouth and replaced it with his tongue. Adam accepted that even more eagerly, purring and grasping handfuls of the back of Septimus's jacket as they kissed. There were entirely too many clothes between them, so Septimus went to work unbuttoning Adam's jacket and waistcoat and shoving them off his shoulders with as much haste as possible.

Undressing always had been the destroyer of passion, but Septimus was so eager to tumble into bed with his lover that he rushed through the process, shrugging out of his jacket and waistcoat and loosening his neckcloth enough to pull his shirt off over his head as if it were on fire. Adam had his shirt off by then as well and had just tossed aside his boots before reaching for the falls of his breeches.

Septimus had no intention of waiting. Adam had settled on the edge of the bed to remove his boots, and in a flash, Septimus knelt in front of him, pushing his knees far apart. Adam yelped in surprise, then laughed as Septimus finished with his breeches, then groaned with pleasure as he tugged those breeches down, allowing Adam's cock to spring free. Septimus's mouth watered with the need to taste and touch. He brushed his fingertips over Adam's thighs, causing Adam to gasp, and moved on to gently tug his balls and grasp the base of his cock. Adam responded like the wanton he was, shifting his hips to give Septimus more, then crying out loud enough to get the two of them in trouble as Septimus closed his mouth around the tip of his cock.

Septimus made his own sounds of pleasure as he sucked and licked the head of Adam's cock, then bore down on him, taking more and more. He swiped his tongue along the underside of Adam's shaft, taking him as deeply as he could, all the way to the back of his throat. It was a feat Septimus didn't even know he was capable of, and it was worth the terrifying feeling that he was about to choke when he pulled back, sucking hard the entire time, and causing Adam to cry out a string of obscenities that would have made the sailors Septimus knew blush. It was so perfect, sensual, and amusing, that Septimus did it again.

Hot jets of semen filled Septimus's mouth and

throat a moment later as Adam came so quickly, they were both startled.

"I'm sorry, I'm sorry," Adam panted as Septimus swallowed, then pulled back, wiping his mouth with the back of his hand. "I should have warned you. I should have lasted longer. I should have—"

Septimus silenced him with a kiss, pushing him to his back on the bed as he did. "You are perfect," he growled as he caught his breath. "And you're young. You'll be ready to go again in no time." He winked, then straightened so that he could remove the rest of his clothes.

Adam wriggled out of his breeches, laughing as he did. The man was pure light and joy. As they rolled together under the sheets, kissing and touching and bringing each other right up to the edge, Septimus decided that he would gladly give up everything to keep Adam in his arms forever.

"There will be another ship," he said, deciding then and there to stay with Adam. "Or, if not, there will be other dreams. We can find a way to be near the sea always, while still being together. All I want is you," he growled his thoughts as he pressed a salve-slicked finger into Adam's hole to prepare him. Adam looked utterly debauched on his back, his legs spread wide, a pillow propped under his hips as if to offer up exactly what Septimus wanted from him. "Everything else is inconsequential."

When he was certain Adam was ready, he pressed into him, slowly, inch by inch. Adam groaned and shuddered as he took him. The play of pleasure and adoration on his face had Septimus's heart slamming against his ribs. The sight of where the two of them were joined as his cock sank deeper and deeper made him ache to fill Adam with a bit of himself. They were two halves of the same soul, destined to be together, and when Septimus began to move with a strength and insistence that had both of them sweating and panting and making sounds of pleasure, he knew he would give up whatever he needed to make Adam happy.

"I love you, Septimus," Adam cried out as he spilled over himself, clenching hard around Septimus's cock as he did.

"Adam, I love you," Septimus gasped as he burst within him. "I will stay with you. I won't take the ship, I won't leave you. I am yours." The words and the emotions pulsing through him were as wild as a storm, and the peace that settled through him as he withdrew and collapsed against Adam was as beautiful as a storm's aftermath. He didn't even feel ashamed or guilty for confessing his love so suddenly. He did love Adam, and he would do whatever it took to keep him.

ADAM AWOKE as the first rays of dawn gilded the windows of Septimus's room with pale light. It felt so right to wake with Septimus's large, powerful body beside him. At the same time, feeling Septimus there racked him with guilt.

What was he thinking, trying to hold the man to him with chains of love? Love was meant to set a man free, not keep him locked tight in a cage where he would be miserable. His conversation with Mrs. Henshaw the day before rushed back to him. He couldn't force Septimus to give up his dreams because they were good in bed together. He couldn't even ask him to forego those dreams for love. Everything Septimus had said to him the night before was beautiful, but terrible too. Septimus would give up the happiness he'd wanted his whole life to be with Adam, but now Adam wasn't certain he could live with that.

As carefully as he could, Adam inched away from Septimus and climbed out of bed. Septimus was so willing to give up everything for him, but it wasn't right. Adam padded around the room, gathering up his clothes and putting enough of them on that he wouldn't shock some poor maid, if he happened to encounter one on his way back to his bedroom. Perhaps it was his passion-addled brain or the haze of morning, but as he sneaked out of Septimus's room and into the hall, Adam was certain that he had to take drastic measures to free Septimus from the obligation the man felt to give up everything for him.

He raced up to his room, washed quickly, then pulled down his old traveling case from the top of his wardrobe. Septimus had said it last night in the throes of passion. He would stay on land, stay with Adam, give up everything he wanted. Adam couldn't let him do that. Septimus had only one offer of employment. He wasn't the only one. Adam had an offer too, an offer that might make all the pieces fall into place. He needed to know more, though, and he needed to know it immediately.

There was only one way to discover what he needed to know, and that was to go to York, to Archbishop Holgate's School, and to inquire after the position Jeremy said needed to be filled. Adam packed all of his things, knowing that if he didn't push himself to set out that very moment, he would lose his nerve, and possibly his one chance to make things right. As soon as his bag was clumsily packed, he hurried out of his room and downstairs, then out the front door, all before any of the servants caught him. The sun was only

2

MERRY FARMER

just beginning to creep above the horizon as he
rushed toward Hull, and if things went in his favor, for
a change, he would know his answer about the school
in York, know which way life would take him, before
sunset.

18

S eptimus was confident in the decision he'd made the night before to stay with Adam instead of sailing to Canton and back. Even though he had made that decision while buried balls-deep in Adam and while gazing down at the man's expression during climax. Who could resist such beauty and such passion? There would be other opportunities, other ways to finance the school, other chances for Septimus to go to sea for shorter periods of time. They had yet to hear back from any of the inquiries into patronage that Septimus had made to friends of his. Everything would work out as it should.

Those thoughts warmed him, along with the morning sunlight streaming through his window, as he awoke. He'd been exhausted and had slept like the dead well into mid-morning. Adam must have still been deeply asleep as well, because he didn't make a single move as Septimus stretched and breathed in the promise of a new day.

A moment later, Septimus realized that it wasn't lack of movement on Adam's part that made the bed beside him so still, it was Adam's absence. He blinked sleep out of his eyes and dragged himself to a sitting position. He could still smell Adam's scent on him, and evidence of everything they'd done the night before was there in the rumpled, soiled sheets. Septimus smiled over it all. He enjoyed a good tumble as much as the next man, but Adam truly relished bed-sports to a degree that Septimus found charming and arousing.

He rose slowly, shuffling to his washstand to clean up for the day. Adam must have risen early in order to be ready to teach Lord Francis and Lady Eliza their lessons. He wasn't on holiday for the summer, as Septimus was. In addition to Lord Malton's children, it was likely that Adam had a thousand items of business to take care of where the school was concerned, now that Septimus had decided not to accept Captain Seabold's friend's offer of a captaincy. They were once again where they'd started in terms of finding patrons for the school.

"You slept late," Barrett teased Septimus as he walked into the breakfast room, implying that he had done very little sleeping.

"And you look as though you've resolved matters between you and Mr. Seymour," Red added with a wink.

Red and Barrett looked to be nearly finished with their breakfast. Septimus sent them a self-satisfied smile, not even trying to dodge their curious looks. "I've decided not to take the offer of a captaincy," he told them as he loaded a plate with the remnants of breakfast from the sideboard, then brought it to the table.

Both Red and Barrett gaped at him as though he'd grown another head.

"But all you've been talking of since arriving at Wodehouse Abbey is returning to sea," Barrett said.

"This captaincy is what you've been waiting for your whole life," Red added.

Septimus sawed into a piece of ham on his plate, smiling out the window at the morning sunlight. "I have come to see that Adam is what I have been waiting for my whole life," he said. It felt good to be honest with his friends, honest with himself. The only reason he'd believe that the only life he could have was one at sea was because that was the only life he'd ever known. The promise of a different sort of life lay ahead of him now, and as it happened, it wasn't so foreign or distasteful as he had once thought it would be.

Red and Barrett continued to stare at him. "You would really change course in the middle of a voyage like that?" Red asked.

Septimus chewed his ham, swallowed, then answered with a smile, "I am sailing into unknown waters, I will give you that. But I believe I have the right navigator by my side. And what joy is there in life if we take the same course year after year? I believe it is time that I try my luck on different shores."

Again, Red and Barrett merely stared at him.

"You say that," Barrett began, grinning as though he didn't quite believe what he was hearing, "and yet every metaphor you just used belongs to the sea. As do you, I'd wager."

"I'm not saying I must always stay on land," Septimus went on, speaking with his mouth full. He was uncommonly hungry after the night's activities. "All I am saying is that I have found something to care about as much as I care about the sea."

"Would that we all were so lucky," Barrett sighed, sending a moon-eyed glance out the window.

"What is this?" Red laughed. "Has Septimus's love story caused you to long for a knight of your own to come riding up on a white steed, to whisk you into a life that you could never have imagined?"

Barrett laughed along with him. "More likely my cock is jealous of Septimus having a regular bedmate, when I can barely remember the last time I had a man between my legs."

Red and Septimus both snorted with laughter at the comment. Septimus couldn't believe how light his heart felt. "Don't let the servants hear you say that," he said all the same. "They'll report you to Lord Malton, who will have all of us walk the plank."

"Anthony would never do that," Red laughed. "I've had a letter from him, by the by."

"Have you?" Septimus asked, mostly focused on his food.

"It came along with several others early this morning," Red went on. "He's completed his business in London and begun his journey home. He should be here within a few days."

"I look forward to meeting him," Barrett said, rising from his place while simultaneously finishing his coffee. "I am mightily impressed with his children."

Almost as if mentioning the children summoned her, Ivy appeared in the breakfast room doorway. The puzzled, troubled look that the nursery maid wore was a stark contrast to the jovial mood among the men.

"Ivy, is something wrong?" Red asked, standing.

"Have you seen Mr. Seymour this morning, my lord?" Ivy asked Red, glancing to Barrett.

Both Red and Barrett looked immediately to Septimus.

Every lighthearted feeling Septimus had vanished. "Is he not in the nursery, conducting lessons with Lord Francis and Lady Eliza?" he asked.

"No, sir," Ivy said, wringing her hands. "We've been waiting since the children had their breakfast, but he has yet to appear."

Worry shot through Septimus's gut, making him wish he hadn't eaten such a large breakfast. "Perhaps he is in his room," he said. There was a chance he'd slipped out of Septimus's bed and returned to his own to wash and dress for the day, but fallen asleep to make up for the night before.

Septimus followed Ivy out of the breakfast room and up to the second floor, but when they pushed open the door to Adam's room, it was empty and the bed was perfectly made.

"I wonder where he could be," Septimus said, his stomach sinking more and more with each moment.

"Oh, that is odd," Ivy said, staring at Adam's wardrobe.

"What is?" Septimus asked.

"Only, Mr. Seymour's traveling bag is gone, you see." She pointed to the top of the wardrobe, as if expecting something to be there.

Deeper alarm gripped Septimus's heart. He crossed the room and threw open the wardrobe, then gasped involuntarily when he saw it was mostly empty. Almost all of Adam's clothes were gone. He checked the shelves and drawers to be certain, but they were empty.

"What the devil has he done?" Septimus hissed, marching past Ivy and out of the room.

"What should I do with the children?" Ivy asked, fretting even more after the discovery.

"I can entertain them for the day," Barrett said as he mounted the top stairs and stepped into the hallway.

Septimus was glad that Barrett and Red had followed him and Ivy upstairs. It gave him the feeling that he wouldn't have to face whatever had happened to Adam alone.

"Did he say anything about paying a visit or making a journey?" Red asked, as he and Septimus headed back downstairs.

"No," Septimus said. He glanced around as they descended the stairs to make certain no servants were within earshot. "We quarreled," he confessed in a low voice. "Adam was hurt that I would, as he saw it, leave him so readily at the first offer to command a ship."

"Does he not understand that you've waited your whole life for this?" Red asked, as they rounded a corner and made their way to the grand staircase.

"He does." Septimus nodded. "But reason tends to fly out the window when love is involved."

"That is certainly true," Red said with a frown.

"I explained that by taking this offer, even though Canton is a long way away and we would be separated for as much as a year, the benefits would help not only me, but him and his school as well. I promised I would return to him. Then the conversation took a passionate turn and I vowed that I wouldn't leave him at all."

Septimus nearly stumbled as Red jerked to a stop and shot out a hand to grasp his arm. Red's eyes went wide with sudden understanding.

"What is it?" Septimus asked, his pulse kicking up.

"You told him in the throes of passion that you would give up on your dreams for him?" Red looked alarmed.

Septimus blew out a breath. "I suppose I did."

"I believe I know where Adam has gone, then," he said, turning his wide-eyed look to Septimus.

"Where?" Septimus demanded, nearly frantic.

Red moved forward again, and Septimus went with him. "I believe the blasted man is trying to be noble."

"How ironic, considering he knows my views on the nobility," Septimus growled.

Red laughed humorlessly. "You mentioned his school, and that reminded me. He received an offer from a friend of his to teach at a prestigious school in York."

"York," Septimus repeated the word as a groan. Adam had asked him about York several days before, asked if he would want to live there. He must have received the offer from his friend before then. It still didn't make complete sense to him. He shook his head. "Why would he fixate on York and potentially travel there when the possibility of acquiring Henshaw house for his own school is so near?"

"Is it, though?" Red asked. "Does he truly have a chance to purchase an entire property of that size, and to furnish it and purchase school supplies as well?"

Septimus let out a breath as they started down the grand staircase. "I will admit, he has encountered difficulties. No one has been willing to become a patron of his school yet. Mrs. Henshaw adores him, though, and has made it known that she wishes to sell to him."

"But can she? Can she truly?" Red asked.

Septimus shook his head as the pieces began to fall into place once more. "The decision is up to her son. We have yet to speak to the man." He paused as they crossed the hall to the front door, then said, "I made the case yesterday that my accepting the captaincy Captain Seabold's friend's has offered has the potential to provide enough income to establish the school. Adam must have changed his mind about the risks and benefits, in addition to his attempt to give me what I want."

"Could you ask Sebold's friend for an advance on projected profits so that Adam could buy the house?" Red asked.

"And then use the rest of the money I would be paid in a year to keep it running, yes," Septimus nodded. "That was my intention. At least, it was until I changed my mind so that we could continue on together."

They stopped just outside of the front door, in the cheery, blossoming summer morning.

"That's it, then," Red said. "Seymour felt he had to leave and go to York to take up this teaching position in order to set you free to accept the captaincy offer."

Septimus frowned. "If he did, then he's an impetuous fool with overly romantic ideas."

Which was, of course, precisely what Adam was. It was the reason Septimus loved him so.

"I'll have one of the horses saddled so you can ride to Hull in search of him," Red said, starting around the side of the house. "If he's headed to York, he'll have to either take a carriage overland or a boat up the River Ouse. Either way, his journey would need to start in Hull."

Septimus stopped Red before he could go far. "Are you daft, man? You know I cannot ride. I'll walk."

Red looked as though he would make some sort of joke, but there wasn't time. Septimus started off down the lane to the road immediately. He mulled over everything Red had said as he walked. It would have been just the sort of sweet, ridiculous thing Adam would do, to abandon Septimus while thinking he was setting him free. Youth had a way of leading men to make rash decisions, particularly when it convinced them those decisions were noble and romantic. As soon as Septimus caught up to Adam, he would wring the man's neck. Then he would kiss him until Adam couldn't dream of running away from him ever again.

Once he reached Hull, however, Septimus realized his search might not be as simple as he had hoped. He had no idea where to begin to inquire whether anyone had seen Adam hire a carriage or a boat. His first instinct was to ask at the post office, the only place where he had any acquaintances at all, thanks to his incessant efforts to check for letters from the Admiralty. The postmaster informed him that no mail carriages had left Hull for York that morning, bidding him to ask at a few of the local inns.

Those efforts bore no fruit either, but one of the innkeepers gave Septimus the name and location of a few boatmen who punted barges up the Ouse to York on a regular schedule. Even so, by the time Septimus made his way down to the water's edge, the sun was high in the sky and time felt as though it were slipping through his fingers, right along with Adam.

"Mr. Bolton!"

Septimus turned, startled that someone would call him by name, and spotted Robert Carver waving to him from farther down the docks at the river's edge. The man smiled and beckoned to him. Septimus was in no mood for idle chit-chat, but if there was a chance that Carver had seen Adam earlier that morning, he would speak with the man.

"Mr. Carver." He nodded as he approached. "By any chance have you seen Mr. Seymour this morning?" He paused, then added, "He is tutor to Lord Malton's children, a young man, blond hair, blue-green eyes." He stopped himself before his description tipped over into lewdness.

"Yes, I know the man," Carver said with a smile. "He's become quite a friend of my mother's, or so I've been told. I have been in Scarborough this last week on a rather exciting bit of business. In fact, I was very much hoping I would encounter you after everything I discussed with my associates in Scarborough. Meeting you like this saves me the trouble of making a trip out to Wodehouse Abbey."

Septimus was stunned to utter silence and stillness at every word that dropped from Robert Carver's mouth. The world around him seemed to hush and pull in to that one moment and the two of them.

"Perchance," he began slowly, "is your mother one Mrs. Henshaw?"

"Yes, she is," Carver said with a wide, fond smile. "I am her eldest son, from her first marriage, hence the difference in names."

Septimus could only nod, his mouth still open slightly, as an array of possibilities exploded in his mind like fireworks. "Adam wishes to purchase her house," he blurted before he could think better of it.

Carver laughed. "Yes, I know. Believe me, my mother has spoken of nothing else since I returned yesterday evening. She is quite adamant that I do whatever possible to ensure the sale goes through."

Another round of fireworks went off in Septimus's mind and heart. "That is good to hear," he said, his voice thick with emotion. A moment later, he steadied himself and shook his head. "There are problems with financing the endeavor," he warned Carver.

"So I hear," Carver said, his expression turning businesslike. "I may have some solutions. And adjacent to those solutions, Mr. Bolton, I was wondering if you were still in search of employment."

Septimus couldn't breathe. It was impossible for so much good fortune to descend upon him all at once.

Then again, as he reminded himself, the wages Carver could offer him as a fisherman were negligible. They certainly weren't enough to allow him to help with Adam's school.

"I am in need of employment," Septimus began slowly, "but I fear I must find something that will pay more than working on a fishing boat."

"How about managing a fleet of them?" Carver asked, a glint in his eyes.

Septimus felt as though he needed to sit down. "I beg your pardon?" he asked.

Carver must have seen how startled he was. He gestured for Septimus to follow him to the edge of the dock and to sit with him on a pile of crates. "My journey to Scarborough was to speak to a Mr. Knopf about merging our two fishing enterprises. A third man, a Mr. Kettering, is interested in joining the business as well. The three of us combined plan to fish the waters of the North Sea and to distribute our catch all along the eastern coast of England and Scotland. But I would need an experienced seaman, both to sail some of the larger commercial vessels and to oversee the large number of vessels we plan to incorporate into the enterprise. When I mentioned your performance at my little competition and your kindness toward Malcolm to Knopf and Kettering, the two men were very interested in your character. I will confess that I wrote to a friend at the Admiralty and asked a few questions about your skill as an officer as well. My friend was impressed, which only confirmed my instincts about you. As such, my partners and I could offer you a percentage of the partnership, if you would be interested."

Septimus was so stunned by the offer that he could only gape. So that was why Carver had taken down names and addresses during his competition. It hadn't been a competition at all, it had been an interview for employment. Perhaps employment precisely when it was needed. Sailing the North Sea was a far cry from voyaging over the length and breadth of the Atlantic, or sailing all the way to Canton and back. By that same token, sailing the North Atlantic would mean he was never more than a few days from home, even while at sea.

"I hardly know what to say, Mr. Carver," Septimus stammered. "It is the sort of offer I never thought to consider."

"I hope you will consider it," Carver said. "I was heartily impressed with your performance at the festival those weeks ago, and equally impressed with your generosity where Malcolm was concerned. And my friend at the Admiralty was explicit about your accomplishments," he added with a clandestine look. "He said it was a crime that you were not given a royal commission in the Navy after your years of competent service, that a man named Wallace egregiously took credit for some of your noble deeds. He informed me of the true story of your heroism. That is what has convinced me you are the man I wish to have working for me."

"I am humbled by such praise," Septimus said, feeling rather like he was drunk. The truth about Wallace's betrayal was known by more than just him and his friends. It was strange and wonderful to feel vindicated at last. "I am grateful about the house as well," he went on, his heart turning to Adam, as it always did.

Before he could say more, a man floating by on a

flat-bottomed barge called up to them, "Oy! You the fellow who's looking for Mr. Seymour?"

In an instant, everything about Carver's offer and the North Sea was forgotten. Septimus shot to his feet so fast it made him dizzy. "I am," he called back.

The bargeman nodded up the river. "He took passage on Jerry Figg's barge headed for York."

Septimus could have wept in relief. He charged away from Carver and down to the water's edge. "How long ago?"

"'Bout an hour," the bargeman said. "There's a chance we could catch up with him, if my boat was greased enough." He held up a hand, rubbing his fingers together.

Septimus's heart sank. He knew precisely what the unscrupulous man was asking for, and he hadn't a penny on him.

To his surprise, Carver marched up to his side, reaching into a pocket in his jacket. "How fast can you row?" he asked the bargeman, handing him a coin.

"For you, Mr. Carver, as fast as the wind."

Carver glanced to Septimus, then nodded to the boat. "After you, Mr. Bolton," he said with a smile.

Septimus should have hesitated, should have questioned the man's astounding generosity, but he didn't. He leapt right into the barge, Carver right after him, and charged to the bow, as if running that way could get him to Adam faster.

The bargeman had only just ordered his men to push away from the dock when a loud call of, "Mr. Carver! Mr. Carver, wait one moment," stopped everything.

Septimus and Carver both turned to find Martin Goddard picking his way down the stairs from the road to the dock. He was clearly in a hurry and stumbled over crates and bits of rope scattered over the dock. His face was pinched with distaste—for the men working on the dock as much as for the detritus he attempted to climb over.

"Mr. Carver, wait!" he shouted again. "I must speak with you about your mother's property. My clients want your mother's house after all, and have agreed to offer payment in the amount of a thousand pounds for the house and surrounding land."

"A thousand pounds?" Carver's eyes widened in amazement.

Every bit of excitement Septimus had felt a moment before twisted into alarm and dread. "Can you go any faster?" he asked the bargeman.

He fully expected the man to ask for more money to get them away from Goddard, and was surprised when the fellow grimaced and said, "I cannot get away from that dolt fast enough." He turned to gesture to his crew to punt faster.

"Mr. Carver, stop." Goddard rushed to the very edge of the dock, teetering a bit as though he might fall into the murky water. "A thousand pounds," he repeated. "They are willing to pay immediately and take possession as soon as possible. Can you honestly say that anyone else is willing to offer you such a price?"

"No," Carver said hesitantly. He glanced to Septimus.

Septimus could only shake his head, his heart bleeding for Adam. Goddard would win after all, damn him. But that didn't mean that there wasn't something else to be done.

He glanced back to the shore as Goddard lost patience with shouting and waving his arms after Carver. He turned to accost the other bargemen instead, as though attempting to get one of them to give him passage so he could chase after Carver. The one bright spot in the ordeal was that Carver did not tell the bargeman to stop or slow down. Carver's brow was knit in thought. Septimus couldn't discern whether that was a good sign or a bad one. All he could do was march back to the bow, glancing ahead as if he would be able to spot Adam ahead of them on the river, and pray they caught up to him before Carver changed his mind about the promises he'd just made.

19

The quickest way to travel from Hull to York was not overland, by mail carriage or other conveyance, but by river. Flat-bottomed barges traveled from the wide River Humber that flowed past Hull, up to the River Ouse, which wound gently through the Yorkshire countryside, passing farms and small hamlets whose livelihood depended on river trade. Since the increase in mills and factories in the last few decades, barge traffic along the rivers had increased tenfold, and Adam was forever fascinated with pamphlets and articles he'd read about plans to expand the river and canal system throughout England, so that goods and people could be transported the entire length and breadth of the land by water.

Adam tried to remind himself of those exciting developments and to find fascination in the many barges he passed as morning stretched on into midday. He told himself he was interested in the cargo of barges laden with glassware and cloth headed down to ports in Hull, or casks of fish and rum heading inland to York, but each of the small trading vessels only served to remind him of the ship on which Septimus would sail away from him. Every curiosity along the river only made him wonder what sort of exotic shores Septimus would see and what kind of trinkets he would bring back from those places.

If he returned at all.

"Cheer up, lad. It might never happen," Mr. Figg, the boatman he'd paid to transport him to York, said as he walked the length of his barge, checking its cargo and their progress.

Adam attempted to send the man a smile. He was merely attempting to be kind, after all. He couldn't know that his glib words actually applied to the situation Adam found himself in now.

Adam sighed and glanced back down the river toward Hull. They were miles away from the town now, miles away from Wodehouse Abbey and Septimus and the deliciously cozy bed he'd left him in. He was miles away from being able to discuss things with Septimus, to talk things through like grown men, and to find a solution that would benefit them both. He could have consulted with Lord Beverley about the entire matter at that. Surely there would have been a better solution to the tangle between him and Septimus and their dreams than absconding from the house in the early morning, like a thief and a coward.

"This was a terrible idea," he sighed, burying his face in his hands. He sat on a small pile of crates along the side of the barge, his feet propped on the edge of the boat, which was a perfect position to curl forward in an attempt to hide from the world and his own, ill-thought-out decisions. "Impetuous," he repeated the word Septimus had used to describe him.

But hadn't that always been the case? Hadn't he always leapt before looking, forming his plan to open a school, then immediately writing to everyone he could think of for patronage without laying out the details of how, exactly, one went about establishing such an institution? Hadn't he taken the position tutoring Lord Malton's children the moment it was offered, because he believed it would be the only position offered to him? Jeremy's letter and the offer from Archbishop Holgate's School proved that was not the case, and that if he'd simply waited, bided his time, and trusted in Providence, things would have sorted themselves. Although, in all honesty, he didn't regret his decision to take the placement at Wodehouse Abbey one bit. Without it, he never would have met Septimus.

Septimus, who was the anchor that his hotheaded impulses needed to force him to steadiness and thought. Septimus, who had the experience to know what was just a dream and what was achievable. Septimus, who kissed him like a fiend and held him like an angel and enveloped him, body and soul. He'd never know the kind of happiness and pleasure that he knew in Septimus's arms. He never wanted to let it go, which was why the idea of letting him fly off to Canton was such a horrible one. Yes, Septimus should be free to pursue his dreams. He should feel free to have his adventures and bring back his treasures. But for Adam to attempt to force him into it by leaving for York was just wrong.

Adam let out a frustrated growl and lifted his head, staring forlornly back along the river. He was an arse—a reckless, impetuous arse.

"Whoa there, lad." Mr. Figg happened to be passing just behind him as Adam made his outburst. "It cannot be as bad as all that."

"I'm afraid it is, Mr. Figg," Adam groaned. He dropped his feet to the barge's deck and stood, needing to pace. "I've made a horrible, cowardly decision."

Mr. Figg grinned, his eyes crinkling at the corners with wisdom. "Running away doesn't sound like such a grand idea after all?"

Adam blinked. "How did you know I was running away from something?"

Mr. Figg laughed. He nodded to Adam's traveling bag, then said, "A man with manners as fine as yours and soft hands, asking for passage to York on a barge carrying herring first thing in the morning, must be running away."

Adam blew out a breath and rubbed a hand over his face, embarrassed over being caught doing something foolish. "I thought it would be for the best when I awoke this morning."

"Had you enjoyed a cup of strong coffee before making the decision?" Figg asked.

"No," Adam admitted.

"There's your problem, lad," Figg laughed. "Never make a decision before coffee."

Adam broke into a weak smile. Mr. Figg might have had a point.

"So what are you running from, if I might ask?" Figg crossed his arms and fixed Adam with a kindly look.

Adam weighed whether he could burden the man with his own, foolish problems. It couldn't hurt to seek the counsel of an older, more experienced man. "I am attempting to open a charity school," he began, "but patronage has been hard to come by."

"Ah, money is the root of all evil, is it not?" Figg said, then nodded for Adam to go on.

"It is," he agreed. "Particularly since I have found

the perfect premises for the school, a house belonging to a Mrs. Henshaw."

"Oh, I know the place." Figg's face lit up. He tilted his head to the side in happy consideration. "That would make a perfect school."

"It would, but I do not have the capital to purchase it at this time, and I am uncertain whether Mrs. Henshaw's son would be willing to sell it to me," Adam explained.

"Have you spoken with Robert about it?" Figg asked. "Your plan strikes me as something he would find worthy of selling for."

Something about the swift and easy way Figg revealed that he knew Mrs. Henshaw's son sent a wave of excitement through Adam, but it was drowned by larger problems.

"My sweetheart has a plan that might bring in a great deal of money for the school," he went on.

"That's something," Figg said with a smile.

"Yes," Adam said glumly. "Something that will take her away from me and place her in potential peril for as much as a year."

Figg looked confused, which didn't surprise Adam at all.

"The offer of employment would take her overseas," Adam explained briefly, then rushed on with, "and I am not certain my heart can withstand it."

Figg's expression changed to one of understanding. "It is all coming clear now," he said with a teasing, yet still kind, look. "You've run away from love."

"And I feel like a muttonheaded fool because of it," Adam sighed.

"Love makes fools of us all," Figg said, reaching out to thump Adam's arm. "That's no reason to run away from it."

"I know." Adam sat on the crates again with a sigh. Figg sat with him. "Between the plans for my school hanging by a thread, and the possibility of losing the truest love I've ever known, I fear the worst."

"And what is the worst?" Figg asked.

The question surprised Adam. He blinked, then answered, "That I will never be able to build something of my own. That I will be forever nothing more than the younger son of an impoverished baron, pitied rather than respected."

"And you wish to be respected?"

"I do." Adam realized the truth of the matter with a rush. "I wish to be respected for my own merit, to be loved for who I am, and not who my father is as well."

"And this sweetheart of yours," Figg said. "She loves you for yourself and wishes to help with your school?"

"Yes," Adam sighed. "And I've made a muddle of things." He rubbed his hands over his face, grimacing at his less-than-marvelous decisions. "I've only ever wanted to be taken seriously, as a man and a teacher, and to help others."

"Every one of us wants to be taken seriously," Figg said, resting a hand on Adam's shoulders. "But even you must admit, running from your problems is not the way to go about it."

"No," Adam agreed with a sigh. He growled with frustration at himself, then turned to Figg. "I don't suppose there's a chance you could turn the barge around and take me back to Hull, is there?"

Figg sent him a regretful look. "Alas, no. But I can return you to Hull by the end of the day if—" He stopped in the middle of his sentence, sitting up straighter and glancing downriver as something caught his eye.

Adam sat up as well, then stood entirely when he saw what appeared to be a wild boat chase. Two barges were tearing upriver at a speed that amazed Adam, considering how slow the rest of the boats on the river were traveling. The one in front was manned by several men who seemed to be putting their all into propelling the boat forward, as a man who could only be their captain shouted encouragement and laughed, as though the whole thing were a lark. The captain of the boat behind it seemed to be having just as much of a laugh over the race.

It was the passengers on the first boat that caught Adam's eye, however. Standing at the very front of the boat, one hand raised to his forehead to fight the sun's glare was Septimus. Adam's heart nearly leapt out of his chest at the sight of his lover. He let out a wordless exclamation of joy before he could stop himself and scrambled over piles of crates and barrels, rushing to get to the back of the barge.

"Septimus!" he shouted, then immediately caught his foot and tumbled to the deck in a pile of arms and legs. He ignored the bruises and scrapes of his fall, lunged back up to his feet, and continued to scramble over the contents of the barge. "Septimus!" he called again, as he clambered up onto a barrel at the very back of the barge, then waved his arms.

Septimus's searching took on a new sort of tension, and as soon as he saw Adam, he dropped his arms to his sides. "Adam!" he shouted over the swiftly shrinking distance between their barges. "Adam, what are you doing?"

"I haven't the slightest idea," Adam called back, too giddy with joy to come up with any other explanation. Septimus was utterly beautiful standing on the bow of a ship—or a boat, at least. He balanced himself with such precision, struck such a noble figure, that Adam's heart felt as though it would leap out of his chest. How could he ever, even for noble reasons, think of leaving such a wonderful man, or about standing in the way of him captaining his own ship?

As their two vessels grew closer, Septimus's expression of joy shifted to a frown of frustration. "What in blazes were you thinking, man? Leaving the house at dawn without telling another soul?"

"I was a fool," Adam called back. "I thought I was doing the gentlemanly thing, pursuing another means of raising the money for the school, and setting you free to take the captaincy."

"Sweetheart, eh?" Figg commented, with a smirk from the aisle between crates behind Adam.

"I do not need you to set me free to do anything," Septimus roared at him in return, giving Adam no time to worry about Figg stumbling across the truth. The boats were close enough now that neither of them had to shout, but Adam could see that Septimus's frustration demanded his full voice. "I do not need you to give me leave to do anything," he said. "I make my own decisions in life, and my decision is to throw my lot in with you, you impetuous fool. We will find a way to finance the school, one way or another. Seabold's friend's ship was just one offer. There is no need to ruin two lives on the suggestion of a possibility of action in just one day."

"I know," Adam called back, "and I never should have left this morning. Only, I wished to explore an offer of employment in York that a friend made and —" He dropped his explanation with a sigh. The whole thing suddenly seemed blatantly ridiculous. "Do you see now why I need you by my side?" he asked, laughing as he did. "I am as like as not to cut off my own ears and sell them before thinking about it, if someone would offer me money for them."

"Daft man," Septimus shook his head. "There are more ways than one to accomplish one's dreams."

"And I demand that you teach me all of them," Adam laughed. "You see? Have I not told you from the start you would make an excellent teacher?"

Septimus laughed and shook his head, both amused and aggravated by him, if Adam guessed correctly. "Come over here and we will discuss things."

"Gladly," Adam said.

He stepped down from the crates and over to the side of the barge, then indulged in one last act of impetuousness by diving over the side of the boat and into the river.

20

Septimus's knees went so weak at the sight of Adam scrambling atop a stack of crates aboard what seemed like the hundredth barge they'd passed on their way up the Ouse, that he nearly fell over. At last, they'd caught up to the rapscallion. Septimus didn't know whether he wanted to kiss Adam or harangue him until he dissolved into a puddle of his own shame for leaving the way he had. He settled for a lesser version of the scolding that Adam deserved.

Which was all well and good until the rash fool dove into the river.

Septimus's heart leapt to his throat. What was his little minx thinking, diving into waters that likely had a dozen eddies shifting this way and that, thanks to the heavy traffic of barges and river boats?

Worse still, Goddard's boat finally caught up to theirs.

"Mr. Carver!" Goddard shouted, extraordinarily peevish as he clambered to the side of his barge as the two boats came abreast of each other. "I must speak with you about my clients' offer for your mother's house at once."

"It can wait," Carver boomed.

At least, that was what Septimus assumed he said. The moment Adam leapt into the water, Septimus scrambled out of his jacket and boots, then dove into the river to rescue him.

The splash of cold as he slipped under the water was a jolt. There was so much silt in the water that even when he opened his eyes, he couldn't see much. The silt stung as much as saltwater, which wouldn't help his efforts to rescue Adam at all. He reached around in the current near where Adam had gone under all the same, aware of the shifting boats closing in with the possibility of crushing them, the pull of the current, and the way his lungs began to burn for lack of air. The only thing that steadied him was when his hand hit something warm right next to him. He grabbed it, then kicked up to surface.

Adam surfaced with him, sucking in a loud breath once his head broke the surface.

"I'm never leaving you again," Adam gasped, surging into Septimus's arms as though they were playing and Septimus's life hadn't just passed before his eyes. "Can you ever forgive me for running off in a fit of haste, albeit well-meaning haste?"

The look of hope on Adam's wet face, the way his golden hair plastered against his forehead, dull with river water, and the sparkle in his eyes—as deep and blue-green as the ocean on a peaceful, sunny day— went straight to Septimus's heart. "You are an impossible fool," he growled.

He then clasped a hand to the back of Adam's head and slammed his mouth against his, kissing him as though they both needed it to live. He pulled them down, sinking beneath the surface of the river as he did, hiding them from the prying eyes of everyone else along the river who might dare to comment. Underwater kissing was devilishly hard, though, and it could only last a moment before he dragged them both above the water again.

"Mr. Bolton, Mr. Seymour, are you well?" Carver called to them from the edge of his barge once they broke the surface again.

"We are," Septimus called back. "I feared Mr. Seymour was in danger of drowning, but he seems to have his breath back now."

The excuse was unnecessary, as no one seemed inclined to comment on the kiss, or the way Adam clung to Septimus with a dream-eyed look. Septimus caught that look and burst into wry laughter, shaking his head. "You are going to be the death of me, I know," he said.

"But at least we will die happy," Adam told him.

Under the water, Septimus squeezed Adam's arse hard. Adam deserved much worse punishment than that, and Septimus fully intended to deliver it as soon as possible. He dragged Adam to the side of Carver's barge, handing him up into Carver's outstretched arms once they reached it. As soon as Adam had been hauled into the boat, Septimus grabbed hold of the side and hoisted himself up with practiced strength. It felt good to be drenched in water again and to feel his muscles work in old, familiar patterns, but from the moment he rolled onto the barge, his thoughts were only for Adam.

"Do you have a blanket to wrap him in?" he asked the bargeman. "Something to warm him?"

"I am perfectly fine, Septimus," Adam said as Carver helped him to sit on a barrel. "You rescued me. You are my hero." He added a cheeky wink that was as like as not to get them all in trouble.

"I would have no need of rescuing you if you

would stop and think for a moment before rushing off in a fit of pique," Septimus scolded him.

"It wasn't pique, it was an idea for—" He stopped as soon as he saw the irritated, sulking figure of Martin Goddard storming up the barge toward them.

"Mr. Carver," Goddard said, clearly exasperated. "Now that this ridiculous fish has been hooked and draw in, could we please discuss the sale of your mother's house?"

Septimus's shoulders dropped as he glanced to Adam.

Adam had narrowed his eyes at Goddard the moment the man interrupted their reunion, but at the mention of the house, his brow flew up. "Your mother's house?" he glanced to Carver. "What house is this?" By the look in his eyes, he already knew.

"Mr. Carver is Mrs. Henshaw's son," Septimus explained, his tone already apologetic. Once Adam heard the offer Goddard's clients had made, his dream of securing that house for his school would be dashed.

"Robert," Adam said, as though fitting the pieces together. "From her first marriage."

"That's right," Carver said with a smile. "I am pleased to make your acquaintance again."

He extended a hand, taking Adam's wet one just as one of the bargemen came forward with a blanket. Septimus took the blanket and draped it around Adam's shoulders, scrubbing him a bit as if it were a towel to bring warmth back into Adam's limbs.

"My mother could talk of nothing but you when I returned yesterday evening," Carver went on.

"I have grown very fond of your mother," Adam started, smiling.

"Enough of this," Goddard interrupted, stomping one foot on the deck, fists balled. "Mr. Carver, my clients are offering you and your mother the exorbitant sum of a thousand pounds for that rotting pile of timber. It would be more than enough for the old woman to live out the rest of her life in the deepest of comfort, and it would provide you with an astounding sum as well. So tell these wastrels to sod off and return to whatever backwoods town spawned them, and come with me to the offices of Hamilton, Bradley, and Associates so that we can take care of the legal aspects of the sale."

Septimus gawped at the man. He hadn't seen such a display of temper since one of the cabin boys aboard the *Majesty* threw a fit after being denied a ration of rum. That lad had been ten years old. Everyone else on the barge, Carver included, stared at Goddard with the same sense of disbelief.

They were all silent until Adam asked, "So you've decided to sell to Goddard's clients?"

Goddard burst into a self-satisfied smile and crossed his arms, staring down his nose at Adam as if he'd finally won a lifelong wager.

That smirk vanished when Carver drew himself up to his full height, puffing out his chest, and said, "No, I have not."

"I beg your pardon?" Goddard gaped at him.

"My mother has informed me of the way you have been harassing her, sir," Carver said. "She has told me tales of bullying and threats."

"The woman does not know what is good for her," Goddard hissed. "A thousand pounds," he emphasized. "When else in your lifetime will you see such a sum?"

"When I have earned it myself through diligence, hard work, and employing the right men to make my enterprises a success." Carver glanced to Septimus.

Septimus tightened his grip on Adam's shoulders. He still stood behind Adam, and when his hands tightened, Adam shifted to glance questioningly up at him.

"Carver has offered me employment with his fishing company," Septimus said, pleased beyond telling that he could make the revelation at such a perfect moment.

"Employment?" Adam asked, his eyes brightening by the moment. "Here? In Hull?"

"Well, in the North Sea, to be precise," Septimus said.

"We've yet to discuss the details," Carver added, "but I've asked your friend to lead up the fleet of fishing and trading vessels I hope to assemble. The men I have partnered with in this endeavor believe we could all make a small fortune." He glanced to Goddard. "Well over a thousand pounds per annum, if we're clever and lucky."

"Carver has offered me a percentage," Septimus told Adam quietly.

"And I may be able to see fit to offer a certain house—to let, of course, not to purchase—as part of the bargain," Carver added.

Adam's shoulders lifted under Septimus's touch as he sucked in a breath of shock. "You would allow me to start my school there?" he asked Carver, his face going pink with excitement. "Without scraping together the money to purchase it or gathering patrons to support it."

"I would still urgently suggest that you find patronage for your school," Carver said. "All schools need patronage. But, as Mr. Bolton and I discussed on the journey upriver, if you would be interested in arranging some sort of joint enterprise by which graduates of your school would enter into some sort of apprenticeship with my company, my business partners and I might be convinced to become key patrons of the establishment ourselves."

Adam's mouth dropped open as he gaped at Carver for a moment, then twisted to glance up at Septimus. "I am so devilishly sorry," he said, hoarse with emotion. "I foolishly thought I could solve the entire problem all on my own."

"Of course you did," Septimus chuckled, patting his shoulder, then finally stepping away as one of the bargemen brought forward a towel for him to dry himself. "Young men always believe they hold the solution to every problem within their own grasp."

"I will never think such a thing again," Adam said, standing and turning to him.

"Yes, you will," Septimus told him with a smirk. "Likely by the end of the day."

Septimus could see all the signs in Adam's expression that the young man wanted to throw himself into his arms and kiss him. All he could do was return the look and wink, praying no one noticed.

"Mr. Oliver, I believe it is time to turn the barge around and return to Hull," Carver said, stepping forward to clap Septimus on the shoulder and to share a victorious smile.

"Pull your boat a bit closer and I can throw Mr. Seymour's bag over," the bargeman from Adam's boat called across.

"I will," Oliver called to him.

"This cannot be happening," Goddard said as everyone began to move, ignoring him. He shoved a hand through his hair, and his eyes went wide with disbelief. "I promised my clients that the property would be theirs within a fortnight. They have begun preparations to take possession."

"You should not have assumed others are as shallow and craven as you are," Carver scolded him. He faced Goddard more fully, crossing his arms. "Did you really think I would sell my mother's land, at any price, to a man who attempted to badger her into the deal, rather than letting it to a kind man with a noble idea who has won my mother's and aunt's hearts?"

Goddard gaped at him for a moment, as though Carver were the one who had lost his mind. He then turned to stomp to the back of the barge, which was close enough to the boat he'd found to chase after them, and climbed back over, muttering to himself the whole way. "Turn around and take me back," Septimus heard him order the captain of that boat.

"Sorry, sir," that captain said with a cheeky smile. "We're heading to York. You'll be able to find passage home once we get there."

"This is an outrage," Goddard shouted as the barge Septimus, Adam, and Carver were on began to turn about. "I demand you take me back at once. I paid you to transport me where I wanted to go."

"You paid me to chase after Oliver," his bargeman laughed. "It was a right good race too. I'll beat you next time, Oliver," he called across as Oliver's barge finished turning and started downriver.

Goddard continued to shout and rail against anyone and anything he could, as Septimus took a seat on the crates beside Adam. The best they could do when surrounded as they were was to huddle together for warmth.

"Poor Goddard," Adam sighed as they slipped down the river, everything suddenly feeling right with the world. "He always was miserable at losing."

"If he continues to deport himself in that manner, it is a condition he will need to grow used to," Septimus said.

Adam laughed with him. Carver was close enough to hear the comment and chuckled in agreement. As soon as Adam was made aware of Carver again, his expression grew more serious. "What is this offer of employment that you spoke of?" he asked, sitting straighter.

The rest of the journey back to Hull was spent discussing the finer points of the job Carver wanted Septimus to do. And the more Carver outlined the details of his vision for the plan, the more Septimus felt in his bones as though it would be the best decision, not just for him, but for Adam and the school as well. There would be quite a bit of sailing involved, particularly when Carver and his associates needed to travel, but Septimus would have more than enough time to spend ashore, helping Adam build and grow his school.

"It is precisely as your mother said," Adam told Carver once they reached Hull and climbed ashore. "Sometimes, when there is a decision to be made between two opposing options, a third choice will present itself which is better than both."

"My mother said that?" Carver asked, accompanying a still damp Adam and Septimus up from the dock to the road.

"She did." Adam nodded. "Your mother is a wise and wonderful woman."

"I've always thought so," Carver agreed with a smile.

Carver helped them to find a wagon willing to drive them back to Wodehouse Abbey. Septimus would have insisted they hire a hack, or some other conveyance more suitable for the son of a baron, as he teased Adam for being. But they both reeked of river water, and Adam's boots still dripped with it. There was a fair chance those boots were ruined. So a farmer's wagon was once again good enough for them.

At the Abbey, the moment they stepped through the doors, right after Red and Barrett made a dozen and one jabs about the two of them looking like drowned river rats, Septimus ordered a bath brought to his room. Adam carefully begged off having one brought to his room as well, saying he would make do with his washbasin, but Septimus had a feeling Worthington saw right through him.

Less than an hour later, the two of them lounged comfortably together in the huge brass tub of warm water that had been brought up to Septimus's room.

"I truly am sorry for rushing out on you as I did this morning," Adam said, as Septimus massaged soap through his hair, as Adam had done for him moments before. "It was silly, to say the least."

"Yes, it was," Septimus grumbled, attempting to sound fierce. "Don't you ever dare do such a thing again."

"Oh, you can rest assured, I will not," Adam said.

He tilted his head back so that Septimus could pour a pitcher of clean water over it, rinsing out the soap. The sight of Adam's elongated neck, the way the water sluiced over his head and shoulders, and the soft sigh of contentment that Adam let out had Septimus as hard as iron. If having Adam as his very own was the prize after all the trouble the two of them had gone through, then it was all worth it.

He set the pitcher aside, then proceeded to run his hands over the strong lines of Adam's shoulders, arms, and back, laying kisses across his wet skin as he did.

"You are a menace," he growled with each kiss, letting his hands slip under the water and along Adam's sides. "An impulsive, impish menace."

"Yes, but I am your menace," Adam hummed, leaning his back against Septimus's chest. "And I always will be, if you'll have me."

"Of course I'll have you, you silly man," Septimus murmured, with his lips against Adam's neck where it met his shoulder. He snaked his hands around the tops of Adam's hips, reaching for his cock and balls, and wrapping his hands firmly around them, as though they belonged to him. Adam gasped and flinched into his touch, then gasped again when Septimus sucked his mark onto Adam's neck. "You are mine, and I will never let you forget it."

"How could I forget something so wonderful?" Adam purred, wriggling his hips against Septimus's aching cock.

That mischievous gesture brought Septimus's patience to an end. "Up," he said, grabbing the sides of the tub to hoist himself out.

Adam stood with him, and for a moment they dripped everywhere as they climbed out of the tub and reached for towels. Drying off turned into more of a chore than usual, as they each tried to dry the other, and grope, fondle, and stroke as they went. They might not have dried off well, but they certainly heated enough to make the water dripping from them turn to steam. Septimus eventually dropped his towel, then pulled Adam's out of his hands and dropped it as well before backing him to the bed.

"Do you know what I have been wanting to do to you since the moment I spotted you standing on that barge?" Septimus murmured against Adam's ear, sliding his hands around to clasp Adam's arse cheeks and pull them temptingly apart.

"Please tell me," Adam said breathlessly, glancing up at Septimus with a coy look. "Better yet, show me."

"I will." Septimus's mouth twitched in amusement as he brought his lips to within inches of Adam's. Adam tilted his head up with a look of delicious submission, his hands grazing Septimus's sides hungrily.

Septimus took a step back, pivoted to the side, and sat on the edge of the bed. He then dragged Adam face down over his knees, then brought his palm down hard over Adam's arse. Adam let out a yelp of surprise that turned into a rich, beautiful laugh.

"Septimus, I am not a child in need of punishment," he laughed.

"Aren't you?" Septimus smacked his arse harder. Adam let out a cry that was equal parts pain and pleasure. "Based solely on your actions, I cannot tell." He spanked Adam again.

Adam's panting and giggles turned into something more than just amusement as Septimus spanked him a few more times. "All right, stop, stop," he laughed. "I have learned my lesson, on my honor."

Septimus pulled his hand away, admiring his handiwork and Adam's bright red arse. Adam's cock pressed hard against his thighs, and he could feel the trickle of moisture that escaped his tip.

"On second thought," Adam said, glancing up over his shoulder at Septimus with a wicked look, "don't stop. Who could have imagined that I was the sort to enjoy a good spanking?"

"I'll give you more than that, you minx," Septimus growled, slapping his red arse a few times more for good measure, then tossing him across the bed.

Adam continued to laugh and wince and wriggle

with his smarting arse in the air as Septimus lunged for the jar of salve on the table beside the bed. When he tried to shift to his side, Septimus held him where he was and pulled his hips up higher, nudging his knees apart.

"This is an extraordinarily undignified position for the future headmaster of a charity school to be in," Adam laughed, then moaned when Septimus pressed a salve-coated finger into his hole.

"You should have thought of that before behaving as though you deserved it," Septimus told him.

"I do deserve this," Adam cooed in a ridiculously wanton voice. "I deserve—oh!" Septimus slipped a second finger into him, stretching him and reaching for the bundle of nerves that would cause him to lose his mind with pleasure. "I deserve every moment of this."

Septimus laughed, removing his fingers, then quickly coating his aching and ready cock.

"Septimus," Adam stopped him just as Septimus was about to drive himself home within him.

"Yes, darling?" Septimus asked.

Adam twisted to look up at him from an angle that would have been comical, if not for the earnestness in Adam's eyes. "I would have let you go back to sea," he said, as serious as could be. "If that was what you had wanted, I would have walked you up to the ship myself, then stood on shore waving to you until you disappeared over the horizon. Then I would have waited every day for your return and greeted you with open arms."

"I know, my love," Septimus said, positioning himself, then pushing slowly into him as Adam groaned with pleasure. "And I would never have taken any captaincy that would have separated the two of us for so long. Not for all the money in the world. You are my heart and my joy. You are my sea and my tides. You are the dream I have waited for my whole life." He moved slowly in and out of Adam with each declaration. "I am so happy when I am with you. Why would I want to give any of that up?"

Adam's only response was a wordless sigh of pleasure as he bore back on Septimus, working with him to bring them the most pleasure possible. It was sweet and sensual, then passionate and all-consuming as Septimus moved harder and faster. He stood on the floor, which gave him more purchase and mobility as he pounded into Adam. He took his cues from the sounds Adam made and when Adam let out a cry that told him he'd found exactly the right angle, he moved as though the two of them were in a race and the prize was pleasure like neither of them had ever known.

It didn't take long for both of them to burst into ecstasy.

"Oh, Septimus, I love you, I love you, I love you," Adam gasped as he spilled a sea's worth of himself across the bedcovers.

Septimus was moments behind, and groaned, "I love you, my darling," as he filled Adam with himself. It was perfect in every way, and as he withdrew and rolled onto the bed, grabbing Adam's spent body as he did, and splayed across the bedcovers with him in a sated embrace, he felt as though he knew what true joy and absolute love was. "I love you with my whole being, my love, and I will be by your side and in your heart for the rest of our days."

AUTHOR'S NOTE

A lot of assumptions have been made about what life as a gay man in the Regency must have been like. Most of these assumptions have been made by examining the laws alone, or by interpretations of primary source documents made by historians in the 20th century that were colored by their own bias. The study of Gay History is an extraordinarily new discipline in Academia that has only just been opening up in the last decade or so. Unsurprisingly, a wealth of primary-source material supports a different view of history than the cold letter of the law—the view that plenty of men conducted life-long same-sex relationships without trouble or interference, even though they had to live quietly for the most part. Historians such as Peter Ackroyd, Matt Cook, Graham Robb, and George Chauncey have begun to paint a picture of gay life before the modern era that is very different from the assumptions academics and lay people made in the homophobic 20th century.

All of that is important to this book—and all of my other M/M Historical Romances—in that the stories I choose to tell and the lives that the men in my books live might not be what you expect to read about in a historical novel. Indeed, you might find yourself tempted to say, "Well, that's not historically accurate!" On the one hand, I reject that perception of historical accuracy. Like I said above, Historians have approached LGBTQ History with a deeply biased viewpoint for the last hundred years or more, so what has been viewed as "accurate" is, in fact, a product of the era in which the research was conducted and the conclusions reached. New research has uncovered so much about the daily lives of gay men throughout history that is challenging the perceived status quo. And there is so much more research to be done. Not just to challenge current assumptions, but to uncover viewpoints we might not even have considered before. As George Chauncey so eloquently puts it in his seminal work *Gay New York*, "Just because no one has gone looking for something doesn't mean it isn't there."

On the other hand, it would be silly to assume that gay men in the 19th century lived completely free and open lives with full acceptance. But you know what? For the sake of this series and the rest of my books, let's take a page out of Daniel Levy's book and imagine an ideal world where homophobia doesn't exist. I am a big fan of Schitt's Creek, and I think Daniel Levy created something magical by portraying a world without homophobia. I have been so touched by his reasons behind writing his show that way and the reception it has received that I've endeavored to do the same thing with the *After the War* series. My aim in writing these books this way is simply to tell love stories—romantic, passionate love stories—without the distraction of prejudice and hate. I don't want my characters to be seen as victims, I want them to be seen as men with lives and hearts and ambitions and hopes. If that means tweaking "historical accuracy" a bit, I'm fine with that, and I hope you are too!

OTHER WORKS BY MERRY FARMER

<u>The Brotherhood – (M/M Victorian Romance)</u>

Just a Little Wickedness

Just a Little Temptation

Just a Little Danger

Just a Little Seduction

Just a Little Heartache

Just a Little Christmas

Just a Little Madness

Just a Little Gamble

Just a Little Mischief

Just a Little Rivalry

<u>The Silver Foxes of Westminster – (M/F Victorian Romance)</u>

December Heart

August Sunrise

May Mistakes

September Awakening

April Seduction

October Revenge

June Forever

<u>The May Flowers – (M/F Victorian with one M/M)</u>

A Lady's First Scandal

It's Only a Scandal if You're Caught

The Scandal of a Perfect Kiss

The Earl's Scandalous Bargain

When Lady Innocent Met Dr. Scandalous

The Road to Scandal is Paved with Wicked Intentions

Scandal Meets Its Match

'Twas the Night Before Scandal

How to Avoid a Scandal (Or Not)

When the Wallflowers were Wicked – (M/F Regency)

The Accidental Mistress

The Incorrigible Courtesan

The Delectable Tart

The Bushing Harlot

The Cheeky Minx

The Clever Strumpet

The Devilish Trollop

The Playful Wanton

The Charming Jezebel

The Faithful Siren

The Holiday Hussy

The Captive Vixen

The Substitute Lover

That Wicked O'Shea Family – (M/F Victorian set in Ireland)

I Kissed an Earl (and I Liked It)

If You Wannabe My Marquess

All About That Duke

Earls Just Wanna Have Fun

All the Single Viscounts

Give Your Heart a Rake

Naughty Earls Need Love Too

And many more! Click here for a complete list of works by
Merry Farmer [http://merryfarmer.net]

ABOUT THE AUTHOR

Merry Farmer lives in suburban Philadelphia with her two cats, Justine and Peter. She has been writing since she was ten years old and realized she didn't have to wait for the teacher to assign a creative writing project to write something. It was the best day of her life. Her books have reached the top of Amazon's charts, and have been named finalists for several prestigious awards, including the RONE Award for indie romance.

CPSIA information... printed in the USA
LVHW...
9781648391101

CPSIA information can be obtained
at www.ICGtesting.com
Printed in the USA
LVHW032114140921
697776LV00004B/78